IDENTITY THIEF

A NOVEL

JP BLOCH

BACON PRESS BOOKS
WASHINGTON, DC
2014

Published in the United States by Bacon Press Books, Washington, DC
www.baconpressbooks.com

Editor and Copyeditor: Lorraine Fico-White
www.magnificomanuscripts.com

Cover Design: Alan Pranke
www.amp13.com

Cover Photo: WiseWanderer

Book Layout and Design: Lorie DeWorken
www.mindthemargins.com

Author Photo: Tristan Robin Blakeman

ISBN: 978-0-9913443-5-2
Library of Congress Control Number: 2014947952

PRINTED IN THE UNITED STATES OF AMERICA

To Tristan, with love

CALL RECEIVED AT 4:27 AM :

"911 Emergency. How may I assist you?"

"There's blood everywhere. Naked and so much blood. Dead."

"Sir, who is dead?"

"I . . . I never wanted this to happen."

"Sir, please stop crying. I need to know what happened."

"Oh God, oh God . . . Christ, please, hurry!"

"Sir, is this person breathing?"

"It's not just one—I mean, yes. I don't know. Just get an ambulance."

"Where are you now?"

"I'm home, damn it. In my bedroom."

"Do you know this person?"

"I told you, it's not just one person. Why can't you listen? Can't you send an ambulance?"

"Sir, I need an address."

"I'm in the Paradise Cul-de-sac, Number 11. I'm . . . I'm Dr. Jesse Falcon."

"Sir, if you are a doctor, you should be able to—"

"I'm not that kind of doctor, you dumb shit. I'm a—I'm a psychologist."

"Sir, please calm down. An ambulance is on its way."

"No . . . Please, no more."

"Sir, please explain what is happening . . . Sir, are you there?"

1 : AKA Jesse Falcon

'M A NICE GUY.

Everyone would tell you I am. In fact, they might say I'm the nicest guy they've ever known. I was vice president of my senior class in high school, and the only reason I didn't run for president was to let a girl in a wheelchair win. At college, three different fraternities invited me to pledge. Junior year, I married my pregnant girlfriend even though I wasn't sure I was the father. Everyone said I should do a paternity test, but I truly believed all that crap about what difference did a drop of sperm make, and a real man did what had to be done.

It was as if I thought I'd get a medal for totally fucking up my life.

I even changed my major from psychology (which I loved) to computer science (which I hated) and decided to forego grad school to support my wife and kid. I always sent my mom a Mother's Day card, even when she called my wife a fuck whore—I guess as opposed to whores who get paid to read aloud from the *Farmer's Almanac*. But then, dear old Mom never put logic above making her point. I always voted, I recycled, and I never ran a red light.

Yeah, that was me. Mr. Nobody, like something you'd scrape off your shoe without a second thought. The perennial best supporting actor. How I felt or what I wanted made no difference to anyone.

Or at least not until now.

The thing is, I have an addiction. I realize that sounds totally lame, like I'm making excuses for myself. Yet, I swear it's the truth. After a while, I couldn't stop. Of course, there are no support groups like AA for people like me. Besides, what would they call us? Identity Thieves Anonymous? It cracks me up just to think about it. I'd be in this roomful of people addicted to stealing other people's identities, but everyone would be on a first-name basis only, so that our identities were protected . . . only which identities? Still, I imagine there'd be varieties of addiction, just like drugs or alcohol. Internet versus credit card identity theft. Using an assortment of aliases versus sticking to only one name. If heroin is the worst drug addiction, stealing the name of just one living person is the worst kind of identity theft. Trust me, it's the most damage you can do—to the victim, to yourself, to everyone. I'm the worst kind of addict. I am the junkie of identity thieves. Sometimes I actually forget I'm not Dr. Jesse Falcon. I'm sure that's a bad sign, too. Even I don't know who I am.

But you know? They say addicts are always blaming their problems on other people instead of taking responsibility for their own mistakes. Well, let me tell you what happened. You decide if it was my fault.

Maybe my wife—deceptively named Betsy, which suggests a much nicer girl—never would've left me if the company I worked for, 21st Century Solutions, hadn't gone belly up. A hundred people went to work one day, only to be told they had an hour to pack up and leave, as if they'd done something wrong. I suppose, though, that the higher-ups had to do it like that, to avoid all kinds of embarrassing crying and shouting and begging and threats.

Anyway, 21st Century Solutions didn't have many solutions up its sleeve after all because there I was, out of work with two weeks' severance pay. My official title had been Support Resources Director, though it would be impossible to explain what I did. Not that anyone would've wanted to know. It's not like kids say,

"When I grow up, I want to be a support resources director." In her dismissive way, Betsy told people I did "computer shit." But I worked my ass off for seven years. I stayed late, I skipped lunch, I worked on weekends, and never took a single sick day.

Yet no matter how many raises I got, my entire paycheck was spent, courtesy of Betsy. There were even a few scary times when we had to empty our pockets and look behind the sofa to put together change for groceries or gas. Beneath the veneer of suburban success, I never stopped panicking over money. The mortgage had been refinanced three times to get cash back to cover credit cards and bills, which had a way of sneaking back, out of control all over again. At champagne cocktail brunches, I'd smile in affinity when people went on about their diversified portfolios or their rollovers, but I only had a vague sense of what they were talking about. I had a two-car garage, mock-Tudor home, yet I lived one paycheck away from homelessness. The only good thing about it was that when other people's investments went down the crapper, I had nothing to lose.

Betsy called herself a stay-at-home mom, which meant she sat around drinking Diet Pepsi while ordering cutesy stuffed animals and fake diamond pins from home shopping networks. Her inertia was such that she must've believed she climbed Mount Everest every time her index finger hit redial on her cell phone. She also made frequent use of her middle finger, which over the years was increasingly extended at me.

In the first couple of years, Betsy helped me change an occasional diaper, and eventually I found out she secretly paid someone to clean the house—but at least it *was* cleaned. Still, our son, Scotty, didn't get the attention he deserved from either of us. Me, because I was always at work, and Betsy, because when she wasn't ordering from QVC, she was fucking her old college boyfriend, Biff. To complete the pathetic little talk show extravaganza, naturally Biff had been my best friend since childhood, and everyone knew about the sleazy affair except me. But then, I'd always been utterly disposable, like a used condom or last year's cell phone.

When I wasn't helping Betsy to live out her days before the TV set, I was bailing Biff out of one jam or another. In fact, the night before my wedding, Biff got stinking drunk and puked all over my mother's favorite chair at two in the morning, and though I was pretty wobbly myself, I painstakingly cleaned up after him. I even gave him my bed while I slept on the floor.

At breakfast the next day, Biff said, "You're the greatest guy in the world."

Well, little did the greatest guy in the world know it, but twenty minutes before exchanging vows, Betsy was with Biff in the church rectory, and they were going at it like bunnies. I didn't find out, though, until a fateful night seven years later, when my unemployment ran out and I still couldn't find a job. Betsy decided this was the ideal time to destroy what remnants of a life I had left. And the rectory quickie wasn't even the worst of it.

"I can't believe this is happening to me," Betsy bitched. She dyed her hair a shade called "Dry Martini," and she seethed as she brushed her bleached electric frizz before her Thomasville dresser mirror, as if even the tangles in her hair were my fault. "To *me*." Her own reflection was like a third person in the room, goading her on.

"What do you mean, '*to me*'?" I said. "Don't you mean to us? *I'm* the one who can't find a job. Betsy, I'm scared. We're down to nothing. Zero. Zilch. I can't even use Visa to pay off MasterCard. The mortgage is overdue. The only thing left is Scotty's miniscule college fund, and I always swore I'd never—"

"Scotty!" She all but spat out the name, as if it were a curse word. "What makes you think he's your stupid asshole son anyway? He looks *exactly* like Biff, in case you hadn't noticed. God, how people have made fun of you behind your back. We even fucked in the rectory twenty minutes before I married you."

I stared at her, unable to speak. I couldn't decide where to begin—that I was just told my son wasn't mine, that he was fathered by my so-called best friend, that Betsy had lied to me all these years, or that she told me in such a cruel way. And it was already the lowest point in my life.

Betsy glared at me. "Biff's never been much good. He's great in the sack, but that's about it. Christ, he still lives with Mommy and Daddy. Did you know he almost had to go on *Judge Judy?* Some bimbo gave him all her money. Daddy, as always, came to his rescue."

"Thank God Biff's all right," I managed to say. I was hurt and angry in the way that makes you grasp at anything to comment on, no matter how irrelevant to the main point.

Betsy absently studied her face in the mirror, turning from side to side and changing her expression, as people in love with their faces often do. "I didn't feel one bit bad lying to your sanctimonious face. You, Mr. Psych Major, should've added two and two. You were *gone* the month I got pregnant, remember?"

"Yes. I suppose that's true. My father was dying, so I came home to be with my mom."

"Whatever. The thing was, I knew perfectly well that Biff had as much husband potential as a skunk. You—you were the good one, the responsible one, the one who would live up to your responsibilities."

"Even though they weren't mine?"

She turned to face me. "You know what I mean. And surely you *knew* all along. On some level. Even you aren't that dumb."

"I—I decided a long time ago it didn't matter."

"Oh, it matters. Because Biff's moving in, and you, my fine fellow, are moving out."

I was stone cold sober, yet I felt the way people have described being on something like LSD. All I could see was this glaring red everythingness before me that seemed to wobble and spin. I didn't know such rage was possible.

I grabbed Betsy's arm; her hairbrush fell to the floor.

"Go on, kill me," she whispered. "Rot in jail for the rest of your stupid life."

My hands shook while she stared into my eyes, never even blinking. She ran her tongue along her upper lip, as if savoring something delicious. It occurred to me that Betsy really was crazy. Her father was a cop who shot himself through the head, and she hated her mother for being what she called mean. So Betsy decided the best way to deal with her unhappy childhood was to destroy other people.

I somehow got past the image of choking her and set my hands down. Looking back, I know Betsy was right. The only reason I *didn't* kill her was because I didn't want to go to jail. It's hard to explain, but sometimes I feel like I'm two different people. One guy does the right thing, while this other guy calls the first guy a chicken shit for not doing the wrong thing that I wanted to do instead. It's as if I know in my bones that the wrong thing is really the right thing, and I'll never be happy until I do what this other part of me wants me to do. Even if I end up in prison or a nut house, I'll finally feel satisfied. The right guy had always been stronger and kept the wrong guy in his place. Yet I hated the right guy and loved the wrong guy.

Yeah, I admit it. I'm not holier than thou. I probably wanted to kill Betsy a million different times. Or Biff, for that matter.

I sat on the edge of the king-size bed, turning toward the wall. I couldn't even look at Betsy. I resisted the urge to rip apart the stupid stuffed animals on the bed—especially this pink hippopotamus with girly eyelashes. I didn't want to give Betsy the satisfaction. Instead I bit my own knuckles until I drew blood.

"We have Biff's daddy to thank once again. He gave Biff some trust fund thingamabob. It's kind of funny, if you think about it. His parents wanted him to move out for years, and they finally figured out the way to get Biff to do *anything* is to give him money. I mean, like, duh." She rubbed a sweet-smelling lotion into her hands, a nightly ritual that always seemed to take forever. "Not to worry, the bills will be covered."

"If you and Biff—I mean, when you and Biff lose the mortgage, don't come running to me. And I still want to see Scotty. I *will* see Scotty." Damn it, there was a big gloppy tear running down my face, just when I needed to be strong. I shook it away in annoyance.

"Oh, as far as Scotty is concerned, you're still his dad. For now, anyway."

It was amazing how effortlessly Betsy issued threats. Keep supporting the kid, or else he'd be told Biff was his father, which among many other things would traumatize Scotty for life. Not only to know a different man was his father, but that the man was Biff—whom Scotty, with a childlike clarity that adults underestimate, never liked.

Don't ask me why, but Betsy and I made love that night. Twice, in fact, and the second time was even better. In the stale nothingness of early morning, with Betsy moaning through some ecstatic dream—about Biff, no doubt—I quickly packed a suit-case, scooped up my laptop, and threw on some clothes. In the mirror, I noticed I had a purple hickey on my neck, my last memento from Betsy. I touched it in a brief flicker of nostalgia.

My first impulse was not to say good-bye to Scotty for now. Not just because of how painful it would be but because I had no idea what to tell him.

Yet I knew I had to see him. I slipped off my shoes and padded quietly to his room. Though I felt guilty about not spending more time with him, Scotty was proving to be an extremely self-reliant child who kept himself entertained through his own imagination. This, no doubt, had to do with his intelligence, which was off the charts. Not yet eight, Scotty was tackling children's books meant for ten- or twelve-year-olds. He also could win video games in less time than it took poor old Dad to get even one level higher. Scotty loved baseball, and he wanted to do a science project on the velocity of an inside curve versus an outside curve.

Probably much of the time he thought he was the parent in the family and Betsy and I were his embarrassingly immature children. He was *too* happy to be by himself, and I worried that he wasn't making friends his own age.

In the dim morning light, I saw Scotty's map of the Milky Way that I had tacked to the ceiling and wall posters of video game characters I did not understand. His glasses were set on his nightstand, where an opus entitled, *Petey Learns to Pitch* lay. Petey, I could see, was a basset hound. Scotty wanted a pup more than anything, but we were waiting until he turned ten. In the meantime, his hamster, Porky, had curled into sleep after playing on his wheel all night.

As I sat on the edge of his bed, I could tell he was awake but pretending to be asleep. I had a passing thought about how people of all ages pretended to be asleep when they weren't, usually for unhappy reasons. Scotty sat up, pretending to yawn; it was doubtful he'd become a professional actor. There was a suspiciously crinkly sound in the sheets, which as a parent I took to mean he was hiding something under his blanket.

I put my index finger to my lips, which he knew meant let's not wake up Mom.

"Hey, Slugger," I whispered. "Let's see what you have here."

I pulled back the blanket, and to my horror, saw a *National Enquirer*. On the cover was a blurry photo of a movie star in a bikini, the headline proclaiming the monumental news that she'd gained weight. A smaller headline chimed that the First Lady was a lesbian.

"What the—"

"Relax, Dad. Mom lets me read them with her. She says you wouldn't like it, so it's one of our secrets." He reached for his glasses. "The pictures are *unfathomably* interesting. That's spelled U-N-F-A-T-H-O-M-A-B-L-Y."

I wondered what other bizarre secrets they shared but decided not to ask. "Did you have any fun dreams?" Scotty sometimes drew pictures of his dreams, which tended to be space adventures.

He shrugged. "Not really." With a studious expression, he flicked on his bedside lamp and turned a page of the *Enquire* that I quickly grabbed and set aside. I wasn't sure what to tell him, but I planned something along the lines of *Daddy will be taking a business trip.*

Scotty craned his neck to see my suitcase in the hall. He looked at me imploringly. "Dad, don't leave," he whimpered, damn near breaking my heart. In his precocity, he already knew what was happening. Some kids knew the word "divorce" by the time they were out of diapers.

"Scotty, I—"

"I know, I know." He reached for his glasses. "Mommy and Daddy don't get along but you still love me, and blah-blah-blah. I *hear* you fighting. I'm not a child, you know."

"I know, son." In spite of myself, I bit my lip to keep from smiling.

"I won't live with Biff."

I thought about asking him why he thought Biff was moving in—besides of course the fact that he was, per Betsy's own words the night before—or what Scotty thought went on between grown-ups. But I decided it was not the best time to get into how babies get made.

"You've never liked your Uncle Biff, have you?"

"I hate him." I was taken aback by the ferocity with which this seven-year-old boy spoke. "He's not my uncle, and he'll never be my dad."

"Just why do you hate Uncle—I mean, Biff, so much?"

Scotty looked away. "He makes fun of my glasses and says no one will ever like me. He says he's going to cook Porky for dinner. He says . . . he says you and Mom had to get married because of me. You know, stuff like that. But only when it's just me and him."

"'Him and me,'" I corrected through force of habit. Then, to make sure, I asked, "Is there anything else?"

He moved his fingers around on the bed in a kind of nervous twitch. "No."

Somehow, I knew he really meant, *yes.* I took his face in my hands and looked into his eyes sternly but with love. "Tell me. Whatever it is."

Scotty was quiet for a long minute. Finally, very softly, he said, "He touches me. You know, like, down there." He pointed to the buttoned front slit in his pajamas. "He says it's the only way I'll . . . I mean, my thing down there, will get big."

Everything I'd been through with Betsy evaporated. It was like wondering if you should appeal a parking ticket and then finding out you're charged with murder. I felt a heartbreak I didn't know was possible. Finally, I asked a stupid question. "Scotty, why didn't you tell me?"

"He's your best friend. I didn't want to hurt your feelings."

"Oh my God." I held my son tightly, mussing up his hair. "I'm so sorry."

"I know." I could feel the breath of his muffled voice against my chest. I think we both cried, but it didn't matter. It was something beyond tears.

Suddenly I let go of him and stood up. "Scotty, you're coming with me. Now."

He sighed with impatience. "Well, obviously."

Scotty knew exactly what to pack and without making a sound. With hamster cage on board, I left a note saying, *Scotty and I are visiting Mom.* That way, Betsy couldn't say I kidnapped him; I was a custodial parent informing the other custodial parent of our son's whereabouts. I had to get custody of Scotty. Sole custody. Biff should rot in jail. But first, I wanted to get us both the hell out of there. I decided as long as I got Scotty to a safe place, I could talk to a lawyer later in the day. It occurred to me that Biff and Betsy would dismiss what Scotty said as a ploy to get back at them. And did I want Scotty to testify in court and be traumatized even more than he already was?

My mom was a decent old broad—or rather, an indecent one—who'd made hating Betsy into a hobby. Besides, I didn't know where else to go on such short notice with no money. Despite all the hours I'd worked, I'd rarely socialized with the people back at my job. I had no real friends.

I was almost at Mom's place when I realized there was something else I should do. Something I had to do to maintain any sanity at all. Making the first illegal U-turn of my life, I drove to the rich part of town, where Biff lived in an imposing, humorless mansion with his snooty parents—although I happened to know they were in the Bahamas. (After all the years I'd known them, they still treated me like a stranger.)

"Wait here," I told Scotty, who was drawing an imaginary picture on the car window.

Biff had the same bedroom he'd always had, which meant I could climb up a tree and a trellis to break in like I always could, especially when we were teens. I knew it was also the servants' day off. Biff would be alone in the house, unless he was fucking some bimbo—or hell, molesting a child. His bedroom itself looked out on the enormous grounds, which included a pool, tennis court, stables, and wooded area. The nearest neighbor must've been a mile away. This served us well during many a boyhood prank. And, I figured, it would serve me well now.

Biff was alone in his designer bed, sleeping away without a care in the world. He fell asleep—or rather, passed out—with his clothes on, including flip-flops. His fancy bedroom was the usual chaotic mess it became after only one day of the maid not picking up after him. (Biff changed his clothes about a hundred times a day.) I stood over Biff for a moment, swallowing back the urge to puke. I wanted some cleansing ritual to erase the feeling of ever having known him. I woke him up with a hard shove.

Biff moaned, but then at the sight of me, he smiled. "Hey. What are you—?"

Gathering everything inside me, I punched him in the face. His skull hit the headboard hard, and I could see his nose drawing blood.

"What the fuck?" He studied the blood while rubbing the back of his head.

I shook his shoulders; his head kept hitting the headboard but I didn't care. "You stay away from my son. Yes, *my* son. If you speak to him, if you get within a mile of him, I swear I'll kill you. And then I'll dig up your grave and bring you back to life and kill you again."

Opening his nightstand, he pulled out a small handgun. "Get out! If you don't, I'll . . . I'll shoot you. And my dad will hire a good lawyer so I won't have to go to jail."

I wisely stepped back, raising my hands in surrender. "Betsy says Scotty looks like you. I'll bet that's why you did it. You really want to fuck yourself. Biff's true love is Biff."

"You shit. You fuck. No one talks to me like that. You're *nothing*, you know that? Nothing." Biff held a Kleenex to his nose as he took aim at me. A shot went off. Either because I ducked or because he was lousy shot, he missed me. I could see the useless bullet burn into a pile of clothes on an overstuffed chair. He leapt out of bed; one of his flip-flops made him slightly stumble. But he quickly steadied himself and took aim.

"Easy now, Biff." With my hands still raised, I stepped toward the window. "You don't want to—"

"All my fucking life you've told me what to do. Always so superior. The good little poor boy. Like we're fucking Goofus and Gallant. Do you know how much I've always hated you?" I heard his pistol click. "Now you're finally suffering, like everyone else. No job, no money, a fucked up kid, a wife who hates you. Oh, and by the way—you're gonna die."

I should've kept my mouth shut, but I couldn't help it. "When have you ever suffered for a minute in your life?"

"Fuck you." The gun was aimed straight at me.

I flinched, closing my eyes. A shot went off; it nearly pierced my eardrum.

I opened my eyes and saw Biff lying on the floor, a bull's eye gunshot right through his forehead. His face was pretty much unchanged. He wore the same indifferent expression he usually wore.

One long second later, I looked over and saw Scotty holding a smoking gun. "Is he dead?" He looked up at me calmly, like any kid asking his dad a simple question.

"Jesus, Scotty. Where did you—I mean, how did you—" I grabbed one of Biff's dirty T shirts to test for a pulse or heartbeat. I'd watched enough TV to know not to put fingerprints on his body. Biff was dead as a rock. The bullet, I could see, went straight through his head to the other side, as if there'd been nothing inside it at all. There was merely a slight discoloration on another of his shirts on the floor, and what you might call a token puddle of blood.

Scotty adjusted his glasses. "It's an easy climb up here. I watched what you did."

I stuffed Biff's T-shirt into my jacket pocket. "I don't mean, 'How did you get up here?' I mean what are you doing with a gun?"

"Biff showed me his gun collection. I stole it when he wasn't looking."

"But how did you know how to use it?"

Scotty shrugged. "Doesn't everyone? I was aiming for his throat. The jugular vein. That's J-U-G-U—"

"But Scotty, why?"

He rolled his eyes. "Get real, Dad. I saved your life, in case you didn't notice. I figured you'd need help because Biff is—I mean, *was* such a jerk. I'm glad he's dead. Now you and Mom can get back together."

"Oh, Scotty." For a minute or so, I just stood there, staring into space. I didn't cry, I didn't reach out to him. I could only stare. I was numb. My son murdered the man who molested him. I couldn't come up with a way to react.

"Since it was Biff's gun, we can stage a suicide," Scotty excitedly offered. "I saw this TV show once where—"

"Scotty, we're going straight to the police." But then I looked at my son, thought about all that would happen to him if I turned him in, and I realized I couldn't do it. Maybe I should've, but I couldn't. I had to think fast. "I mean, no, we're not. And we're also not 'staging a suicide.' Christ, where did you learn to talk like that? It's too risky. We're going to have to clean up instead and get rid of the body."

Scotty smiled with admiration. "Whatever you say, Dad."

My not quite eight-year-old son. A murderer. Sexually molested. I would deal with that later.

Fortunately, Biff's head fell onto more scattered clothes, which meant there was no bloodstain on the carpet. I wrapped Biff's body and bloody clothes in a bed sheet and threw it out the window, aiming carefully so that it didn't get caught in the tree. I put both guns in my jacket. Though it grossed me out, I wiped the nosebleed from his Kleenex on the bed to mix with the trace of blood on the headboard. Then I wiped it all away. It would look like he had a nosebleed and tried to clean it up. I knew where Biff kept his passport in his dresser. I got it out and pocketed it. Next, I got his wallet from the floor and took out a credit card. On his laptop, I made him a reservation for that day to fly to the Bahamas. I took one of his suitcases and packed it with his passport, wallet, and some clothes and tossed it out the window next to Biff's corpse. In spite of myself, I laughed a little when the suitcase landed on his groin.

I sent his parents an e-mail saying I (meaning Biff) was on my way to join them. "Biff" confided that he needed to get away from Betsy. He told them that he agreed to move in with her because he was afraid to stand up to her since she was such a bitch, but he really wanted nothing more to do with her. I next sent a message to Betsy from Biff, saying that, I, "Biff," would be joining my parents to milk them for more money but would be in touch soon.

I signed it with all of Biff's love.

Next, I wiped away any trace of fingerprints except for objects I knew Scotty and I hadn't touched and picked up all the shell casings. I made sure our shoes had left no discernible imprint in the carpet.

Scotty studied me intently throughout, especially when I stuffed the body into the trunk of my car. As we drove, I found a large, empty fast-food box by the side of the road, put the guns inside the box, and tossed it into a town litter can. By the time anyone would want to find it—if such a day would come—the guns would be long gone into a landfill. We drove to an old dirt road. I buried the body deep into the woods, carefully arranging leaves and sticks in a natural, random-looking way on top. I knew that burying bodies in the woods was pretty common as murders go, but Biff hated being out in nature, so searching the woods was unlikely to be a top priority. I drove to another area to bury the suitcase. I made sure our footprints and tire treads were covered over.

Done at last, I wiped my brow for the sweat. "It's off to Grandma's."

"Dad, you're the greatest." Scotty smiled at me. Oddly enough, I found myself tickling and roughhousing him, and he giggled like he always did.

Ironically, though, all that happened did nothing to take my mind off of money.

Instead, I realized I needed money more than ever before. Divorce, custody, maybe even a murder trial down the road. And Biff's parents could take on twenty of me in court with one hand tied behind their backs. I knew my mom had some money stashed away. She'd sold my childhood home for a handy profit and moved into a small, pricey condo. But I'd never borrowed from her before and especially now couldn't bring myself to ask. She could end up being an accessory after the fact.

I told Mom nothing about Biff, other than that he and Betsy planned to live together. It would be a while before all the dots could possibly be connected. First, there'd be a missing persons report, then there'd be a search for the body, and so on. The dots were likely to connect to Betsy or me and not Scotty. I'd go to jail for Scotty without thinking twice, but I was damned if I'd let him live with Betsy as sole parent. Scotty gave me his solemn promise to say nothing to Grandma or anyone else about all that had happened. I completely trusted him.

I barely nibbled on the microwave breakfast Mom insisted I needed. Her condo, like my childhood home, was homey in a trailer park sort of way. Mom liked dollar store paintings of babbling brooks and placid deer and wooly covers for Kleenex boxes and toilet paper.

She called Betsy an A-Number-One Cunt right in front of Scotty, who said, "Dad, if Grandma says 'cunt,' is it okay if I do, too?"

My mother thought this hilarious, but before I could respond, she asked me to get the morning mail from the mail stand in the parking lot. And it was there, among the grim bills and hysterical sweepstakes offers, that I saw a pale blue envelope addressed to a Dr. Jesse Falcon, presumably the condo's previous owner.

I started to toss the envelope into the recycle bin, but when I saw it was a credit line offer, I couldn't resist opening it. Apparently, Dr. Jesse Falcon was my polar opposite. A new nationwide bank was pleased enough with his credit rating to offer him a twenty-thousand-dollar line of credit. There wasn't even a disclaiming asterisk. I made sure no one was watching and tucked the envelope into my pants pocket.

If you've ever been in a car crash, you know the feeling: you spend the rest of your life wishing you left the house two minutes later or didn't make that wrong turn. I could've thrown away the envelope. Yet, in the moment, I couldn't. It just wasn't meant to be. I had the answer to my prayers, as far as I was concerned. Not that I'd literally prayed, but sometimes living in hell is its own kind of prayer. I know it sounds unbelievable, like when people on trial for murder say they don't remember firing the gun, but it really did feel like someone else was doing this instead of me.

I plunked the useless mail on the kitchen table. Scotty, I saw, was reading my mom's *Enquirer* on the front lawn. "Mom, I'm curious. Who owned this place before you?"

Mom drank her morning black coffee as if it were straight whisky. "He was some shrink or professor or something. In a big hurry to move across the country." She chuckled to herself. "He must've really stepped in a pile of shit."

"How could you tell?"

"Oh, he was so full of himself. That kind of snooty jerk makes nothing but enemies. He'd yawn when I asked him questions, and when I said I might plant flower boxes in the front windows, he said in this uppity way, 'Yes, I imagine you're the type.' I mean, what the hell was that about? 'The type?' Who the hell hates *flowers*, for God's sake?"

"Betsy doesn't like flowers. Allergies."

"Figures. She has an allergy up her ass, if you ask me. Didn't I *tell* you ten years ago to get a paternity test?"

"It was eight years ago. And yes, you did. I was a wild, impetuous youth, and never paid heed to my wise elders."

"Cut the crap. I assume you'll sue that frigid whore for custody? If it were me, I'd sue her just for getting in my face. Do you need money?"

"I'll be fine, Mom. But thanks."

"Look, if it's your asshole male pride, we can make it a loan."

"Really, I'll work it all out. Go be a nice grandma. Bake some cookies."

"*You* go bake cookies, Sonny Boy. I'm watching my NASCAR races today."

Feeling the torn, folded envelope crinkle in my back pants pocket, I felt like I couldn't get to my laptop fast enough.

Stealing Jesse Falcon's identity was not the nicest thing I've ever done, but it was by far the easiest. I have considerable computer skills, but a child could've done it. I would've preferred stealing money from Biff, but obviously that was likely to get me caught. Besides, was it really stealing if this Jesse Falcon never even knew he had the money in the first place? After all, I had every intention of paying it back.

First, I did a search for "Jesse Falcon" plus "psychologist." Within seconds, I was browsing through his web page from a nearby university. I struck gold with his online vitae, which included his all-important social security number. It was the type of arrogant, absentminded mistake that people who think they are invincible often make. The university also had a union contract available online, so I looked up how much Jesse Falcon would've been making.

Then, since my mother told me he'd moved cross-country—the university, like many bureaucracies, was slow to update its website—I did another quick web search and found him to be in private practice. This gave me his current office address and phone number, in case I needed it later. Obviously, I wanted the twenty grand to come to me and not to him.

Next, for thirty bucks, a people-search website gave me a history of where he'd lived, his credit rating—superb—and any criminal charges—none. I knew how long he'd been married, the name of his one child, Sabrina, and where *she* lived and what she did for a living.

This same source also told me what bank he patronized. Conveniently for me, his accounts were all in another new nationwide bank that had branches everywhere. At the bank website, I clicked on the "I forgot my password" box needed to access the checking account. This required two test questions to make sure I was who I said I was: What was the name of "my" daughter, which I already knew was Sabrina, and what was the name of "my" dog, which I knew from Jesse Falcon's web page was a bull dog with the pretentious name of Jeremy. I soon had Jesse Falcon's checking account number and samples of his signature from photocopies of cancelled checks. I next set up a free, all-purpose e-mail account that supposedly was Jesse Falcon's. And at a website that specialized in genealogy, I got a copy of Jesse Falcon's birth certificate.

Finally, I filled out the online application for twenty thousand dollars. I watched a computer-generated dot spin around for a nervous minute or two before getting the ecstatic message that this other bank approved the twenty-thousand-dollar credit line. I—or rather, Jesse Falcon—could use it as a checking account, direct deposit, or debit card. I checked the box for direct deposit, since I couldn't wait for anything to get mailed to me.

Maybe I was rationalizing, but Jesse Falcon's online photo minimized any guilt I was feeling. He had one thick eyebrow arched higher, and the corners of his lips turned down in an ironic grin, as if he thought he were James Bond or something. He'd also written a conceited blurb in which he described himself as an "intellectual" and a "passionate lover of fine wine and living life to the fullest." There was even a pompous quote from Virgil in the original Latin: *Audentis fortuna iuvat.* Upon searching for an online translation, I learned it meant *Fortune favors the brave.* I imagined him as one of those professors who always singled out a student to bully, to show how superior he was.

Offhand, I couldn't find out why Jesse Falcon quit his job and moved so far away. My guess was that he knocked up one of his students. But then, I didn't need to know that right now. Though I was new to breaking the law, I intuitively embraced the criminal golden rule to keep things simple. Don't tempt fate unless you have to.

I told my mom I was getting a settlement with 21st Century Solutions. I don't think she believed me for a minute, unless her saying, "When it comes to bullshit, you take after your father," was a vote of confidence. But she had a firm belief in people making their own beds and sleeping in them. Mom took it for granted that all people were louses and considered this sad fact of life to be none of her business. She cut me more slack than she did other people, though sometimes I thought if I ever really got in trouble—like if I murdered someone—she'd say something like, "You did the crime, so do the time."

But my mind was not focused on Mom or for that matter, murder. Instead, I went straight to a divorce attorney. I needed to do what seemed perfectly normal under the circumstances. Plus I might need a lawyer in a big way down the road. And so it all began.

Whatever else happened, I faced it like a man. I have to keep telling myself that. And I did learn one important lesson. The biggest mistake you can make is thinking you know who you are.

2: Dr. Jesse Falcon

"LOOK AT ME," she kept saying, like a little girl wanting her daddy to watch her jump rope. "Look at me." Only she wasn't a little girl, and nobody was jumping rope. I was screwing the daylights out of her, thrusting so hard I worried that the rubber would slip off or break. "Jesse . . . why . . . can't . . . you . . . look . . . at . . . me?" she blurted out between thrusts. "Are . . . you . . . thinking . . . of . . . your . . . wife?"

Truth be told, it wasn't like I *never* looked at the woman inches below me, I merely wasn't relentlessly staring at her with every cell of my being. How could I explain that no, I wasn't thinking of my wife. Sad but true, my wife Esther would be the last person I'd be thinking of at a time like this. I just didn't want this woman I was with to get the wrong idea. Supposedly she understood that our relationship was purely recreational. For the record, she even had a husband. But sure enough, she was starting to want what is obnoxiously referred to as "more," or putting the relationship on "another level," which always conjured an absurd image in my mind of all the couples in the world occupying different steps on a long, long stairway, with hell at either end. Lesbianism notwithstanding, sometimes I wondered if women would be capable of orgasm if things like bridal magazines and china patterns ceased to exist. Or maybe I cheated with all the wrong women.

It was ludicrous to feel like I had to change the subject in the middle of having sex, but I did. Tactfully, I put my index finger to her lips. "Shhh," I said. But instead of turning things down a notch, she coyly put my index finger in her mouth, indicating with an arch expression that she understood the signal for "blowjob." This may have been seductive in different circumstances, but since we were already naked and *fucking*, it didn't make sense. It was like handing someone a gift, and then after they opened it, saying to them, "I have a gift for you." Subtle she wasn't. A control freak she was.

"Are you pretending my finger is your husband's?" I asked, giving her a taste of her own medicine. "And I don't mean just his finger."

It was fortuitous that precisely at that moment, we both came.

Afterward, she sat up, reaching for her panty hose. "You don't like me at all, do you?" she asked, her supple leg extended in midair as she yanked up her stocking.

"You don't like *me*. You only think you're supposed to." I zipped up my wool suit pants over my boxers. "You're projecting your disdain onto me."

She gave her hair a quick comb out with her fingers, fastening her blouse at the same time. "I don't get what you mean."

"Yeah, you do. You think what you're doing with me is bad. That makes you a bad woman. You convince yourself you quote-unquote *like* me, which transforms you into a good woman. A victim of love and all that bullshit."

She slapped me hard across the face.

Just as suddenly, as if she had multiple personalities, she put her hands to her mouth, horrified by what occurred. "I'm sorry," she said. "I overreacted."

I rubbed my jaw where she slapped me. "You always overreact. You wouldn't know what to do if you didn't overreact. On your tombstone, they should write, 'She's overreacting.' But I'm used to it."

"Oh, you . . ." She tisk-tisked, as if resigned to her fate. "Honestly, the things I put up with." For an instant, it was like we were a married couple ourselves.

I put my thumb under her chin and gave her a quick kiss. "You need to go."

"I know, I know." She distractedly reached for her coat and purse. There was a knock at the door.

"Dr. Falcon," said my receptionist. "I'm sorry to interrupt, but your next patient has been waiting now for ten minutes."

"Bring her in."

"It's a *he*, remember?"

"Oh, right. Bring *him* in." I turned to my female patient who had occupied the past hour of my time. "Same time next week, Mrs. Goldstein?"

"Yes, Dr. Falcon. Thank you. I'm really making progress." She winked at me. It was such an obvious, arch wink that she might as well have put up a billboard announcing to the world that we were fucking. Fortunately, my receptionist was one of those modest, not very bright people who had the decency to realize she wasn't very bright, so she never paid attention to anything that wasn't part of her job description.

My next patient was the biggest schmuck I had ever met in my life. It was always the same song and dance about how nobody liked him because he was superior to other people. "My good looks intimidate people," he would say. "And my intellect." I'm not the best judge of male looks, but he seemed to me to be pretty much an average looking young man, and as for "intellect," he read science fiction. Big deal.

Yet even had he been the most riveting conversationalist I had ever encountered, my mind would have been elsewhere. Mrs. Goldstein was becoming a major pain in the ass. My wife, Esther, said she would leave me if I cheated on her again—and what is more, that she would take me for every penny I was worth. Esther herself made good money as an interior designer. In the year since our hasty move cross-country, she'd already landed several upscale clients. But, she said, it was the principle of the thing. The principal of the capital interest was more like it.

What Esther didn't realize, of course, was that when you make an adult feel like some teenager on probation, it isn't long before he starts doing exactly what he isn't supposed to do. She thought she was being *so patient and understanding* to give me another chance after I got in hot water for having an utterly consensual affair with one of my graduate students back at the university. The school wanted the whole thing kept quiet, naturally. No college wants to advertise: "Come to Acme U., where the professors have sex with students." When they fired me, the cover story was that I wanted to "pursue other opportunities." I thought about suing them since I had tenure, but the father of the grad student was a real blabbermouth, and it would have ruined my reputation forever if I made even the slightest wrong move.

Esther and I decided to make a fresh start cross-country. I'd set up a private practice as a psychologist, while Esther would build a design clientele. Fortunately, money was not an issue. We sold our home and income properties for a decent profit, and I also had a solid monthly allowance from my trust fund. It wasn't enough to buy Esther the Hope Diamond, but if business was slow, we could still get by. And, as it happened, business had not been slow at all for either of us. I'd invested my inheritance from my father wisely and conservatively. There was a handy retirement to look forward to. Our one child, Sabrina, recently finished her MFA and was teaching sculpture at a rarified liberal arts college. Finally, she was off the family payroll. Esther may have seen herself as Mrs. Martyrdom, but even when we first dated, I was never faithful to her. She knew what she was getting into. I happened to love sex. Excuse me for breathing. As a psychologist, I knew as well as anybody that supposedly this was indicative of deeper issues, and some people even would've called me a sex addict. But I didn't buy into all that addiction talk. *Everything* was called an addiction. For openers, if there were three hundred million people in the United States, then logically it would follow that there were three hundred million television addicts.

Really, the only problem was Esther. If she wanted to fool around with other men, I wouldn't have minded at all. Occasionally, I wished for a different wife who was into couples swapping and that kind of thing, but that wasn't for me, either. I liked casual sex, and I liked having mistresses. I didn't want Esther involved in what I did with other women. In some cultures, that's considered perfectly normal.

However, mine was not one of those cultures. After years of suffering in what she erroneously called "silence," Esther made her ultimatum. We would start over in a different place, and I would keep my pants zipped up at all times. Literally, at all times. Esther, you see, didn't exactly suffer from nymphomania. She could've worn a T-shirt that read: "I have a headache." We hadn't shared the same bed for years. She claimed it was because she couldn't be vulnerable with me, knowing what I was really like. Vulnerable, schmulnerable, if you ask me. Sex is ecstatic. It's *fun*. What did being vulnerable have to do with it? To me, vulnerable was when you got robbed at gunpoint or had a fatal illness.

I was a good boy for about two weeks. Soon, I started having lunch-hour quickies in hotels with girls who hung around hotels. I fooled around for a month or so with a divorced woman who lived in our neighborhood. One of my patients made a play for *me*, which I resisted for about five minutes before succumbing to my natural urges. Naturally, I did not neglect to say it was a normal phase of the process to be attracted to your therapist. She sensibly decided to terminate treatment, though in a mischievous moment I referred her to a lesbian therapist. (I later saw them holding hands at an outdoor table of a wine bar.) There also was another patient who ended her first session early because she said she felt attracted to me, which was flattering. And another who, after we got it on, threatened to blackmail me, which was not flattering at all. In the end, she said the whole thing was boring her, and she wanted to go live with some guy in Barcelona. She settled for a few thousand, and Esther was none the wiser.

Enter Mrs. Goldstein—or should I say Linda? We had similar marriages, and we also had similar sex drives. I did manage to interject some actual therapy, and anyway, her insurance paid for her visits, so what was the problem? Linda, of course. She started saying how it was hard to have sex with someone without developing deeper feelings, etc. And somehow I was supposed to do something about this. Like what? Divorce Esther and let her take me to the cleaners? And who said I wanted to marry Linda Goldstein? Certainly not I. In her delusional state, Linda believed that the only thing standing in our way were our marriages. That kind of monolithic thinking is never a good sign. The tepid affair was like a snowball rolling down a hill, getting bigger and bigger until no one could control it. Life as I knew it would be over.

"So, Dr. Falcon," said my boring male patient. "What do you think?"

"About what?" I had no idea what he'd been talking about.

He laughed. "You headshrinkers are all the same. Always bringing it back to the patient. Oh, I'm wise to you, all right."

I feigned a cough, for want of anything else to do. "As you were saying?"

"I think I was right to say that if she didn't go out with me, it was her loss."

"Yes, good for you."

As we shook hands good-bye, he reached to give me a hug. I stopped him by patting his shoulder.

My next patient was like an X-ray of the patient before. All his morbid doubts and fears were right there on the surface, all gooey and quasi-suicidal. Everything was always *so* serious. "I honestly do believe in God," he said, in something less than a convincing tone. Unless believing in God made people into zombies.

"Just the other day, some old lady at the pharmacy was screaming about how she was ninety years old, and she shouldn't have to pay for her twenty different prescriptions and how she couldn't open the bottles herself and how nobody cared. And I thought, 'There has to be something more to life than this. There has to be a God.'" After an interminable pause, he added. "What do you think, Doctor Falcon?"

To be honest, I had no idea if there *was* more to life than either dying too young or dying too old. But when you're a shrink, you're supposed to act like you're president of the Life Fan Club.

"What matters is what you think," I offered pleasantly.

"I don't know what to think."

The way he said this, you'd have thought he was saying, "But the sun will be going out for good in a matter of minutes." Maybe what made me a good shrink was this element of detachment. I honestly didn't know why people believed that what they thought was so damn important.

"Well, you've posed the question to yourself. That means you'll find an answer."

"I want my life to mean something, to make a difference."

"It will. Be patient." I smiled warmly. "I'm afraid we're out of time."

Driving home, the traffic was impossible as always. It was well after six by the time I walked in the front door. Our house was spacious and got a lot of sun, and Esther had decorated it with her fanatical good taste. Everything was white or else a very pale color, as if every room was coated in talcum powder. But you couldn't touch this and you couldn't break that, so I never experienced relaxation when I came home.

Esther, who worked a good deal of the time at home, was there to greet me, if you could call it a greeting. "Hello, dear." She smiled as if her teeth were ice cubes and condescendingly offered me her cheek to kiss.

I kissed it. "Hey, babe," I said.

"I already ordered dinner," she said. "Take-out Thai."

"You and your coconut sauce."

"Sweet and savory go well together."

Esther was one of those people who thought every decision she made had to signal her superb taste and urbane demeanor. If she went to heaven when she died, she'd rearrange the clouds. There were times I wished I could analyze her to see if there was a human being beneath the millions of pronouncements she lived by. But there was no way into her. Even if she sat there humming while reading *Architectural Digest*, she seemed to be someplace else.

"Fine. Thai, whatever." I hung up my coat and rummaged through the mail. There was a letter from the grad student I'd left behind, which I was sure Esther already noticed. Not in the mood for rehashing all that, I tore the unopened letter to pieces, which I tossed in the wastebasket like confetti. "Sorry to disappoint you, Esther," I said.

She shrugged quizzically. "I don't know what you mean."

Okay, fine. I was too drained for an argument. Besides, I noticed that a letter from some unfamiliar lender company had arrived by certified mail.

"What's this?" I asked Esther.

"Oh, I signed for it. I have no idea."

Thinking that the certified element was a publicity gimmick—to make sure you would read the contents—I tore open the envelope and read the somber letter within:

Dear Dr. Falcon:

Your current balance of $20,000 plus $1,500 in late penalty fees is now past ninety days overdue. This means that payment is due in full.

You have made no effort to contact us, and we had to locate your new address ourselves. To avoid further action, please pay the amount due in full today. There is a $10 service charge for all payments made online or over the telephone.

"Esther, did you do this?" My day-to-day business matters were handled by my accountant, who happened to be my kid brother. I knew I could trust him. Every business quarter, he sent me a breakdown of my finances down to the penny.

Esther reached for her designer reading glasses and studied the letter. "Of course not. You know I don't spend that kind of money without talking to you first." That much was true. Maybe because it was her job to buy other people pretty things, Esther shopped for our own home only as needed. Once a room was done, it was done. And she wasn't extravagant when it came to things like travel, clothes, food, or jewelry, either. She didn't live like a pauper, but she was the same sensible girl I married straight out of prep school twenty-five years earlier. Having grown up around money—and a family who conservatively hoarded every penny—she found extravagance to be vulgar.

But you know? I couldn't help noticing the unusual satisfaction she took in the letter—the way she scrunched her mouth to keep from smiling. I was a bad person in her eyes, so I deserved to have bad things happen to me. Hers was a classic passive-aggressive personality. She left it to the rest of the universe to condemn me for my wrongs against her. Over the years, I occasionally dreamt that she'd poisoned me, and then I'd wake up and see her at the breakfast table, drinking her coffee and staring into space.

The Thai food arrived. I didn't feel like eating. I called the credit company instead.

"Hello, my name is Tiffany, may I have your account number please?"

"Good evening, Tiffany," I said. "I'd be happy to." I thought I would keep things as friendly as possible, to get them straightened out quickly. I always imagined people who worked at these kinds of jobs to be like nasty kids in a reform school, who would do all sorts of nonsense if they didn't like you.

After I rattled off the incoherent account number on the letter, Tiffany read what was obviously a generic message on her computer screen. She read aloud in a choppy, phonetic style, over-pronouncing her words as if she had no idea what they meant. "Please be informed that your account is over ninety days past due. If you do not make a payment immediately, legal action may result. The total amount you owe is—"

"Yes, but you see, I don't owe this money. It's a mistake—"

Tiffany would not be deterred. "The amount you owe is twenty thousand dollars, plus one thousand five hundred dollars in late penalty fees, plus a fifty dollar service charge. How will you be making a payment this evening?"

"I won't be making any payment because I never spent the money. I don't even know who you people are. And I've never been late with a bill in my life."

"Are you saying, sir, that you are not Dr. Jesse Falcon?" She read off my social security number, my former address, and my current address.

"Yes, but I sold that other property *before* you say my account was opened. I can prove it. Really, it wasn't me."

"One moment, please." She put me on hold. Annoyingly, there was a recording of someone like Robert Goulet singing, "The Impossible Dream."

After what seemed an eternity, Tiffany came back on the line. "I spoke to my supervisor, sir. She said we could mark your account as 'pending further investigation.' This means that what you need to do is show us proof that this account was never yours. Things like cancelled checks with your signature, proof of address, and a notarized letter will help. You may want to speak with an attorney, though hopefully that will not be necessary. You will have thirty days to provide us with this information."

"Thirty days from *when*?" The letter, though it just arrived, was dated ten days earlier.

"From today," she said brightly, which I took as a good omen.

"So you will not contact me in the meantime?" Though I had nothing to hide, threatening certified letters were a hassle I could live without, not to mention that I didn't want to have to explain all this again to some other minimum wage ninny.

"No, sir, we will not."

After getting off the phone, I ate some room temperature Thai food in silence. Esther was equally taciturn in the living room, looking over some possible sofa fabrics for a client.

The next morning, I was not at all pleased to see Linda waiting for me at my office. "I have to talk to you," she said.

"Mrs. Goldstein, you are not scheduled until next week."

I looked meaningfully at my receptionist, who said, "I know, Doctor, I already reminded her."

"Doctor, please, this is an emergency." Linda hissed through clenched teeth.

"Very well," I sighed. "But my nine o'clock should be here soon."

I didn't know what to expect from Linda, but as soon as I closed my office door to find out, my receptionist buzzed me, stating I had an urgent call.

"Hello, my name is Mark," said the voice from the credit company. "I am calling to collect a debt—"

"Mark, look at my account," I said, in a more forceful tone than the night before. "It should say, 'pending further investigation.'" I went on about my talk with Tiffany, and how I would be sending out the materials requested.

"Yes, I am familiar with accounts pending further investigation. But I see no PFI designation on your record."

"No *what?*"

Linda nuzzled me; I pushed her away in annoyance.

"PFI—pending further investigation."

"That's impossible."

"Sir, all I am showing is that your account is over ninety days past due. How would you like to make a payment today?"

"I'm calling my lawyer." I slammed down the phone. "Now, *Mrs. Goldstein*, what do you have to tell me?" I nearly shouted.

Linda stared incredulously. "Why are you being mean? I've left Marty."

I could all but see my insides crash to the floor. Marty was her husband of twenty years. "What do you mean, left him? You mean you're maybe thinking about possibly leaving him?"

"No, I mean I left him. I told him last night it was over. That I'd found someone else." She wiped away her tears and blew her nose into a Kleenex.

"And who did you say this someone else was?" I grabbed her arm so hard she begged me to let go. But I didn't.

"I didn't tell him, I swear." She twisted free of my grip, rubbing her arm in self-pity. "Marty said he would *kill* this other guy." She feebly and nervously touched my cheek.

I felt like she was crowding me, and resisted.

"Why are you mad at me, Jesse?"

Clearly, things were not going as she expected. Yet as she nuzzled her leg against mine, damn it if I didn't get aroused.

"Look, Linda, do what you want with your life, but I'm not interested in changing mine. Do you get it?"

"Of course, Dr. Falcon."

We both laughed in spite of ourselves.

"Okay, we have maybe five minutes." I loosened my belt. "But after today, this is *it*, do you understand?"

"Of course, Dr. Falcon."

She unzipped my fly and got down on her knees.

The instant I was done, she walked a few feet to my office water cooler and drank two mini-cups of cold water, one right after the other. Some women found the taste of semen repulsive, which always annoyed me. If they liked giving blowjobs so much, what was the big deal? It made no sense.

"I'm pregnant," Linda said.

"Somehow I knew that was coming." As I caught my breath, I turned away from her and looked out at the city. "I want nothing to do with it. Assuming it's mine."

In a fury, she threw her wet paper cup at me, though it landed only inches in front of her. "Who the hell else's would it be? My dumbfuck *husband's*? Christ, give me some credit. Rubbers aren't a hundred percent, as I'm sure you are old enough to know."

"Don't ruin my carpeting. Look, I'll pay for half the abortion. Deal?" I offered my hand hopefully.

"Abortion? *Abortion?*" She narrowed her eyes as if she suddenly was this great moralist.

"Yes, abortion. As in, terminating an unwanted pregnancy. Ever hear of it before?"

"I'm having this fucking baby, damn it. I'm not getting any younger, and this is my one chance for happiness."

"So go and be happy. But not on my dime."

In the end, I needed my receptionist plus the building security guard to remove Linda from my office. She alternated between cursing me out and crying like a helpless baby every step of the way, but luckily for me she never spilled the beans about the kid. I hoped against hope that she took the hint that I had no intention of becoming a father again.

I got two more calls that day from the stupid credit people. So I called my brother, my lawyer, and the police. Before long, the situation degenerated into a limbo of endless and contradictory letters and phone calls, each more pissy than the one before.

From my brother, I learned that someone claiming to be me got that damn twenty thousand dollar credit line, put it into my account, and withdrew the money. But there were what the cops called additional legal complications to the case that they would not specify. Then there was a tug of war between my local police and the police where I used to live as to whose jurisdiction it was. Soon the FBI got involved. Then the FBI got uninvolved. One day I got a voice mail from the out-of-state police saying they had apprehended the person who did it, but when I called to find out who it was they said there was no record of this and I must have misunderstood the message. The most I could get out of the local police was that there were several persons of interest but not enough evidence to prosecute anyone. I called my lawyer about the possibility of suing all the cops and the FBI for incompetence, but he talked me out of it.

"Be patient," he told me. "They'll find who did it. Give them a chance to build their case. Besides, the debt's been removed from your account. They know it wasn't you who spent the money."

Everyone—even Linda Goldstein—kept saying this to me, until I wanted to strangle somebody. "Let's see how *you* feel if it happens to you!" I screamed at my lawyer. "It's like . . . it's like a form of rape. Someone thinks they can use my good name to get money that doesn't belong to them. What if he does it again?"

"Jesse, I think you're taking this a wee bit over the top. Would you really rather get raped than lose a few bucks? Yes, a *few* bucks, given your total net worth. And anyway, you didn't even lose any money."

"Fuck you. Fuck everyone." I hung up on him.

Since the address the credit people had was that of a condo we'd used as income property before selling it, I wondered if the crazy old lady I sold it to was involved. According to the cops, she wasn't.

"She's quite a character," said one of the officers. "Every time we talked to her, she'd raise her right hand and swear that she'd never stolen anything in her life. She has all these bumper stickers on her car about supporting your local police. There's a record of her filing a report with the postal service that she wasn't receiving some of her mail. We're not sure she even understands the situation."

Next came the real kick in the balls. It turned out that since I myself did not lose any money and because I didn't owe the credit jerk-offs anything, the entire case was dropped.

"Keep an eye on your finances at all times," said the local police, inanely. "Maybe the identity thief will strike again."

I was so pissed off I could hardly see. I wanted to say something like, "No, I think I'll sit back and let this scumbag drive me to the homeless shelter." But I managed to contain myself, and said instead, "Yes, I'll speak to my brother, my accountant, and make sure nothing fishy happens." As if I hadn't already done this.

Someone pretended to be me. I could scarcely comprehend how angry it made me.

Whoever it was, I hated him so much that I would get up in the middle of the night and pace the floors in rage, fantasizing things like setting his body on fire or stapling his dick to a desk. I knew he had to be some lowlife scum. Sometimes I even imagined killing his whole family in righteous punishment. Maybe I'd saw off their heads. Maybe I'd keep the identity thief alive. He'd have to live with his guilt. They probably were all on drugs, on welfare, on everything that spoiled life for decent people like me.

From her separate bedroom, Esther either slept through my torment, or would care only to the extent that I had woken her up by walking too loudly or knocking something over.

"Damn it," she would say, "you're a shrink. Surely you must know how to handle this better than you're doing?"

"Eat shit," I'd reply. "This is the worst thing that's ever happened to me."

"If that's true, then you really are a spoiled little piece of shit."

"Ha! Look who's talking about being spoiled. When have you ever had to worry about anything in your shitty life?"

"For starters, when my husband fucked everything on the planet with tits."

"Oh, yada, yada, yada."

In the middle of all this was some asinine shrink conference that I'd already arranged to attend. Everyone wore name tags—I hate name tags—and scurried about like millions of amoebas. I couldn't begin to concentrate on what any of the speakers were saying. Listening to some idiot drone on in a carpeted hotel stateroom, I experienced true claustrophobia for the first time in my life. I could feel my damp, white dress shirt sticking to my stomach.

There was a speaker whose English was incomprehensible, but everyone had to soberly nod as he spoke, as if we understood a single word. Finally someone else got up to speak. With a big smarmy smile, he began by saying how he didn't need a mic because he was sure everyone could hear him. For some reason speakers were always saying that, as if it made them superior beings who were *so self-confident* speaking in front of groups.

I stood up, wiping the copious sweat from my forehead. "Yeah, we hear you all right," I said. "But why don't you shut the fuck up?"

The room was silent as I took my leave. I spent the rest of the conference in my hotel room, watching stupid TV shows and drinking scotch straight out of the bottle. I didn't even try to find a whore, that's how lousy I felt.

Hardly adding to my bliss was the omnipresence of Linda Goldstein. The absurd thing was, she was still my patient. She refused to terminate treatment or accept a referral and threatened to report me to the APA if I didn't let her see me once a week.

"How have you been since last week?" I asked her on one such occasion, my voice filled with sarcasm.

"Oh, simply dandy," she replied, with a malicious, exaggerated smile. "I'm a forty-year-old woman soon to be divorced, pregnant by another man who wants nothing to do with me. Oh, and did I forget to mention that if the divorce doesn't settle PDQ I'll get nothing because the ol' tummy will start to bulge, and Marty's lawyer will bust me for adultery? What am I supposed to say, that I accidentally swallowed a watermelon?"

I firmly leaned forward in my swivel chair. "You could tell your husband the child is his and propose a reconciliation, Mrs. Goldstein."

"Or you could tell your frigid, asshole wife that she's going to be a stepmama."

I rolled my eyes in exasperation. "I've told you like a gazillion times that Esther will take me to the cleaners if she finds out I've been cheating again. The best I can do is skim a few grand off the top. She's not dumb, you know."

"Why no, she's a genius. After all, she married *you*."

"Linda, in all seriousness, what are you going to do? If you take me to court, I lose everything, and you won't get a dime."

"There's your *future* income, smarty-pants." She crossed her arms smugly, as if having played the ace of spades. "And anyway, maybe you can hire a better lawyer than Esther and not lose your shirt, like you keep saying."

"You don't know Esther."

"Thank God for small miracles."

I could feel my face fluster. "Can't you leave me alone*?*"

"No. I love you." Linda jutted out her chin in defiance. Apparently, part of her neurosis was that she literally believed love conquered all.

I stomped over to her, not sure what I would do, but too angry to sit still. As she recoiled, Linda fell over backward in her chair. I did not bother to help her up. For whatever reason, she set the chair back in its place before standing to face me.

"That chair cost me a lot of money," I said. "Be careful with it."

I thought she would cry. Instead she started screaming at me. It was like, flip a coin, will it be crying or screaming? "How could you hit me? I'm *pregnant*, damn it. And with your bloodline, the loin of your flesh."

"I *didn't* hit you. Hello, we live in the physical dimension of the universe. This is a desk, this is a chair—"

"No, but you were going to hit me, I could tell."

She came at me, aimlessly flailing both fists. I easily grabbed her hands and held them hard. "See what a sick fuck I am?" I hissed at her. "Do you really want to be with me?"

There was a moment of showdown between our eyes.

"No, I guess not." Her icy tone came as a relief. She let go and gathered up her purse and coat.

Glory Hallelujah, she was finally getting the message.

"You always win, don't you?" she said, as though I'd done something illegal.

"Yeah, right. My life is one great victory after another. I reign supreme over time and space." I reached in my desk for a bottle of whiskey and took a swallow. I hated that stupid desk. It was this steel and glass contraption that only had one drawer. But Esther had picked it out because it was very trendy, and I guess even though she hated my guts, I deserved nothing but the best. "Let's hear it for me."

"You really are a prick." Linda gave me the finger.

"This session is on the house," I called after her, as she took her leave.

I felt the relief you feel when a bad tooth gets extracted. The worst was over—or so it seemed—but I still needed to heal. Apropos of this, I went to a fine hotel, found a girl, did what I had to do, and was the better for it.

For dinner that night, Esther served take-out Indian. She kept complaining that the food was neither spicy enough nor sweet enough, to which I replied that perchance the food was hinting at something in regard to Esther herself. She picked up a full container of *pindi chana* and threw it at me. Fortunately, I ducked out of the way. Esther always stormed off to her bedroom and slammed the door shut. I was supposed to go running after her and beg her to let me in to talk to her. Well, that worked for about ten years before I got sick of it.

In hindsight, the most obvious characteristic about Esther was her lack of spontaneity. Everything she said or did was premeditated somehow, even if only a split second in advance. She was incapable of manslaughter; only first-degree murder would do for her. Not that she murdered anyone exactly, though hopefully you get the idea. Had I noticed this sooner, my life would've turned out much differently.

For the moment, all I could do was look at the mess of jazzed up chickpeas on the floor. I wondered how long Esther would brood before she came downstairs to clean up the mess she had made.

3: AKA JESSE FALCON

ONCE YOU STEP INSIDE the door called "Crime," all sorts of things happen to you.

It'd been a few months since I stole Jesse Falcon's ID for money, plus covered up Biff's death, which I kept telling myself didn't count as a crime. But that was only the beginning. I never had a dull moment again.

Late that first morning at my mom's condo, I went to a divorce lawyer. Someone back at 21st Century had praised her divorce attorney, so I figured I'd try the same one. Plus the lawyer in question, R. Ondine Washington, was a woman, and I hoped that would create sympathy for me in court. I didn't even call to make an appointment. I put on a suit and tie and went straight to Ondine's office. I was too anxious about Scotty to wait. I told Mom to take good care of him and to hide him if she had to. She replied that I didn't have to tell her that and to stop treating her like an idiot. Of course, she thought I only meant that Biff or Betsy might come for him. I wondered if I would ever tell her what Scotty did.

But I also left the condo because I had too much nervous energy to burn. I'm one of those people who, once in a stressful situation, will deal with it sooner instead of later. When people say to me, "Don't worry about such-and-such, it's not today's problem," I have no idea what they mean. How do you sit back and watch TV when your world is falling apart? Not that I was scared, exactly. Oddly, I seemed stronger than I ever had before. It reminded me of those vampire movies, when someone reluctantly drinks blood for the first time and it makes them wise and powerful in a way they never knew possible. After a lifetime of always losing by following the rules, I thought that by breaking them, I might win for a change. For once, I'd give my bad guy side a chance to show what he could do.

There was a secretary posted in front of Ondine's office, but Ondine's door was half-open, and I could see she was eating a sandwich, her stocking feet up on the desk. I ignored the secretary's warning not to enter Ondine's office, and Ondine herself gave me an icy scowl as she said, "Yes, may I help you?"

I mentioned my former work colleague, who turned out to be a personal friend of Ondine's. Her next appointment was not due for a half hour, so before long, we were talking like old friends. She even offered me half her sandwich, which I politely declined. Ondine was a pleasant-looking, plus-sized woman with an easy laugh and a razor-sharp knowledge of divorce law. I liked her right away. The most prominent feature of her office was a large poster of Sojourner Truth.

I left out the minor detail of Biff being dead. I almost slipped up and said he was going to the Bahamas, though I caught myself in time. As far as Ondine knew, Betsy and Biff could've been screwing the daylights out of each other that very moment.

She did, however, shake her head in disgust when I told her about Biff and Scotty and scolded me loudly for not paying better attention as a father. However, Ondine added that a couple of police detectives owed her a favor, and she would have them put a tail on Biff without mentioning Scotty's name.

"Attorney-client privilege," she said. "But obviously this creep can't keep diddling around with children."

"Of course not," I agreed. But I quickly realized this could complicate Biff's disappearance in a fortunate way for Scotty and me. The cops were unlikely to drop everything to figure out who killed a child molester. And Biff's parents would probably rather see him missing or dead than bringing this kind of publicity to the family name.

"I know some reporters, too." Ondine winked at me.

Thus far, Betsy had not called my mom about Scotty. Probably Betsy was too busy shopping on TV for something to wear when her beloved Biff returned to her loving arms. But I knew Betsy well enough to know that at some point she would strike back with all the might she could muster. She seldom retreated into a defensive mode. Instead, she kept the offenses coming, even if they were totally untrue. Winning, to her, was more important than how she played the game. Still, Ondine gave me more than a little reason to hope.

"As the father of record," she explained, "the laws of our state give you a certain toehold. Normally the biological father can still make a strong case, especially if he is now cohabitating with the biological mother. Even if Biff denies the sexual abuse, he certainly won't want it coming up at trial. And if the cops find other kids he's abused, that will pretty much be that. I doubt Scotty will have to testify."

Ondine stretched and yawned. "As for you, my good client, ever hear of getting a job yourself? Not to mention a place to live. Your mother's condo is too small for the three of you. Though I assume Grandma loves to babysit?"

"As long as she can watch pro wrestling. I already told you, I *have* been trying to find a job. For over a year, ever since I got laid off."

Ondine was unsympathetic in a way that nonetheless communicated that she cared. "You know computers, right? Set up your own online business."

"In what?"

"In whatever. Keep it clean. No Russian prostitutes. It shouldn't cost more than a hundred to be convincing. And maybe you'll make some money. Fancy that."

"When you say, 'a hundred,' do you mean—?"

"A hundred thousand, of course."

I could tell the question did not interest her. I hoped my fear did not show. "Oh . . . why, yes, of course. I can do that. Thank you for thinking of it."

"And as for a place to live, first let's see what we can do about the house. Maybe we can use it as a bargaining chip."

"Sure, maybe." But in truth I was disgusted at the thought of Betsy "trading" Scotty for the house. Even if she would do it, I didn't like what it said about the mother of my son.

"And as for Scotty," Ondine continued, "I will contact Miss Betsy Wetsy and tell her that you are filing for sole custody. By the time there's an initial hearing in a week or two—let's say a month at the most—make sure you have a lil' ol' income. Or at least be credibly moving in that direction."

"Ondine, I swear, you must be an angel." I had no idea how I was going to pull it together, but of course I couldn't tell her that.

"I wouldn't go that far." She smiled. "Although my retainer is only thirty."

Having caught on to the lingo, I knew " thirty" meant thirty grand. I had to think fast.

"Tell you what, Ondine," I said, without missing a beat. "Let's call it twenty grand now, and I'll have the rest by the end of the month. Most everything is tied up. You know—Betsy, one thing or another."

I think she knew I was full of it, but she let it slide. Money messes were doubtless a common occurrence for a divorce lawyer.

"Sure," she said. "And the full thirty no later than this Friday. The end of the month is too long to wait. Otherwise, I keep five, and give you back fifteen." Fortunately, it was a Monday, and when you're truly desperate, a full business week to get it together can seem like a gold-paved path with a rainbow at the end.

"By the way," she added, "I only take certified checks."

For some reason, her insistence on an honest check was the first time I felt guilty about what I'd done. My shoulders gave a quick shiver, which I hoped she didn't notice.

"I'm here until four every day," Ondine said indifferently. "Fix the knot on your tie."

I obeyed as I took my leave, saying to the secretary, "It's a nice day, don't you think?" I figured it best not to alienate anyone who might have to be on my side. The secretary feigned intense concentration on her computer, ignoring me.

About a block away was a new branch of the new national bank Jesse Falcon had his accounts in on the other side of the country. The bank had changed ownership so many times that the previous bank—now defunct—was still featured on the awning, while the new bank had to make do with a paper banner in the front window. Unless through some bizarre coincidence the teller I got happened to know the real Jesse Falcon, there was no reason for the teller to think I wasn't Dr. Falcon. Every day, thousands of people passed themselves off as someone else. Why shouldn't I be one of them?

Still, I was nervous as I opened the glass door to enter and hoped to God it didn't show. In a way, I empathized with the fine old building, with its high, copper ceiling. It was as though one hostile bank takeover after another had cost the building its dignity.

"I need to see ID," the teller said, after I asked for a bank check for twenty thousand and showed her a printout of my approved credit line.

Naturally, I'd expected to be asked for ID. And all I had was a photocopy of Jesse's birth certificate, which was not officially stamped. But time was of the essence. I figured I had nothing to lose by trying. Besides, I'd already worked out a cover story or two in my head. Ironically, now that I was a criminal I was finally using my psychology training. Quickly studying the teller—a middle-aged, sympathetic, lonely looking woman with no wedding band—I decided how to proceed. I intuitively knew that a cover story should not be overly rehearsed. Improvisation came in handy if you had your wits about you.

I smiled warmly as I handed her the birth certificate. "Please don't take this the wrong way, ma'am, but you remind me so much of my mother."

She studied the photocopied birth certificate, but I could tell I'd pleased her. "Surely this isn't all you have?" She grinned back at me.

"Someone stole my ID." I leaned forward, as if taking her into my confidence. "Someone is writing bad checks in my name. The police were no help—"

"No, they never are, are they?" She shook her head in sympathy.

"I guess not, no." I smiled with a sad irony. "I desperately need money to cover myself. That's why I got this emergency credit line. If you bring up my record, you'll see I have a spotless credit history. Until now." I ran my fingers through my hair to signal a touch of despair and got all choked up, as if ready to cry. "My wife is pregnant. With *twins*. We *need* this money."

Deeply moved, the teller patted my hand in a motherly way that my own mother never did. "Well, I really shouldn't . . . but

what the heck. You have an honest face. Let me see the birth certificate." She smiled understandingly. For several tedious minutes I
stood there while she photocopied the birth certificate, withdrew
the money for the check, painstakingly counted it twice, gave me
a receipt, gave me back my own copy of the birth certificate, and
typed up the certified check I requested. I had to repeat how to
spell "Ondine," which rattled my nerves. I wanted to get out of
the bank as soon as possible. But then, I would've been anxious if
the story I'd told her had been true, so I hammed it up a bit more.
Then she got a phone call, which lasted less than a minute though
it felt like a hundred years.

"Here you are, Dr. Falcon." The teller handed me the check.
"And best of luck. From your mom."

For a second, I didn't know what she meant, until I remembered what I'd said.

"Thank you so very much," I replied, glancing at her name-
plate. "Lizabetty, I am forever in your debt. Or should I say
Mom?" Having methodically practiced Jesse Falcon's pompous
signature, I signed the check in the teller's presence and neatly
folded it in my suit coat pocket.

I was a far better liar than I'd ever known I was, probably because I'd never really lied much before. It was as if at birth everyone was awarded a certain number of lies they could use through
life, and since I was only beginning to tap into my supply, it was
in mint condition.

A very attractive girl stood near me as I walked toward the
exit door. She had exceptionally beautiful long hair. But I made
a point of not noticing her much, in case my old friend the teller
was watching. The door was all of twenty feet away, and I knew
I'd feel immensely relieved once I made it outside.

There was a loud bang. All the bank chatter instantly stopped. For a fleeting, hopeful instant I thought it might have been a flat tire or fireworks. But obviously—as Scotty would have said—there were no fireworks or flat tires in banks. With a terrible sinking feeling, I realized it was a gunshot. It sounded like it was aimed at the ceiling.

"On the floor!" I heard a voice cry out, and as I instinctively obeyed, I saw three men in ski masks sporting machine guns. The pretty girl was lying near me; our eyes met. The door, the wondrous glass door that meant freedom, was maybe ten impossible feet away from me. Technically, it was the second time that day that someone was trying to kill me.

A security guard took aim at one of the thieves and was immediately shot down in a deluge of bullets. The poor guy jerked about as if he was being electrocuted, and his blood splattered in all directions. I got a sticky spray of red on my suit sleeve, and it gave off a salty smell.

"Give us all your money," said one of the robbers to the terrified customers, waving around his machine gun while one of his partners approached the tellers. Lizabetty, the teller who helped me, called the robber a hooligan and attacked his face with pepper spray. But her timing was off, and the robber shot her down. Another female teller in the next window burst into tears while the third robber was shown his way inside the bank vault by yet another woman who I assumed was a bank officer.

Fuck, I thought, with the machine gun poised an inch from my face. I handed over the check.

"Damn it," said the robber. "What do I look like, a check-cashing service? I want *cash*. Clean, no-fucking-around cash." He said this as if I were a delivery boy who brought him the wrong sandwich from the deli. "Goddamn certified bank check. Sit up. Are you a cop?"

I felt like I was in one of those dreams in which you need to speak, but you can't. "Uh, no," I managed to muster, scrambling to sit.

"Now stand up." He pointed the gun a fraction away from my nose, and again, I immediately obeyed. "Me and you are going to cash this here check."

Since he and his pals were already robbing the bank vault, I didn't see why he needed to cash my check so badly, but I guessed that twenty grand was, after all, twenty grand. Maybe, too, he wanted to prove he was in charge.

I almost tripped over one of the people lying down as the robber led me relentlessly by the necktie to the teller's window. The crying teller trembled as she took the check and gave the robber twenty grand plus everything else in her drawer. The teller methodically gave me a slip of paper, which I signed, "Dr. Jesse Falcon." I was careful to use Jesse Falcon's writing style. Then she stamped the check "void."

"A doctor, huh? Guess your fancy-shmancy wife ain't gettin' no mink coat after all," the robber said, pleased with his sarcasm.

"No, I guess not." I didn't know if he wanted me to smile—kind of one guy to another—but I decided not to.

"Hey, what are you lookin' at?"

"Nothing, nothing at all." Yet in spite of everything, I was looking toward the pretty girl. Though a total stranger, she seemed the one source of comfort in the world.

"You're really full of lip," said the bank robber. "Mr. Fancy-Talk Doctor."

It's hard to know what to say or do when a machine gun is

pointed at you, but the task is not made easier when the conversation doesn't even make sense. In truth, I'd said almost nothing, so how was I to keep this lunatic from killing me? I had a fleeting memory of a grade school bully who used to do this—he'd say anything to keep you off guard and scared.

"I, uh . . . um, I'm sorry."

"*Sorry?* Don't make me laugh. You rich doctors—you're never sorry for anything."

He aimed his gun, and I heard a ringing in my ears that seemed to drown out all other sounds. Time seemed to no longer exist. A burning pain came so intense I had to leave my body to escape it. My teeth chattered from a coldness that seemed to permeate the entire world, and I knew I was dying or maybe was already dead.

"Dr. Falcon?"

I was so weak that merely opening my eyes felt like I'd just finished the decathlon. It took a while to adjust to the light; in fact, it actually hurt. There seemed to be vague blotches of ugly colors everywhere, as if refuse from a nightmare had fallen off a phantom garbage truck. In the background was a terrible noise of people scurrying around. I wanted it to stop.

"I'm not Dr. Anybody," I hoarsely managed to whisper. Whoever was speaking to me said, "Hmm. There's no indication of memory loss on the chart." As I turned to look, I saw it was some sort of doctor or nurse; it took an extra moment to focus enough to tell that it was a woman. I figured she was a doctor because nurses usually were not this detached in how they spoke to you. But what was I doing here?

Then I remembered. Identity theft, bank robbers, gunshots. "Yes, I'm Dr. Falcon."

"Do you know where you are?"

"I'm guessing a hospital. It doesn't look much like heaven."

"Yes, quite amusing." The woman faked an unconvincing grin. "According to your chart, you are very lucky. Of the four bullets that struck you, only one struck major organs. Two bullets were removed from your buttocks and the last grazed your elbow. That was three days ago. Your stomach and spleen were salvageable, but you will be on a restricted diet for one month. You should be able to go home in a week." She looked at me as though I should kiss her feet for bothering with me. "Any questions?"

I rubbed my sore elbow. "Yeah, as a matter of fact. How'd I get shot twice in the ass?"

"Because God is just." It was the unmistakable voice of Mom, who'd entered the room—that is to say, my curtained-off half of the room. "And you never could tell your ass from your elbow."

"I'll be going now," said the indifferent doctor.

I was connected to a bunch of tubes and monitors, but the first thing my mom did when we were alone was punch me in the nose. "How dare you," she began, "stick me and your own son—your *own son*—in such a crapper full of shit." She double-checked that the bed on the other side of the curtain was empty.

"I—"

"Don't even start with me. Don't even *try*." She sat down on the one chair and took out a Butterfinger candy bar from her purse. "No, you can't have any," she said, reading my thoughts. "You have to eat all this fucked up shit like farina for the next month. Serves you right. But I wouldn't give you some anyway. I don't give candy to two-bit criminals."

I realized I'd turned a corner in my life because instead of feeling nothing but guilty for having been caught, I was equally curious to know how much she knew. "What do you mean, Mom?"

"That 'Who, me?' look didn't work when you were five years old, and it doesn't work now. What made you think you could steal someone's identity? And the asshole who used to own my own home? How stupid are you?"

I was relieved that at least she didn't know about Biff. "Did you—?"

"Of course I didn't tell the cops." She angrily munched on her chocolate. "Oh, great. You think your own mother is a snitch. Even when you were teething like there was no tomorrow, I let you suck the milk from my tits. And look at the thanks I get. Am I a canary? Do I flap my yellow wings and sing away the day to the cops?"

Despite how rotten I felt, I was salivating for a bite of candy bar. "But how did you figure all this out?"

She finished the last bite and tossed the crumbled wrapper in the wastebasket. "With something called a brain, though I realize you were born without one. I knew you went to see that shyster lawyer. When you didn't come home by evening, I called her. She said you went to the bank. The TV was going bananas over this big local bank robbery, so I figured it was just your lousy luck to be there. At first I thought you were stupid enough to rob the damn place. But I figured I should find out what was what before asking the cops anything. I looked up the last web pages you went to on your computer. Yep, that's right. You, the great computer whiz, didn't delete the wookie-cookies or whatever the hell they call them. Dr. Jesse Falcon! Are you nuts? They told me you were here. Anyway, I called the nephew of this nice lady who's my neighbor. He works for the crummy town newspaper, and he told me that Dr. Jesse Fuckhead Falcon was shot in the bank robbery. One of those bank robbers was turning you into

Swiss cheese when the cops broke in and shot him right through his dumbfuck head. That's what saved you. A teller ID'd you as the Good Doctor. When you're out of this dumpy hospital, you should light a candle in a house of worship and thank the good Lord God."

"Where's Scotty?"

"With me, you idiot. What did you think, that I sold him to pirates? My neighbor is watching him now. A nice, law-abiding old bag like his grandma. I don't want him seeing you this way. I don't know if he should see you ever again. But his mother is such a fuck, I suppose you're the lesser of two evils." She took out a nail clipper from her purse. "Hold out your hands."

I obeyed, as she clipped my fingernails. "You should always maintain a clean appearance. Surely I raised you to know that much."

"What should I do, Mom?"

"Get the hell out of town, dummy," she replied, cutting my nails neatly to the quick. "Let's see if it blows over. I'll keep Scotty for now. We'll tell him Daddy's busy. It's not like Betsy McBitch is dying to take care of him. We'll tell the lawyer lady that you're setting up a job someplace. I threw your laptop in the trash—in a plastic bag full of Porky's stinking hamster shit and piss litter. If the cops come around, I'll pretend to be some senile old lady. I already complained to the post office about not getting my mail, just in case."

"Uh, what about, you know . . . money?"

"I paid the lawyer her retainer and then some. Why couldn't you take money from me in the first place? I'm your *mother*, damn it. What made you think you could get away with any-thing? Criminals are smart."

I looked at my freshly clipped nails. "I'm smart. You always said so."

"I didn't say it so you'd become a *crook*. I thought you'd be a doctor. Someone who'd take care of his poor, weak mother in her old age. Someone I could've been proud of."

"Apparently I have a strong spleen. Isn't that something to be proud of?" I noticed my morphine drip was running low. I buzzed for the nurse, who quickly filled it back up.

"Are you feeling any better, Dr. Falcon?" asked the nurse.

"He's a dear," Mom answered on my behalf, smiling pleasantly.

"I've never understood your sense of humor," Mom complained, after the nurse left. "Now, Don Knotts, he was funny. Anyway, I have enough money to take care of Scotty. And I'll give you five G's to settle yourself in and find a J-O-B. Then that's *it*. I'm not cashing in another annuity to keep your stupid, penny-ante criminal ass out of the slammer."

"I have to get my stuff."

"Like hell you do. I moved your car to a scrap heap. You'll never see it again and hopefully, neither will the cops. If anything comes addressed to Jesse Falcon, I'll burn it. I already burned your clothes and suitcase, except for one change of clothes, which I left with the nurses. And don't do anything stupid like calling me on your cell phone. One time, your louse of a grandfather—" She stopped herself from continuing.

"What about Granddad?" I sat up in bed, anxious to hear more.

"None of your damn business. Your grandfather is in heaven, where good people go."

"I love you, Mom."

She grunted dismissively. "Yeah, right. Tell it to a pile of dog shit. Tell it to your prison cellmate when he wants to make you his sweet little mama's boy."

The week went by in a haze of morphine drips, nurses male and female who reminded me of flight attendants, and snooty doctors male and female who confused me with other patients.

Technically, I couldn't get discharged without someone to pick me up, but since I supposedly was a doctor myself, the hospital finally relented and said I could go home in a cab. The problem was that I had no home. A nurse helped me get dressed, since I was still in a lot of pain. The same nurse was about to call me a cab.

"Jesse!" a melodious voice called out. I turned, and saw . . . who was it? Oh God, yes. It was that pretty girl at the bank robbery. I recognized her beautiful long hair. A sight for sore eyes, as the old saying goes. Only what the hell was she doing here? I had a passing thought that my mother somehow arranged it to make fun of me later.

"Jesse, thank God you're alive." The girl kissed my cheek. "Is it okay if I give you a hug?"

"Uh, sure." She hugged me warmly but with an awareness of my injuries. "Nurse, I heard you calling a cab. Please cancel it. I'll drive Dr. Falcon home."

When the nurse left, I opened my mouth to ask about a million questions, but the girl beat me to it. "No, of course I don't *know you* know you. And yet, the way we looked at each other during the robbery. I can't explain it—the life and death of it all. It was so . . . so everything all at once. When you got shot . . . I don't even have the words for it. I went to the police and found out your name and that my prayers had been answered. You were still alive. I can't explain it without sounding like some lunatic, but I *had* to see you. And I knew I would."

Out of everything I'd been through, was something positive occurring? Maybe life was a trade-off. Something bad happened—or in my case about a million bad things happened—but then along came something good. Or at least something that *seemed* good, which was more than could be said for Betsy and Biff. I figured I had nothing to lose. Even if I never saw her again, I'd get a free ride from the hospital. Of course, she thought I was Jesse Falcon, and I had no idea how to handle that. But one thing at a time. For now it was simply a free ride home. Or so I told myself.

"By the way, what's your name?"

We both laughed. I didn't know if we were embarrassed or something else.

"Sequoia," she said.

"And does Sequoia have a last name?"

"Falcon, of course." She laughed again. "Just kidding. I'm Sequoia Vargas."

Sportingly, she held out her hand for me to shake. I properly shook it.

"So, Jesse, where is home?"

Good question. Now all I needed to do was invent an answer. "I was house hunting when—you know."

"But where were you staying?"

"With . . . uh, my mother." Talk about a mood breaker.

But Sequoia just smiled; she had a beautiful smile. "Am I right in guessing that Mom is not Miss Congeniality?"

I rolled up my shirtsleeves; it was warm in the hospital, but Mom left me a long-sleeve shirt. "Let's just say getting better is going to be a challenge living with my mother."

"Don't you at least need to get your clothes? Your car?" She felt my forehead to make sure I didn't have a fever.

"No wheels at the moment. And as for my clothes, my mom destroyed them. That's one of the reasons I went to the bank. We had a fight about . . . I guess you might as well know." I sat down on the hard, lumpy hospital bed, gesturing for her to sit next to me. I clasped her hand and mustered up the most sincere expression I could. "Sequoia, I have a seven-year-old son, Frankie"—I didn't want to give her any name that could lead to my real identity—"And I'm separated from my wife. I really *am*. Do you believe me?"

"I probably shouldn't. But yes, I believe you, Jesse."

I turned away, as if in private sorrow. "My mother thinks my soon-to-be ex-wife should have custody of my child. I want custody myself. My wife is . . . I guess I have to say it. She's a heroin addict."

"Oh my God." Sequoia squeezed my hand in sympathy.

"I've told this to my mother a million times, but she doesn't believe me. My wife has her wrapped around her little finger. My mother's very, very traditional. She believes that children belong with their mother, period."

"I think that's very unfair. A child belongs with the best parent." She tenderly rubbed my chest. "By the way, what kind of doctor are you, Jesse? If it's okay to ask."

"That's perfectly all right. I only recently finished my PhD in psychology. I've been job searching. In fact, I missed three interviews because of everything that happened."

Pain pills did little to keep me from getting physically aroused. And for some reason, all the lies I was telling were making me harder and harder. Then, out of nowhere, we fell into a kiss, with that dizzy feeling that makes it seem there is no other choice. It was easily the best kiss I'd ever had. I felt weak and strong at the same time as we made out on the hospital bed. It seemed that my ride home came with a bonus prize.

Sequoia sat up on the bed, combing her hair out of her face with her fingers. "I have a plan," she whispered. "You come home with me. No strings, no expectations. We get you a suit or two for a job. If we end up hating each other's guts, you can look for a new place at the end of the month. Hopefully, you'll have a job by then."

Catching my breath, I feigned deep consideration. "Okay, Sequoia. Sure." I don't know what I would've done had she not made this offer, but I tried to make it seem like I was weighing a dozen different options.

"Oh, Jesse, I don't even have the words. To say I feel wonderfully happy sounds corny, and yet . . ." She put her head to my heart as I stroked her long hair.

Sequoia didn't deserve to be hurt, and I thought about telling her the truth right then and there. Only what if she was some undercover cop? Or at least *went* to the cops after hearing what I did? After all, Sequoia did seem so very, very nice. Like she'd never even had a sip of wine. Like it never occurred to her that people didn't always tell the truth. All my life I'd let my inner good guy rule, and now that I finally met a nice girl, my inner bad guy was in charge. I guess that's why some people are called losers.

Sequoia drove like she was taking a driving test. No speeding past amber warning lights for her. At stop signs, she came to a full stop, looking both ways even at four-way stops. The radio *very* softly played harmless, light pop rock. Still, the ride was an opportunity for her to supposedly learn more about me—where I supposedly did my graduate work, supposedly how I got married—and also for me to find out more about her.

"I was an orphan," she said, pleasantly humming along to the innocuous music. "My parents died when I was nine."

I stroked her knee for want of knowing what else to do.

She stopped at a light about to turn red. In the side mirror, I could see the driver behind us swearing at her.

"I was an only child. I moved in with my aunt and uncle. They had no other children. So they adopted me, and yes, they loved me like their own. I'm sorry if I sound impatient. It's nothing personal, Jesse. Please understand. I've been telling this story all my life, and . . . I don't know, with you, I want to keep things happy. My birth parents would want it, too. People treat me like damaged goods, and I'm tired of it."

"May I ask how they . . . uh, died?"

"There was a fire."

I could see the question made her uncomfortable—even a little impatient, after telling me why she didn't want to go into details. Well, there was plenty of time to talk about the past. And she certainly was more forthcoming than I'd been. "So do you work?" I asked, changing the subject.

"I'm very fortunate. I have a trust fund that my parents set up for me. But I like working with kids. I volunteer at the city children's art center a few days a week."

"That must be fun."

When she turned on her blinker and looked in the rearview mirror to change lanes, her concentration made you think she was flying a space shuttle. "It's very challenging. Kids in the twenty-first century. It's all video games and special effects. It's hard to interest them in the idea that they can draw a picture themselves. The kids I work with have all been labeled slow, or ADD. A couple of Asperger's. A lot of them come from—you know, not very nice families."

"I see," I offered sympathetically. "You must be a patient person. Patient and giving."

Sequoia was distracted, though. "A parking place! Have I died and gone to heaven?"

We parked in front of a building that was a plain, five-story rectangle; I was seeing that Sequoia disliked anything fussy. Still, it was in an upscale neighborhood. It also was in the dead center of the city, and as my mom seldom left the suburban tranquility of her condo, it was unlikely she'd bump into me. She lived about a half hour away, but it might as well have been on the moon.

As Sequoia got her mail in the lobby, I noticed that her name was not on her mailbox in the foyer. "Is that on purpose?" I asked. "You know, keeping your name off the mailbox?" In a fit of protectiveness, I wanted to lecture her on identity theft, of all things.

Sequoia sighed, sorting through what appeared to be a typical day's assortment of bills and junk mail. "Reporters. To this day, they hound me." She paused at an envelope.

I saw that Sequoia's name and address were handwritten, though there was no return address.

"Oh, no," she said. "Not again."

My slightly sinking feeling at the thought of getting within a million miles of a reporter gave way to concern. "What's wrong?" I asked.

She flashed her beautiful smile. "Nothing. An old nuisance, that's all. Go ahead and look around," she said, as we entered her apartment. "I trust you. I need to finish reading my mail."

The apartment featured white walls with black furniture that had white accents or black walls with white furniture that had black accents. I'm no interior designer, but I couldn't help noticing the complete absence of colors. Nothing was even gray or tan. Her own artwork on the walls consisted of black-and-white lithographs; her salt-and-pepper shakers were white and black, respectively. For that matter, I realized she was wearing a white blouse with a black skirt and black high heels. I sneaked a peek into her clothes closet, and sure enough, everything was black, white, or black and white.

"Cool pad." I smiled at her as she sat at the white desk in the living room.

"I'm nuts for black and white, in case you were wondering," Sequoia said cheerfully. "I even try to *eat* black and white. White asparagus, never green. White seafood and poultry or else beef charbroiled to black. Black and white sundaes. Marble cake."

I sat on the white couch. "That's . . . uh, interesting."

"I know exactly what you're thinking." She sat down close to me and put my arm around her. "That it's some sort of weird thing because of my parents." Before I could speak, she added, "Look, I've been in therapy. I'm not OCD or XYZ or anything else. For your information, I've *always* preferred black and white. It's who I am."

"Sounds good enough for me." I kissed her passionately, and she responded. By the time the long, deep kiss ended, I was a pile of mush. Somewhere in the corridors of memory was my mother's admonishment for me to move far away, but I couldn't begin to consider leaving Sequoia for a second.

"Should we make love now, or are you hungry?"

I had the passing thought that she asked what had to be the happiest question a man could be asked. "I can only eat farina for a month."

"It's white, what a happy coincidence. I'll spoon feed you like a little baby." She quirked an eyebrow in a cute, dirty way.

We went at it three times in three different ways in less than an hour. With Betsy, I was lucky to get it three times a decade. Wasn't there some old saying about how it's the nice women who were the most ravenous in bed? Sequoia was solicitous of my wounds whenever we changed positions; I literally thought I might cry. In the haze of making love and pain pills, I slipped in and out of a dream in which Sequoia would reach into my gunshot wound and pull out a baby, a little girl we named Jessica. I know that must sound weird and gross, but the dream itself was beautiful.

Sequoia nudged me and fought to catch her breath. "I guess we should take you clothes shopping. After that, we'll pick up some farina at the market around the corner."

"Sounds like a plan." She stood up, innocently naked, and padded her way to the master bathroom. "I like to bathe alone. I hope you don't mind."

"Whatever." I lay in bed, savoring the ecstatic aftermath. A newspaper on the nightstand caught my attention. I read the headline story, "Counter Spy Ring Grows Larger." Big surprise. There was some huge corruption scandal in the federal government, and all sorts of lifers in the CIA turned out to be selling secrets for years to China and the Middle East.

Suddenly, I had an idea.

Ondine didn't realize how right she was when she said I should start an online business. Obviously, getting a job as Dr. Jesse Falcon was out. I might as well have turned myself in to the cops. But being myself wasn't landing me a job, either. Sequoia's modest lifestyle was typical of some people who were set for life. She could afford not to work, but certainly she didn't want to live with a bum. Nor would I get Scotty back without an income. It seemed a matter of logic to use my computer savvy one more time to get money from Jesse Falcon in order to get my online business up and running. After all, thanks to the bank robbery, I was back down to zero. Ondine had suggested I spend a hundred grand, but in what seemed like a moment of restraint, I decided to see what I could do with the twenty grand I wanted in the first place. I considered myself ironically moral, like an alcoholic who usually drinks scotch thinking he was on the wagon by drinking beer instead. I rationalized that banks were insured against thievery, and wealthy people had a way of landing on their feet. Anyway, I told myself that once my business was in the black, I'd redeposit the money, and no one would have to know who I was or where I was. And simply hacking into his account to make a withdrawal was a hell of a lot safer than walking into a bank.

So in the moment, I told myself I was doing the best thing, the practical thing, the only thing. Honesty was an overrated concept, about as useful as my old Boy Scout merit badges. I really had no other choice. As for coming clean with Sequoia—or for that matter, going low profile, like my mom said—the newspaper headline gave me the perfect out.

Looking back, I realize something else. I fell in love with Sequoia at the same time I fell in love with crime. I already missed the surge of power I'd felt when my phony credit was approved or when that poor bank teller bought my story. And as nice as Sequoia was, something about her seemed a perfect fit for this new guy I was turning into. She'd be the honest one, and I'd be the one with all the crazy secrets. It was the opposite of life with Betsy. It balanced things out.

The master bath was shiny and black, and Sequoia stepped out of the bath like a dripping wet Venus. It'd started raining hard, and the pelts of water against the window made it seem like all the world was clean and wet. I gently helped to dry her off with a huge black towel. Then I stepped into the shower. Sequoia demurely did not comment on my hard-on. "Don't get the hospital dressing too wet," she said instead.

I turned on the hot jet spray of water but almost instantly turned it off.

"Sequoia, I have to tell you something."

She shrugged as she towel-dried her hair. "Sure." I put my hands on her shoulders and set aside her towel. We could barely see our reflections in the steamy mirror.

"You're not in pain, are you, Jesse?"

Damn, she was sweet. "It's not that at all. I . . . I just have to say it. I'm doing special work. For the government. I'll need to set up a cover job. Something online to give me flexibility. But as for what I really do . . . You can't ever ask me. It would put you in danger. And I may have to . . . you know, go away sometimes. And very suddenly." Sort of like Pinocchio's nose, once again my sexual arousal grew with each lie.

Sequoia burst out laughing. "You're kidding, right?" I hoped my serious expression communicated that I wasn't.

"I'm working as a psychologist, that's all I can tell you. I was handpicked by a special branch of the government."

She put her hand to her mouth. "My God, you're serious. What about the bank robbery? Was that—?"

"A shitty coincidence, nothing more and nothing less. I had to be low-key and not fight back. It would've compromised my cover." Out of habit, I rubbed the steam from the mirror with my hand. The mirror steamed right back up again.

She leaned down and kissed the gauze and tape on my stomach. "My brave Jesse. You will be careful, won't you? I couldn't take—

I mean, if something happened to you"

"I'll be fine, Sequoia. And I promise I'll never deceive you again."

The best time of my life was beginning.

4: DR. JESSE FALCON

EVERYTHING I'D BEEN THROUGH seemed like an hors d'oeuvre on a toothpick, compared with the main course of fricasseed crap about to unfold.

Another twenty thousand was stolen from me. The first twenty thousand involved that phony line of credit, so it was fairly easy to deal with. This meant it only took about fifty calls to the cops and the credit company dopes to get the matter straightened out. But the next twenty grand was an electronic withdrawal from my actual money. Whoever did this had a lot of chutzpah. The good news was that the cops got involved. The bad news was that the cops got involved. It was a repeat of the same power struggles, contradictory communications, and downright incompetence of the previous interlude. Phone call after phone call, letter after letter, and to date anyway, none of it made a damn bit of difference.

Everyone treated me like shit. I'd call the cops or the bank or my lawyer and get these smarmy lectures about how worrying doesn't solve anything or that the most important thing was to stay calm. And here I thought the most important thing was to get my money back. Silly me. When I'd lose my temper—and I'd lose it a lot—the dope on the other end of the phone would repeat the same meaningless bullshit that pissed me off in the first place. Or they'd say they'd talk to me once I calmed down.

Pretty soon things really started to get intense. An electronic withdrawal for fifty thousand dollars from a matured CD. A second such withdrawal for yet another fifty grand. The FBI got on the case at this point, not that it made any difference. One moment they'd say what a serious crime this was, and then the next they'd remind me that relatively speaking it was small potatoes given other cases that took priority and how hard it was to prosecute identity thieves. All the usual garbage.

Time marched gallantly forward through all the manure. Linda Goldstein got increasingly pregnant.

I simply wanted to close out my accounts, but the FBI said to keep them open, in order for the culprit or culprits to get caught. The problem was that the bank could not trace the withdrawals either, which meant my stolen money would take a while to get replaced. The bank kept telling me to be patient. The FBI said the same thing. So did my lawyer, who I fired and replaced with another lawyer who told me the same thing.

Patience, I learned, was not a virtue. It's a sign of impotence and cowardice, a booby prize for people too stupid to expect much out of life. I wanted what was *mine*. What was there to be patient about?

The worst part was telling Esther about the money. After all, she did have a right to know. She couldn't care less that I was flushing myself down the toilet. No matter how fragile I was, I never missed an appointment with a patient, so what difference did it make if I'd been broken into a million pieces?

"Why are you letting this happen?" Esther asked when I told her about all the legal red tape I had to contend with. "I've seen you practically kill to save fifty cents." We were in the so-called family room, which featured the one TV in the house and what Esther called casual furniture, which meant you were allowed to touch it without getting your hand chopped off.

"I'm doing what the FBI *said* to do, I've already explained that."

Esther sighed like the smug martyr she was. "I guess you've become an old man. The Jesse I married wouldn't let anything come between us and our security."

"Well, the Esther I married wasn't such a hateful bitch with those awful frown lines around her mouth."

"*You* put them there." She glared at me like a harpy, which probably meant that as soon as I wasn't in the room she would cry.

"You're right, I live to ruin people's lives. I ruined your life, I ruined my life, and—" I stopped myself before mentioning Linda Goldstein.

"No, you don't live to ruin anyone's life. You just *do*. Because you're incapable of thinking for one second that you're not the center of the universe. Or should I say that your cock is not the center of the universe?"

"Well, it sure as hell is not the center of *your* universe."

"Oh, blah-blah-blah. Look, when you pass out in front of the TV, at least try to keep the volume down."

She was right. I'd adopted a wonderful new habit of passing out in the living room with the TV on. It was part of my new lifestyle, thanks to my identity thief. I slept maybe two hours a night. I'd grab a candy bar on my way to work and call it breakfast and lunch, and then barely pick at whatever home-delivered crud Esther called dinner. I stopped showering every day and instead, doused myself in cologne. I stopped working out at the gym. Something about the monotony of exercise was way out of sync with my endless anxiety. My fantasies of what I wanted to do to this identity thief became so violent, I'd bite my hands to try to keep my feelings under control. My fingers developed calluses from biting into them. And my feet developed blisters from pacing the floors. I got pulled over twice for speeding. Fortunately, no one figured out it was road rage.

Most of it is a blur, but I remember one night when, in a stupor on the sofa, I was shaken awake by Esther.

"The TV is too goddamned loud," she shouted. "Do you even know it's on?"

I stared at the TV screen. It was one of those true crime shows, and some guy was confessing on tape to the cops about killing somebody or another.

Esther shook her head in disbelief at what transpired on TV. "Look at that murderer, sitting there with his hands folded on the table. And he's animated, smiling and raising his eyebrows, like he's talking about the weather."

I was nodding off again but managed to stay awake. "Serial killers are still human. He still has to do something with his hands. His facial muscles aren't paralyzed. Does Miss Manners say there is a correct way to discuss chopping someone into bite-sized pieces?"

"Go fuck yourself," Esther said. "Pass out some more. I'm turning off the TV."

The sudden silence and darkness of the TV screen scared me to death. The never-ending noise inside my head got worse when there was silence. I needed more sounds. Otherwise, there was nothing to blot it all out.

Finally, I went to a psychiatrist (fancy that!), who prescribed three different anti-anxiety meds. They took the edge off, but that was all. My bad daily habits continued. The labels on my med bottles warned me not to mix the pills with alcohol, not that I let it stop me.

Yet in the midst of all this hell came an unexpected ray of light. After a long and typically exasperating day, I drove home and was greeted by the most therapeutic person I could've seen.

"Dad!"

It was my daughter, Sabrina, a lovely young woman who was my pride and joy. Maybe life wasn't all bad after all.

We hugged warmly and kissed on the cheek. She had lovely long hair, and I gave it an affectionate muss.

"Jeremy sends his love." Jeremy was our bulldog, which Sabrina kept when Esther and I moved across the country. Esther secretly hated animals and mumbled something about how weren't we too mature to still have a dog? As if it brought shame to adults to own a pet. It was Esther who insisted on giving him the dumbfuck name of Jeremy, and in fact she said we'd have to get rid of him unless we kept that name. Over the years, she would maybe about once a month condescend to pat him on the head.

"Jeremy's an old grouch, and you know it. What are you doing here? Did you lose your job?" We strolled to the living room, which Esther furnished with uncomfortable chairs that had these squiggly wooden things on the back. The squiggles reminded me of how much I hated Esther.

"Oh, by the way, Mom is consulting with a client this evening. The only time they could meet." This was cause for neither alarm nor elation; Esther's clients often were unavailable during the day.

"I don't suppose she left a message for me?"

"Hmm. No. How funny, now that I think of it."

Sabrina knew nothing of the troubles between Esther and me. It was the one promise to each other that Esther and I had kept. As far as Sabrina knew, we were Romeo and Juliet.

Sabrina sat next to me on the ramrod stiff sofa. "To answer your question, I'm on semester break, you big old dummy. I figured I'd kill two birds with one stone. I wanted to come out here to see you guys plus do some research at the art museum. They have this great collection of Byzantine tapestries. I'll bet you've never been there, have you, Dad?"

I sighed. "Art. You know I don't get it."

"Don't worry, I get it for both of us."

She gave my hand a warm squeeze. Thank God there was one

person in the world who appreciated me. "Are you hungry? Thirsty? Tired?"

She laughed self-consciously. "I'm fine, Dad. Let's wait for Mom to get home." She squeezed my hand harder. "But there is something I wanted to tell you. Before we both tell Mom. I mean, you are a psychologist, and probably . . . well . . ."

"Sweetheart." I put my hand on her shoulder in concern. There had been something about a young man she told us about a while back, claiming that he was the love of her life and all those naïve, sappy things. That his name was Cole Colton or was it Colton Cole? It sounded like the name of someone from a comic book or soap opera. He was studying business or law or something; I forget exactly what. Sabrina, for all her beauty, intelligence, and talent, had a way of attracting blah people. All her girlfriends through high school and college, not to mention her boyfriends, were among the most boring people I'd ever met, and believe you me, as both a professor and shrink I've met some mighty boring people. Esther and I hadn't even met him yet when just as suddenly they broke up. Sabrina never went into detail and blandly claimed it had been a learning experience. Though far more amiable than her mother, she shared with her mother an inability to recognize anything negative, as if sworn to secrecy that the world sucked. But maybe she finally was going to confide in me.

"I . . . I . . ."

"Whatever it is, we'll get through it," I said. "Are you pregnant? Did someone—" I stopped myself, unable to say out loud the terrible thought that a man did harm to my princess.

Sabrina sniffled. "It's nothing like that. I was in a bank robbery. I almost got killed. Oh Dad, I know I'm lucky to be alive, but I saw people getting shot to death. I didn't say anything because I didn't want you or Mom to worry. I thought I could get over it. I mean, I should be *grateful*, right? Nothing bad happened to me. I didn't even have any cash to give them. But I can't help it. I keep having nightmares. I can't sleep. Every time I hear a loud noise, it all comes back."

Bank robbery? In my old city? Could it be—?

"Which bank, sweetheart? When?"

She gave me an odd look, confused that this would be my first question. She told me the date and location. Yes, this had to be the private police matter that I was not told about when I first reported the credit-line theft. My mind and heart raced. Sabrina was an artist, after all. Maybe she noticed something the cops missed.

"Were there any suspicious characters in the bank?"

She pulled away from me and frowned. "Dad, they were *bank robbers*. They wore ski masks and carried machine guns. I'd say that's pretty suspicious, no?"

"Not *them*." I gave a dismissive gesture with my hand. "I mean, among the customers. Did anyone seem shady to you?"

"Dad, why in the world are you asking me this? Why would I notice the customers? Okay, I admit it. I thought one guy was very cute. I'm sure he's dead, the poor man. He got shot as the cops arrived to kill the robbers."

"But he seemed *nice*? Like, on the level?"

She shrugged. "Well, yeah. I guess."

"Damn it."

"Gee, thanks, Dad. You've been a real comfort."

I reached over to hug her. "I'm sorry, sweetheart. Your Mom and I knew about the bank robbery because of our accounts. But I . . . I mean, it comes as such a shock to think you were there."

"*And* that I could've been killed?" she interjected, with a hopeful expression.

"Well, yeah. Of course."

Esther entered through the foyer and joined us in the living room. She had her rolling briefcase and wore one of those sexless suits and blouses she liked so much, with a matronly pin on her lapel. I thought she looked so depressingly prudish. If, for some reason, scientists decided to invent an anti-arousal for men, they could've distributed this image of Esther. No man could stay hard at the sight of it.

"Hello, dear, how was your day?" Esther offered me her cheek to kiss as she fell into character for the benefit of Sabrina.

"Okay, I suppose, but I missed my Estie-Westie." I subtly licked her cheek as I kissed it, just to gross her out. If Esther ruled the world, body fluids would've been illegal. Kicking off her high heels, she ordered us take-out Hunan for dinner. Then she poured herself a sherry—for some reason, it drove me crazy that she drank sherry— and joined us in the living room. The liquor tray was the same color that the furniture was. Everything was all nice and matchy-matchy. Esther was unable to resist moving the throw pillow I was sitting near to its proper location, silently intimating that I, in my unbelievably careless cruelty, had let it slide over a couple of inches. My training told me that Esther's obsession over minutia was a projection that something deeper bothered her. I couldn't even begin to guess what it might've been.

"I guess it's a small world," I said as cheerfully as I could. "Esther, dear, it turns out that our Sabrina was in a bank robbery. You know, *our* bank?"

Esther did not get the hint. She carefully set down her sherry on a blue coaster. "Oh, my poor darling." She nudged over to Sabrina on the couch, turning her back to me as she stroked Sabrina's back. "Tell me everything."

Sabrina looked at me imploringly. "Dad, would you please . . .?

"Of course, sweetheart. I'll break it to your mom as easy I can." I cleared my throat. "Esther, our darling of a daughter had to lie there and watch helplessly as innocent people got shot to death. At the time, she didn't want to worry us, but she can't get over it. I think she feels guilty for surviving. She keeps having bad dreams. And now she wants our help."

"Oh, my poor Sabrina." With a worried frown, Esther held her close to her chest.

"Of course," I continued, "when I asked her if anyone else in the bank looked suspicious, she drew blank. Wouldn't you just know it? My own *daughter* was there, but she's no help whatsoever. Though she did go gaga over some guy."

Sabrina looked over at me, as if unable to believe what I was saying. "Dad, what are you talking about? Mom, is there something wrong with Dad?"

"It's merely your father's way, honey. He feels so bad for you that he's . . . well, *angry*." She patted Sabrina's back and shot me the meanest look I ever saw. "We know you did nothing wrong. We want you to feel better, that's all. To . . . to, you know, um, toughen you up a little. That's all your father's trying to do. And I know he's very sorry for upsetting you. Isn't that right, Jesse dear?"

If I had to listen to another second of Esther's sanctimonious shit I would go out of my mind. "What the hell are you talking about, woman? All I know is that my money—*my* money—is . . . was . . . Ah, forget it."

For a moment, no one said anything.

"Well, your dad has been under a lot of stress at work," Esther finally said.

"Yeah, that's it. Stress at work." I went to the liquor tray and poured myself a triple scotch, damn near downing it in one gulp.

My cell phone rang; irritated, I got it out of my jacket pocket. "What the hell do you want?" I said to whoever it was.

"It's me, you prick," Linda said. "I can't live anymore. I—I've left a note. It explains everything."

"Aw, fuck." I mouthed to my wife and daughter: *a patient.* "Well, where are you?"

"I'm on the roof of your office building." Desperate as she was to die, Linda thought nothing of telling me her exact location. I hate it when phonies take up my time, but welcome to my world.

"Okay, I'll be right there. Don't do anything until I get there. Do you promise?"

"Yes, I promise."

"Sorry, gang. I have a suicidal patient."

"I'm curious, Dad. Do you always say 'Aw, fuck' when a patient wants to die?"

"Yes, it's a new technique. It's called Fuck Therapy."

Esther laughed bitterly. "Well in that case, I'd say that you've been—oh, never mind. Tell us about your love life, Sabrina dear. Are you going to make us grandparents anytime soon?"

Before Sabrina could say anything, I interjected. "I hope so. I hear babies are selling for a tidy profit on the black market." I knew this would deeply offend Esther's conventional sensibilities. She sat there with her mouth open, though I could see Sabrina bite her lip to suppress a giggle.

I slammed the door behind myself and drove back to the office I'd just left. Lucky me.

I found Linda on the gravel roof of the building, the night city lit up all around her. From a distance, the few rooftop lights made her seem filmy and electric. And she was wearing a mink coat. But this was no romantic liaison. Linda stared despondently at the street twenty stories down, but when I called out her name, she turned, waved and smiled. Like she was Miss Universe. Then as an extra added attraction, she opened her fur coat, which revealed her naked body. Her only articles of clothing were these high-heeled sandals that had little daisies on them.

Talk about desperate. Her message seemed to be: *Fuck me now or I'll kill myself.* I'd always been proud of my virility, thank you very much, but still—to jump off a building unless you get some? I wanted to walk away and leave her there. The news headlines would've read: "Woman Flashes, Takes Own Life." But this was the building I practiced in, she was my patient, she was pregnant, and my wife was Esther. I realized I couldn't take any chances.

"What do you want, Linda?" I rapidly, yet calmly, walked toward her.

"What do I *want*? What do you think I want?" She let her fur coat fall down to the gravely rooftop. I could see the goose bumps on her skin from the cool night air.

"Look, I'm here." I held out my hand to her. "Let's go downstairs to my office."

"And we'll . . . well, *you know*?" she asked demurely, as if too pure to say bad words, while what appeared to be tears of joy streamed down her cheeks.

"You mean, 'fuck?' Sure, what the hell?"

My attempt to lighten the situation appeared to backfire. With fists clenched and lower lip curled, she shrieked, "That's all I am to you, isn't it—a fuck? You took advantage of me." She pointed at me accusingly.

"Oh, horseshit, I did. Let's get your coat on, you must be freezing." I reached down for the worn mink coat and grabbed her arm to bring her toward me. I draped the coat over her shoulders and slid it across her torso. As I tried to slip her arms inside the sleeves, she kept trying to take off the coat. It was as though she thought whether the coat stayed on or off determined her fate. I heard a sleeve rip as we struggled. For an instant, the soft mink went across my eyes, and I couldn't see what was happening.

I yanked the coat from my face and easily grabbed it away from her. But, looking down, I saw that Linda had tugged us to the edge of the roof. The safety wall around the rooftop came up to my knees and Linda's waist. Ominously, I heard an ambulance speeding through the traffic lights below.

"You bastard!" Linda cried, trying in vain to push me over the ledge. "You're going to pay." I stopped her with one hand to her face, which she kept trying to punch off. After maybe ten seconds, I grabbed her arm yet again, to lead her away from danger.

Unfortunately, she rammed her knee in me below the belt. I managed not to let go of her, but I was caught off guard, to say the least. Linda charged at me, and her daisy-sandaled right foot got caught in the lip of the wall. As she struggled to free herself while trying to push me over, she lost her balance. She sort of somersaulted over my chest and fell over the edge. Linda didn't scream exactly. Instead, she made a long groan of clumsiness, like someone overreacting to stubbing a toe. The mink coat lay on the roof, worse off for its ordeal.

Scooping up the mink, I briefly thought about making a run for it. But I dialed 911, gave my name, and said an ill, naked patient of mine fell off the roof of the building after a struggle. It was only then I noticed that she didn't fall all the way to the pavement; a ledge about three stories down broke her fall. I pretended to sound overjoyed by the possibility she might still be alive. I hung around to show my so-called concern and looked up from my tenth floor office window as the cops and paramedics walked out to the precarious ledge and lifted her body inside.

I called home and explained I was following the ambulance to the hospital. This was only partially true. First, I made a brief stop. I wanted there to be nothing to link me to much of anything, so I threw the torn mink coat into a pile of plastic bags near a Goodwill dumpster where some homeless person no doubt would find it. This seemed to me smarter than throwing it in the river. Things thrown into water or buried in the earth have a way of turning back up. This way, by the time the coat was found—assuming the police would ever look for it—it would have changed so many grubby hands, it would prove nothing.

I spent about two hours in the waiting room before a doctor came out. I already knew that Marty, Linda's estranged husband, was out of town, so the attending physician spoke to me, since I was her doctor.

"Well, things could be worse," he said. "Mrs. Goldstein is in a deep coma. She may or may not wake up. But she *is* alive."

"What a miracle." I hoped I sounded convincing.

"And her baby is alive. We had to deliver it immediately. The child's a good month premature. We've all got our fingers crossed it'll make it."

I pretended to smile. "Out of curiosity, is it a boy or a girl?" I thought it odd that the doctor referred to the baby as an "it," as if Linda had given birth to a guppy. Not that I was shedding tears of joy at being a father again.

"A girl."

"Gee, that's great." I, of course, would've made the same statement if it was a boy. I never understood why people had to say they were happy about a baby's sex, whether it was a boy or a girl. Of course, a lot of everyday customs struck me as ridiculous.

I saw a couple of uniformed cops walking toward me. One was a fairly young man, and one was a much older man.

"Dr. Falcon?" asked the younger man, though he did not wait for me to answer. "We have a few questions for you." I got the impression that the older man was his senior partner and was training him. Yet the older man seemed primarily interested in his paper cup of hospital coffee.

"Of course." I gestured that we could all sit on the vinyl waiting room sofa.

"You can sit, but we prefer to stand," he said.

As a psychologist, I knew that they were trying to put me in a vulnerable position by towering over me. I pretended not to notice. "Fine, I'll sit." I sighed with exhaustion. "It's been a long night."

The younger officer asked me what happened. I knew that what I said would determine my future existence. "I was at home with my wife and daughter. My daughter lives out of state, and we were having a nice little reunion. Mrs. Goldstein called me on my cell and said she was on the roof of my office building, ready to jump. Naturally, I hurried over."

"Why didn't you call the police?"

"She said she would jump for certain if I did," I lied. "It all happened so fast. When I got to the rooftop, I saw she was nude, except for her shoes. I tried to lead her away, but she kicked me hard in the groin. She tried to push me over but fell over herself. Then I called 911."

"Are you saying she wanted to push *you* off?" asked the young cop.

The old cop sipping his coffee scrutinized him with a frown.

"Yes. She was very disoriented. She kept calling me Marty. Doctor-patient confidentiality prohibits me from saying much, but she was very, very unhappy. Mind you, even though she was pregnant, which should give you an idea. My groin area is somewhat bruised, if you want pictures or anything."

"That won't be necessary," the old man said, speaking for the first time. "This one's open and shut. Though if she wakes up, Dr. Falcon, you may want to charge her with attempted murder."

"Thank you, but she's been through quite enough, and her new little girl will need her."

"We could tell right away by the way she landed that she wasn't pushed," said the old cop, though the younger one gave him a dirty look. I inferred that the older cop thought his partner was over-zealously suspicious of everyone and that he would keep him in check.

"Do you know how to reach Mr. Martin Goldstein?" the young cop asked.

"I imagine at their home." I was careful to say nothing about the impending divorce. I wondered if they were trying to fool me and would try to open my sealed record from when I was professor or do a DNA test on the baby.

Yet as the days went by, there really was nothing more to it, provided that Linda didn't wake up. Or, if she did, maybe she wouldn't remember what happened, or I could say she was being delusional. Of course, a lil' ol' thing called a paternity test could've put an end to my theory, but maybe Esther would think the baby was so goddamned cute she'd go easy on me.

I had a brief moment of insanity in which I thought about approaching Esther about adopting the baby without saying who DaDa was. Thankfully, I got over it in a hurry. Marty Goldstein, once found, kept tearful watch by his wife's bedside every evening after work, frequenting the non-denominational chapel to pray for his preemie daughter's survival. Maybe the Goldsteins would have a happy ending. And as far away from me as possible.

If only things had gone more smoothly on the home front.

When I exhaustedly arrived home that first night, Sabrina was already asleep from jet lag. Esther, though, had waited up to tell me, "Don't think I don't know what really happened. Or that I don't know *enough*, anyway."

"My patient's alive," was all I offered in reply, hanging up my coat. Unless Linda had talked to Esther at some point, I was reasonably certain Esther did not know anything. She was on a kind of fishing expedition, hoping to trip me up in a lie.

Esther stared ahead blankly. "I don't know what's wrong with me. I was raised to have self-respect. My parents worshipped me."

"Well, that's what's wrong with you."

"You always have some smart answer for everything, don't you?"

"Not really. It's simply that you're not as smart as you think."

Esther marched toward me and spat in my face. Then she silently marched to the kitchen, to put the three plates, three forks, and three glasses we used for our takeout dinner into the dishwasher. This probably took her thirty seconds, but she said, without turning to look at me, "You've always been *such* a help around the house."

"Well," I replied, "you've always been *such* a lousy lay."

She stared at me soberly. "Why do you hate me?"

"Because there's nothing to love."

I could hear her mumble, "What a dickhead," as she stormed off to her bedroom. Sabrina knew we slept in separate rooms, though she thought it was because of my snoring instead of Esther's frigidity.

The morning after the Linda incident, I woke up early to go through some papers on the identity theft case. Through an amazing coincidence, the papers had turned into tiny, confetti-like pieces since the day before. My, could Esther have possibly had something to do with it?

I completely lost my cool with Esther for the first time in front of Sabrina, accusing my wife of plotting to drive me crazy. Esther put her hand on her hip to reply there was no need for her to drive me crazy since I already was and things pretty much digressed from there.

"I didn't tear up your stupid papers!" Esther shouted. "You must've done it. When you were . . . you know . . ."

"You mean drunk? You mean strung out on meds?" In a fit of sarcasm, I threw a couple of handfuls of confetti over my head. "Look at me, I'm crazy."

Esther stared at me sadly, like I was a teenager beyond redemption. "I know you're embarrassed. Because you can't remember doing it. You honestly can't."

"Oh, well, aren't you so wonderful to find it in your heart to pity me? Quick, call the Pope. There is a living saint among us."

To my horror, Sabrina grabbed her suitcase and said, "Dad, I don't know what's happened. I don't even know you anymore. And I don't want to know you." She refused to hug or kiss me good-bye, and rubbed salt on the wound by letting her mother do so. "Oh Mom," she said, "please let me know if I can help. Come and visit, if you'd like."

As soon as Sabrina left, Esther said, "I need to get out of here. I'm going for a drive."

"Hopefully off the edge of a cliff." I couldn't resist.

I expected some bitchy reply, but she stood there for a minute. "Never mind," she said. "It's not worth saying."

After falling asleep on the couch, I woke up and thought to go to Esther's bedroom, to see if she'd returned. I felt like shit—drunk and hung over at the same time and woozily depressed from my meds. I opened her door and found her in bed, reading some decorating magazine as if nothing unpleasant had ever entered her world. Sometimes we'd have huge fights, but if someone called, she'd answer the phone with a lilting, smiling, "Hel-*lo*," as if she were in the midst of feeding the goldfish.

She took off her reading glasses. "Don't come near me. I'll call 911."

I rubbed my eyes for my headache or hangover or whatever it was. "Relax, Esther. I'm not going to hurt you."

She breathed in and out with fear. "Then what . . . what do you want?"

I sat down on the bed, looking deep into her eyes. "I want . . . I want you to stop slamming the door. I mean, I want to stop making you slam the door. I mean, I want life to stop making me make you slam the door." Totally out of nowhere, I started to shiver. But it seemed more like I was a reptile shedding its skin, cleansing all the poison from my life.

"It's always someone else's fault, isn't it? You always . . . oh, come here." Esther was crying. She held me until I stopped shaking, which took about an hour. As much as I hated to admit it, there was still a glimmer of something between us. I remembered the girl I married. I could see her before me. All the mutual hate was gone. I realized in that moment that we really were *married*—only death would part us.

We made love for the first time in years. She was never a particularly demonstrative or inventive sex partner, but as the old saying goes, it was the thought that counted.

Esther fell asleep in my arms as I stared at the blank ceiling, trying to remember the last time I was at peace. All at once, I realized something that felt like the heaviest weight of all time. *Oh my God*, I thought, as all the fear, dread and anger returned.

As a psychologist, I wondered if stress was impeding my long-term memory. But as just another schmuck, I wondered how I could be so stupid. That lunatic Linda. She told me she had a note that explained everything when she called me that ill-fated night. Yes, she most definitely said that, no matter how hard I tried to tell myself I was imagining things. Was the note in the long-gone mink coat? Did some homeless person find it and throw it away or turn it into the cops? Did the cops have it all along? Or did Marty have it?

Turning away from Esther, I curled up like a fetus as one awful possibility after another went flashing through my mind. In her sleepiness, Esther put my arm back around her.

"Stay put," she murmured. "No more running away."

I kissed her forehead. "I love you, Esther." Her drowsy smile said the same thing in return. It should've been one of the nicest moments of my life. But all I could think of was that motherfucking letter. Then I remembered about the identity thief again, unable to decide which terrible thing to obsess about the most.

5 : AKA JESSE FALCON

SEQUOIA WAS BRINGING ME A JOY I never thought possible. Corny as it sounds, I became a firm believer in love at first sight. Our life together was one of those amazing spells in which everything you say and do feels like making love. When she gave me her fortune cookie over some take-out Chinese, it was as if she'd given me her heart. And when the fortune said something like, "You have a secret admirer," it was as though God blessed our union.

I did notice that Sequoia was extremely unsentimental. Not that she wasn't affectionate, but she refused to have photos of us on display because she claimed it was a cliché and did not care much about things like birthdays or talking about how long we'd been together. Still, one on one, she was extremely kind and present. And given her childhood, I figured she had good reason not to trust nostalgia.

Maybe love at first sight was the only kind of love there was. Maybe first impressions never did go away, and you either loved, liked, or hated someone from the moment you met. Looking back, I think I always hated Betsy, but in some crazy way that made me feel sorry for her, especially when she got pregnant. And Biff was always a nut job.

Yet at the same time that my life had never been better, my life became more and more of a lie. I missed Scotty a whole lot, and though I know it sounds wimpy beyond belief, I felt guilty lying to Mom. Supposedly, I was living low profile someplace else, exactly like Mom said I should do. Mom had temporary custody of Scotty, and the only time I found out what he was doing was when she'd call me, using one of her friend's phones. I decided that even e-mails were too risky. Plus, of course, there were all the crimes and lies I was hiding from Sequoia. Yet in a strange way, that didn't bother me as much. I couldn't comprehend our not staying together no matter what happened.

One of the more inconvenient situations was the fact that I periodically had to go away for a day or two on "government business" to make that particular lie look good. I would fly to Washington, DC—I very quickly racked up bonus miles—and would stay at an inexpensive hotel I'd found that had no frills but was bug-free. I'd kick off my shoes, loosen my tie, and watch TV for a day or a weekend, miss Sequoia so badly I'd thought I'd lose my mind, and then gratefully fly back home. Sequoia once asked if the government couldn't do better than the cheap hotel I stayed at, and I told her I couldn't discuss why I always stayed there.

Obviously, I also had to keep Sequoia completely out of the divorce, since she thought I was Dr. Jesse Falcon. I told her I didn't want her to have to get involved or worry about any of it at all. That much was true. I got a PO Box for all my correspondence with Ondine.

My original plan to take only $20,000 more from Dr. Jesse Falcon proved naïve at best. Besides getting my website going, there were Scotty's living expenses, which I insisted on paying for, plus my own, as I refused to be supported by Sequoia. It's funny how relative life becomes. I told myself that I'd done a highly moral thing when, thanks to substantial advertising contracts and benefit options that Sequoia helped me set up, I got my online business going for a mere $85,000 of the $120,000 I'd stolen to date. As for what the business was, it was Sequoia who came up with what she saw as the perfect solution. And she could not have known, on that happy day, how life-changing her brainstorm was.

"What do you think?" she asked me, showing a mock-up of my possible homepage.

I leaned over into the laptop and saw the title: Ask Dr. Jesse. It would be a kind of online "Dear Abby," only I'd offer answers to four menus of information: Personal Advice, The Facts about Sex, Mental Illness Guide, and Physical Fitness. There was even a subheading that read: "The Psych of All Trades."

Of course, I really wasn't a doctor of any kind, but it was only natural of Sequoia to want to capitalize on the assumption that I was. "Um, it's great, sweetheart. But I have to be *extremely* low-key, remember?"

Sequoia made the funny face she'd make when some minor problem emerged between us. "Ah yes, all those government secrets. Don't worry, I didn't mention your last name. And I can set up a small business to own the copyright."

"Still, even 'Jesse' is too much."

Sequoia tapped her index finger to her lips. She was a quick thinker. "What about 'Dr. Know-It-All'? Or 'McShrink'? Or maybe 'Free Psychology'?"

I thought about it. I did, after all, originally want to be a psychologist. Way back when, I was a straight A student. There also were all sorts of books and websites I could get accurate information from. And it seemed poetic justice to finally live out my dreams without Betsy's lies spoiling them.

"McShrink," I decided.

"Great! We're in business. I already looked up the legal wording for our disclaimer, so no one could sue for bad advice."

"Great!" I parroted back, though in truth that hadn't even occurred to me. Sequoia was not only incredibly easy to love, but she made an excellent business advisor.

It was then that we launched the website. Sequoia already had an alias she used for investment reasons and that was the only name that appeared on any contracts. She also was the webmaster. We advertised on a bunch of other websites and fairly quickly I began getting e-mails from people seeking advice.

From the first e-mail I received, I never consulted any of the textbooks I thought I'd refer to. Instead, I relied on my gut. Or what I really mean is that I relied on my inner bad guy. I advised people to do the kinds of things I'd always wanted to do but never had the nerve. It was as if every time I'd stuffed my anger, it turned out to be a bank deposit of sorts, and now I was ready to cash in on all that pent-up energy by helping others. I didn't assume people would follow my advice, but—except for the occasional slimeball—I thought that the people who wrote to me needed to feel like someone was 100 percent on their side. I was their online life coach egging them on to tell whoever was bugging them to fuck off.

Dear McShrink,

I'm a 5' 7" woman who weighs 140 pounds, not excessive for my height. Yet my boyfriend says unless I lose weight, he'll break up with me. His best friend is always there to back him up. They get drunk and call me a fat slob. What do I do?

Badgered

Dear Badgered,

Your weight is fine. Tell your boyfriend that his best friend must be secretly in love with him because there's no other reason why he should care how much you weigh. Say this to the best friend as well as everyone you know he knows. Then breakup with your boyfriend. But before you do, go through all his drawers and fill them with lard. Don't forget the glove compartment of his car.

Dear McShrink,

My mother-in-law hates me. She hates that I have an outside job, she hates how I care for our kids, she hates everything I do. My husband never stands up for me. He just sits there while she tells me that everything I do is wrong. Help!

Wit's End

Dear Wit's End,

How you choose to live your life is up to you and is nobody else's business. If your husband can't say at least that much to his mother, divorce the wimp, and find a husband who has balls. In the meantime, when your mother-in-law pulls her crap, do something harmless but effective, like throw a bucket of water over her head. Tell her you'll be doing things like that from now on until she starts minding her own business.

Dear McShrink,

My live-in girlfriend insists that I support both of us, even though she makes as much as I do, and we have no kids. She says I'm not a real man unless I do this. Her paychecks go into a separate bank account I'm not allowed to touch. Is this normal?

Desperate Guy

Dear Desperate Guy,

It is far from normal. Insist on getting married, then immediately divorce her and sue her for alimony, since she makes more money.

PS: If it's safe to assume you have a dick, you're a "real man" in the eyes of the law.

Dear McShrink,

My ex-boyfriend has been diagnosed psychotic, but he's gone off his meds and refuses to take them. He's been acting very strange and keeps calling me. Please help.

Scared

Dear Scared,

Stop whatever you're doing right now and do this instead: Change your phone number, report the ex-boyfriend to the cops, get a restraining order, move, if at all possible, (with no forwarding address), and get a license for a handgun and learn how to use it.

Dear McShrink,

My family is very close, but I'm gay, and at twenty-five, I'm still afraid to tell them. I think they'll disown me. What should I do?

Closet Guy

Dear Closet Guy,

If your family isn't even willing to talk about such a big part of your life, then you aren't "close" in the first place. Turn the tables. If they disown you, hire a lawyer and sue them for psychic trauma.

These and other answers quickly garnered far more attention than I could've predicted. Very quickly, our advertisers reported significant increases in web hits and sales, and before long I was making much more money than I thought possible. Any number of blogs or magazine blurbs started speculating on who "McShrink" really was. There was even a joke on *The Tonight Show* about it. My anonymity remained integral to my mystique and popularity. Once, when I was buying flowers for Sequoia, the flower vendor laughed and said something like, "What happened, did McShrink tell you to make up with your girl?" I laughed back and said that was exactly what happened.

Soon, there came TV offers. Acting as my agent, Sequoia explained that my anonymity was key to my popularity. "Besides," she added, "Dr. McShrink wants his advice to be received with no bias whatsoever. So that people learn to trust the truth." Popular talk shows fell for the gimmick. I put lifts in my shoes to be taller than I was and padded my arms and stomach to seem huskier than I was. I'd arrive wearing a ski mask—a bit ironic, under the circumstances—and say nothing. They'd put a sack over my head and electronically disguise my voice, and in silhouette behind a curtain, I would field questions from the audience. I'd usually end with a standing ovation.

Book contracts were soon underway. I had money saved to start a new life, and I was approaching having enough money to pay back Jesse Falcon, which I still had every intention of doing. To keep things simple, I figured I'd do it in one lump sum.

I not only enjoyed the material success but the fact that I

was having an impact on people's lives. In a way, the gimmick wasn't really a gimmick at all. I felt appreciated for who I truly was, without the paraphernalia of what I looked like, what I was wearing, or all the crap that was going on.

To find my true self, I had to make myself a total secret.

Ondine knew about McShrink and never told anyone due to attorney-client privilege. She was proud of me and told me so. Ondine never questioned why I chose to be an anonymous online shrink, she only cared that the idea worked. Nothing about Jesse Falcon ever came up with her. She got the judge to agree that all divorce proceedings would be sealed, since secrecy was integral to my livelihood. Further, Betsy would only be told I had a computer-related job of substantial income, given her likelihood of retaliation. I told Mom nothing about Sequoia or my specific website, only that I was doing well with "computer stuff" and hopefully could soon take custody of Scotty. I thought Scotty would love Sequoia, once I figured out how they could meet. Even though I'd promised Sequoia I'd never deceive her again, I realized that at some point I'd have to at least tell her my real name. Probably I could get away with it by saying it was part of my government cover.

In the meantime, Biff became an official missing person. His wealth worked against finding him. He had the money to be anywhere. And let us not forget his last alleged message to his parents—courtesy of me—stated that he needed to get away from Betsy. The police told Biff's parents that as part of the investigation they needed to be told there were allegations that he was a pedophile. I would've expected his parents to at least feign outrage at the suggestion, but oddly they said something about how Biff was always a troubled boy and to please be gentle with him when he was found. As I thought more about it, I realized that keeping themselves utterly blameless in the eyes of public was more important than anything else. Even the *suspicion* of being a child molester branded someone for life. Or in death, for that matter.

Betsy told Biff's parents about his being the real father of Scotty. They wrote her a check—for a hundred grand, I think—and had her escorted out of their house. Betsy being Betsy, she yelled and screamed that Biff couldn't possibly have wanted to get away from her, and why would anyone be afraid of her because she certainly was no monster. Her anger turned to self-pitying nobility before long, as though she were Penelope waiting for Odysseus to return. The reason was obvious. She needed to behave in ways that did not make the cops suspect her of bumping off Biff for dumping her. Mom, for her part, was sure that Betsy had knocked off Biff. But it was Mom's nature to sit back, amused, and let the cops figure it out for themselves. Ondine thought it was funny that Betsy had been jilted.

So, with head held high, Betsy kept fighting for sole custody of Scotty.

As for me, I briefly appeared at the cop station to be interviewed about Biff. They only asked me questions about Betsy. I told them that Betsy was crazy but surely not capable of murder, if that's what they were getting at. Besides, Biff had always been a coward, so it didn't surprise me that he disappeared. I added that I doubted he was dead. I offered to give them my DNA. They said it wasn't necessary for now. That "for now" did a number on my nerves. It told me I wasn't totally ruled out. Still, I tried not to let it show. Nothing came up about the last time I saw Biff, or what might've happened to Scotty. Was it police incompetence or part of a master plan? It was impossible to know.

I was not surprised when Betsy asked to meet me at a trendy coffee house and when I agreed to do so, that she'd discuss reconciliation. The notion of having a career never occurred to her. She took it for granted that she would spend all her days being pampered by a man.

"It's best for Scotty," Betsy said to me, with a big smile, as though everything was great between us. "He needs *both* his parents." She took a loud sip of her upscale latte; one thing about Betsy was that she made no apologies when she liked something.

Scotty already told the judge that he'd rather live with me, and Betsy knew this. I decided to be a gentleman and not remind her. She may not have been Mother of the Year, but it must've hurt her deeply to hear what Scotty said.

I stared into the steam of my unadorned cup of decaf. "Betsy, please. Don't insult my intelligence. Or yours."

"A child needs a mother."

"A child needs *love*." I stared at her without any fear of her temper.

She threw her gourmet oatmeal cookie at me. "Now you're saying I don't love my son. Daddy is always nice, while Mommy is . . ." She paused, as if unable to continue.

"A selfish bitch?"

"Bitch—I mean *Biff* is his father. I wanted to right a wrong. What's so selfish about that?" Now she was practically screaming.

"And get laid in the bargain."

She smiled with superiority. "How dare you! I cheated with Biff for *years*. If I only wanted sex, I could've kept doing what I always did."

You'd have to know Betsy to understand she was dead serious in defending her morality thusly. It dawned on me that what made her more irritable when I lost my job was that I was around the house during the day. There was less opportunity to cheat on me.

"Well, maybe you should've kept fucking Biff, instead of trying to live with him. I'm sure he's not dead. He wanted to get away from you." Just when I was feeling that for once I was winning the unspecified contest between us, I clumsily spilled my coffee on the table.

As I reached for a bunch of paper napkins, Betsy said, "Ha! Good one. You've always been such a . . . such a loser."

"Then why want me back?" I shoved the coffee-stained napkins to the corner of the table.

"I told you. For Scotty."

"Okay, let me make sure I have this straight. First you sacrificed yourself so that Scotty would have Biff, his biological father. Now you're sacrificing yourself so that Scotty has me, his non-biological father that he had in the first place. Is that about right?"

She slammed her hands on the table, utterly out of patience. "Biff is gone, remember? Look, I thought I could go about this in a nice way. We're getting back together, and that's all there is to it."

"Not in a million years." Damn, it felt good to say that. I only wished I could tell Sequoia about it.

"You're right. It'll be more like five seconds from now." She looked as if she could kill me with a snap of her fingers. Maybe that she already had. "You'll be moving back in today. I have all sorts of plans for you, *Dr. Jesse Falcon.*"

My insides fell into the soles of my feet. I couldn't even speak.

"At a loss for words? Don't worry, I'm sure you'll have plenty to say when I tell you how the rest of your life will be lived. After all, I *know* you have lots of money, Dr. Falcon." She stood up and grabbed my necktie as that bank robber did, like I was a dog on a leash. "You think you're such a good person, and I'm some piece of shit. Well, if I'm a piece of shit, so are you. It's like you're St. Bernard shit, while I'm one of whose—whatdoyoucallits? You know, those yappy little dogs? Anyway, your shit is tons bigger than mine."

"I don't know what you're talking about." I carefully disengaged from her grip. It occurred to me she might be taping the conversation, so I was careful to say nothing incriminating. "I'm not moving in with you, I'm getting custody of my son, and I don't know why you keep calling me Dr. Fallon." I made a point of mispronouncing the last name.

"*Falcon*, you know the name is *Falcon*." She slammed her coffee spoon on the table. "Look, I found this guy who's a computer whiz. I had him hack into your accounts."

In spite of myself, I was intrigued. "In exchange for . . .?"

"Never you mind. Anyway, I know you've been stealing money from this guy's bank account."

I tried to think of a comeback but couldn't. I was grateful that apparently she hadn't learned about McShrink, which, thank God, was launched from Sequoia's computer.

"Don't you get it, Doctor Dearest? Think of the team we'd make. The guy I hired couldn't figure out how you transferred the money. He couldn't get past your firewall thingie or whatever it is. But you could show me. You could set me up to steal some other rich fuck's identity, and we'd really be in business. We'd be millionaires. Hell, billionaires. Or even—well, whatever it is that comes after billionaire."

No doubt everyone wanted to be rich, but the naïve, awful way Betsy proposed the concept actually made me feel sorry for her. "I don't believe a word you're saying. But for the sake of playing along, what about this computer guy?"

"I paid him off, duh. From the cash I got from Biff's rat shit family. He's some computer geek. He reads comic books, even though he's like thirty. He's from Outer Mesopotamia or someplace, and he needed a wad of cash to pay someone to marry him to get a green card. He'll never say a word. But you see, now I can blackmail you and you can blackmail me. The only thing to do is get back together."

"You should be a marriage counselor."

"Look, this isn't a joke."

I took a bite of the cookie Betsy threw at me. "Even if what you're saying were true, what would I have to blackmail you with?"

Betsy licked a fingertip of foam from her latte. "I killed him."

I thought I must've heard wrong. "Killed who?"

"Biff, of course." She looked at me in this uppity way. I felt like an amateur at dishonesty next to Betsy's utter calm and resolve. Granted, I was not winning any prizes for truth telling as of late, but Betsy clearly lost what little ability she'd ever had to be honest.

"You did *what*?" This was getting too weird. I didn't know if I should find out more or run for my life.

"Shh. Be quiet. I purposefully picked a public place to keep your reactions in check, but you still have to control that temper of yours."

"My temper? Do you have any idea how you—"

"Look, there's plenty of time to work out our personal differences. We have our whole lives ahead of us. But there you have it. I'm a murderer. Or do they still say 'murderess'?"

For a short while, we both sat there.

"Well, don't you even want to know how I did it?"

I suppressed a perverse urge to burst out laughing. "Sure, Betsy, tell me."

"Well, I know they can trace where you looked on a computer, so I went to the public library for the first time since I was like ten years old. I looked up poisonous berries in a book—I was careful not to check it out—and found the exact same berries in the park by our house. I put them in his Long Island iced tea." She hastily added, "Biff had no intention of dumping me. That was his macho bullshit. I dumped *him* right after you moved out. He refused to leave me alone. I was . . . I was like a prisoner in our own home. He wouldn't take his eyes off me for a second. Finally, he fell asleep, and I snuck off to the library."

I nodded my head to signal validation of her words. "I see."

"A girl is free to change her mind." She bent her wrist, as if gossiping. "Think of it as putting an animal to sleep. A very horny animal. Biff didn't even suffer when it happened. He was in the middle of saying how much he'd always adored me."

"What did you do with the body?"

"I dissolved it," she quickly replied. "You know, with acid, I forget what kind. In the bathtub."

"What about the bones?"

"I put them in a big sack and went back to the park. I gave the bones away to a whole bunch of stray dogs."

"That certainly was clever of you. And very kind to the dogs."

Betsy flustered with pride. "Well anyway, now you have the goods on me, too. So you see, I'm really not trying to trap you. I truly want you back."

Clearly, Betsy was far crazier than I'd thought. I had to keep her away from Scotty more than ever.

I looked at my watch. "I have to go," I lied.

"But what about everything I said?" She scrunched her nose, as if she'd proposed we do something harmlessly naughty like eat an entire chocolate cake.

"I have to go," I repeated.

"I'll be waiting to hear from you," she called out, as I briskly left the coffee shop.

Well, I thought, *what would McShrink do now?*

Ondine was on vacation for two weeks. But Sequoia had to know everything. It had all gone too far. If Sequoia still wanted me, we would move someplace far away, hopefully with Scotty. If I had to run away or even, yes, go to jail, Scotty would be okay living with my mother.

As I made all these plans, there was an unexpected sense of relief at the thought of returning to a life of honesty. The good me, the real me, was making a comeback. In a way, I had Betsy to thank; I didn't want to end up like her myself. I wondered if that was why I stayed with Betsy all those years. Like it or not, she made me be a good person. Whereas the minute she split up with me, I became a criminal.

Still thinking like McShrink, I realized that before I talked to Sequoia, I had to know about her past. How did I know what she could or could not handle? I not only had to tell her the truth but do it in a way that caused the least emotional damage. And anyway, wouldn't it be good for me to know more about this woman who I decided was the love of my life? We were crazy in love, but I'd been assuming that at some point she'd tell me more about herself. She was as secretive as I was, if not more so. She never brought up anything at all.

It was my turn to go to the public library. I looked up newspaper articles from when Sequoia would have been about nine. Sure enough, a very successful brain surgeon named Dr. Clement Vargas and his wife, Gabrielle, burned to death in a house fire.

But Sequoia neglected to mention that the fire was determined to have been arson. The arsonist had never been found. Not only that, she had a sister and brother who died in the fire. Sequoia, the oldest child, was away at a sleepover with a friend. There was a very sad picture of her being given a piggyback ride by a police officer to cheer her up. According to what I read, she was going to live with her father's sister and her husband.

Their names were Dr. Jesse Falcon, and his wife, Esther Vargas Falcon. They had a daughter named Sabrina.

Normally—whatever normal was anymore—I might've gone into a state of shock over this piece of news. But the roller coaster of high highs and low lows these past months made my discovery seem like, "What's next?" I wasn't someone who could be trusted, so why should anyone else be any different? Maybe everyone I encountered from now on would be crooked, as if crooks found each other through some weird magnetic force. The woman I loved obviously knew I was not who I said I was. Why was she going along with it? And why help me?

I had no idea what to say to Sequoia—whether I should confess about myself first or what. But by the time I arrived at what I'd come to think of as our apartment, I realized the situation was such a mess it didn't matter. I had to start *someplace*.

Sequoia greeted me with a long, deep kiss. I let myself savor its sweetness before easing her away. It crossed my mind that, depending how the conversation went, it could be the last kiss I'd ever get from her.

"What's my name?" I used that deadpan, non-judgmental tone I remembered from my college classes in psychology.

Sequoia frowned, like a mother wondering if her child had a fever. "Are you serious, Jesse? I don't get it."

I took out the rolled up photocopies from my coat pocket and tossed them on the floor. The black-and-white news stories looked eerie on the squares of black-and-white tiles. It was like Sequoia's whole life was entrapped in lurid news stories.

"Dr. Jesse Falcon and his wife Esther—" I could feel myself sweating.

"Stop!" Sequoia shrieked, looking this way and that for a way out. She tried to pry me away from the door. When she couldn't do it, she looked up at me pleadingly.

"Jesse, everything is perfect. Please, let it go."

"No." I had no right to assume such an unwavering posture, but I did. "Talk. Tell me."

We stared at each other, neither of us speaking. Finally, she said, "I've always hated lying. Even though I do it all the time. I have to, and I'm good at it. But I guess not as good as I thought." She took me by the hand and led me to the white sofa to sit down. But she remained standing, as if we were playing charades.

"When I saw you in the bank, I felt like I knew you all my life. *Honest.* When I realized you were using my uncle's name, I had a million questions. But when I saw you again at the hospital, none of those questions mattered. Yes, I have many secrets. But I have nothing to hide. I promise."

"I'm not Jesse. I'm—"

"*Yes, you are.* You are because I say so. Because I can't . . ." Sequoia turned away from me, and with her hand muffling her voice, she said, "My father beat my mother to death. I'm sure of it."

Though I wanted to touch her, I decided it best to give her space. "How do you know?"

Sequoia paced about the room with jittery hands, still never looking at me. "He beat her for years, probably before I was even born. I know that he pushed her too hard and killed her. He set the house on fire. He was a medical doctor, so he would've known how to make her body look . . . you know, like she died in the fire. And he took my sister and brother with her, to make it look good. I'm sure he meant to escape. That's what he was like. But the fire must've spread too quickly. I cried and cried. But I knew deep inside me that I'd wished him dead. It was like God was punishing me for my evil thoughts by taking away everyone. Then, when I got older, I hated my narcissism. I mean, it wasn't about me. My poor mother. My sister and brother. Gone forever." She lowered her head in shame.

"It's natural for a child to feel like the center of the universe," I said, still not moving toward her. "Sequoia, I have to ask. You're sure your father set the fire?"

She looked at me and gave an odd little laugh. "You mean did I do it? I was *nine*. I was into Ken dolls and girl's soccer. I was at my best friend's house when it happened. Her mom was making us Rice Krispie treats when the news came over the TV. My entire whereabouts were accounted for, given when the fire must've started. *Okay?*"

For some reason, this broke the tension in the room. We laughed and made out for a while, ending up in the bedroom. I completely believed everything she told me, so I thought it only fair that I told her all about me while we fucked. I left nothing out. I guess that's one way to break it to someone gently. "Now . . . Betsy . . . has . . . me . . . in . . . a . . . corner." I panted through my thrusts.

"Not . . . necessarily," Sequoia replied. "She . . . sounds . . . crazy."

"That's . . . why . . . I . . . can't . . . trust . . . her."

"My . . . poor . . . Jesse . . . and . . . poor . . . poor . . . Scotty."

"I'm . . . not . . . Jesse."

She clasped her hands around my neck. "Jesse . . . suits . . . you."

"Okay . . . then . . . I'm . . . Jesse."

After we went at it a few times, I nuzzled my body next to hers. It was just sort of taken for granted that everything was our special secret.

Suddenly I remembered something she still hadn't explained.

"So Jesse—I mean the real Jesse—and Esther took you in? Then who is Sabrina Falcon?"

Sequoia moved her finger along my chest hairs, making it into a little game. "Their pampered little princess of a daughter. Even when we both got interested in art, they'd buy me smaller sets of paints than they did for Sabrina. Isn't that petty? We were both about the same age. Sabrina would break things around the house and say I did it. Jesse and Esther had awful tempers. They'd yell at me until I wanted to disappear. I still crawl out of my skin when people start yelling, even when it's not about me."

"You told me they loved you like their own." I stroked her shining hair.

"We both said a lot of things, didn't we?"

"Yeah. Life would be much easier if it were illegal to tell the truth."

Sequoia laughed out loud. "You're probably right. Anyway, when I was fourteen, they were going on about what a saint my father was and how ashamed he would be of me, and I couldn't take it anymore. I told them he was a wife beater and murderer who started the fire. I was very calm when I said it, as if . . . as if I lived on some other planet than they did. Esther slapped me across the mouth and said I was not to slander her brother ever again. Jesse said that I must never repeat this story or it would bring shame to his reputation. I had a trust fund, plus an inheritance coming to me when I turned eighteen. I wasn't help-less. I was old for my age. I went to an attorney and became an emancipated minor. I enrolled myself in a Swiss boarding school and traveled. Esther and Jesse said they never wanted to speak to me again, which was fine with me. It turned out that Jesse had skimmed a little off the top of my trust fund and was ordered to return it. I guess what goes around comes around."

"I *will* pay him back." I nuzzled as close as I could along her body, yet no matter how close I got, I kept wanting to be closer.

"Fine, but don't feel you have to do it for me."

6: Dr. Jesse Falcon

"**Y**OU SHOULD CHANGE YOUR NAME, JESSE. You and Esther and even Sabrina."

It was my lawyer on the phone. He was explaining to me that a common practice among victims of identity theft was to change their names. I knew that telling me to change my name wasn't the same thing as telling me to chop off my dick, but still, it seemed ridiculously unfair. Why should I have to go through all that nonsense—not to mention my wife and daughter—simply because law enforcement was too incompetent to solve my case? It really pisses me off when I have every right to be pissed off but someone tries to calm me down, as if the only real problem was that I was pissed off. I said as much to my lawyer, who calmly went on and on about how these cases were very complicated.

"Well, your asshole is pretty complicated, too." I hung up the phone.

"What is it now?" Esther came toward me, rubbing my shoulder in sympathy. I clasped her hand. It was amazing how close Esther and I had become. Maybe all those years of simply staying together were worth something after all. Esther kept all the identity theft documents for me and said that I could only look at them once a day. I had to admit it was helping a little. Too bad I couldn't fully appreciate such happy turns of events. Only about an hour earlier, my accountant brother told me that another hundred grand had been withdrawn from my investments and placed in an offshore bank in my name. After popping a couple of extra happy pills, I called the FBI and was put on hold for forty-five minutes. I hung up and called my lawyer, whom I also hung up on. As I thought of it, probably the thing I did most anymore was hang up the phone on people.

I explained to Esther about changing our names. She tried to make light of it.

"Well, that's not so bad, is it? I never cared for 'Esther' anyway. Maybe I could be Sophia Something. In honor of Sophia Loren."

I popped another pill. "I know you're trying to help, honey, but I don't know how much more I can take." Of course, the missing suicide note thing was also destroying whatever sanity I had left, but I hadn't told Esther anything about it. It was so nice to have a real marriage again that I didn't want to mess it up. In fact, I'd only had one hotel quickie since we'd kissed and made up—something of a record for me.

"I suppose we should call Sabrina," Esther said.

"Yeah, whatever."

She clasped my hands. "Jesse, please. However hard this is, we need each other now more than ever. I don't want to sound like a nagging wife, but you're still taking too many pills and drinking on top of them. You of all people should know how bad that is."

"Look, you said you were going to call Sabrina. Do it already." In times of old, this kind of remark would've set Esther off, but now she looked at me with an understanding sadness.

"What do you think our new names should be?"

"Mr. and Mrs. Fred Fuck." I went to the front door. "I'm going for a ride."

"You really shouldn't be driving, dear, when you've—"

"I'll be fine."

I thanked God I was a psychologist when I called Marty Goldstein from my car.

For the heck of it, I'd already inspected every square inch of the rooftop but was hardly surprised that Linda's tell-all suicide note wasn't sitting there waiting for me. I knew that it could be virtually anywhere. But since the cops took my word for what happened, they did not dig deeply. I thought the note might be in Linda's purse, which presumably had been inside her car when she decided to go psycho on the roof. She was one of those women who practically lived out of her oversized purse. And from what she told me about Marty, he was such a schnook that it might never have occurred to him to go through her belongings for clues about her bizarre behavior. From Linda's descriptions, he was the kind of man who had to ask for instructions for how to make a peanut butter sandwich. Apparently, though, Linda had been true to her word and never told Marty about us. Now what I needed to do was get Marty to let me look inside her car and purse. And if it turned out he already had the goods—doubtful though the possibility was—I was prepared to make a generous offer.

I went to the hospital one evening, relatively certain Marty would be keeping vigil by Linda's side. Indeed, the voice message at their home—apparently, he'd moved back in—informed the listener that, "This is Marty, and I am either at work or at my angel wife's bedside. Please leave a message and send a prayer." However, to get to Linda's room, I had to get past the snooty nurse receptionist, who said that only immediate family was allowed to see Mrs. Goldstein.

"I'm her psychologist." I showed her my credentials in my wallet. "I want to see how she is, and also how her husband is doing. I understand he's here."

"Are you also Mr. Goldstein's psychologist?" She held a pencil to her chin, tapping it lightly as if to express her utter control of the situation.

"No. But I'm here to see Mrs. Goldstein."

"Mrs. Goldstein is in a *coma*, sir."

"Well, so are you."

She flustered, her head trembling and her chin quivering. "I beg your pardon, sir."

"Look, you fucking bitch, I'm fucking here to help." I pounded my fist on the counter. "I'm going in there or expect a lawsuit from the APA."

"Just one moment." She disappeared behind a cubicle and came out a few minutes later with another woman, though the other woman didn't say anything. "Okay, you may go in," said the nurse receptionist, handing me the room number on a slip of paper.

"What do you want me to do, kiss your ass?" I stormed off to the elevator.

Through the glass partition where Linda lay motionless, I saw a stumpy middle-aged man with thick glasses and very little hair left, though he insisted on featuring what few remaining tufts he had. He was exactly how Linda described him. I could also see Linda, who, in her state of deep slumber, looked more attractive than when her bizarre personality was in force, which detracted from her appeal. There were machines and tubes everywhere. Marty was holding her hand and sobbing. "Our little girl, Linnie, is home with her grandma," I heard him say. "Linnie's a fighter, just like her mommy. She fought to live. You can do it, too."

Frankly, I imagined Linda normally fought to remember how to tie her shoe, but I did not think this the opportune time for such sarcasm.

I tapped sympathetically on the glass and entered. "Mr. Goldstein? I am Dr. Jesse Falcon. I thought it was time we met." I extended my hand.

Marty ignored my hand and gave me a hug instead, burying his head in my chest. "Oh, Dr. Falcon, Linda spoke highly of you. I'm so sorry she caused you such unhappiness with her tragic action."

Disengaging as quickly as I could from the hug, I could see how Marty would've been impossible to live with. Linda may have been way over the top, but at least she had some spirit for living. Marty was one of those utterly nerdy types who took wild guesses at what life was supposed to be like. I'm tempted to say his ability to make money was rather like those autistic people with a genius for music or math, except I don't wish to insult the autistic, whose achievements are sincere.

"No need to worry, Mr. Goldstein—"

"Marty." He smiled with a melancholy air.

"Okay, Marty. As I was saying, it is part of one's training as a psychologist to learn how to cope with these . . . these . . ." I feigned a mighty grief that I was swallowing back.

"I know, I know." He patted my hand. "Please, have a seat." He gestured to the second chair in the room on the opposite side of the bed.

"I heard you say your little girl is home, safe and sound."

"Yes, she's beautiful. She looks exactly like her mommy. Our first child. But then, you already knew that, I'm sure."

"Oh, I'm sure she has some of her daddy in her, too."

Marty permitted himself to chortle. "Let us hope not." Self-consciously, he touched his balding head.

"How are you doing, Marty?" I frowned for my supposed concern.

"Hanging in there, Dr. Falcon. Thank you for asking. It's been hard going to work every day and then coming here in the evening. I don't get much R and R. But my mother's been taking care of the baby. Grandma is also a wonderful cook and housekeeper. So it hasn't been *too* bad."

God, talk about a man of depth. He thought all I meant was how was he budgeting his time or whatever. I mean, *hello?* Your wife tried to kill herself and is in an irreversible coma, and you have a daughter who will never know her mother. And though doubtless it was an ordeal to come to the hospital every evening, apparently he never missed a single minute of work. I wondered if the only reason he cried about the situation was because of the time it took away from things he'd rather be doing.

"How are you *feeling*, Marty?"

"Oh, you mean how am I doing like *that*. Sorry, Doctor. I've never been in therapy. I don't know too much about it. I guess I'm okay. Really, I only want Linda to wake up."

"Of course you do." I nodded my head with understanding. "Have you wondered much about why Linda . . . well, what she did?"

Marty looked away. "No, why should I? I mean, what she did was wrong. Why would I want to know more about it?"

"You've never even been curious?"

"I figured you were the expert on that. You're her doctor. I know from watching TV that you can't tell me anything she tells you."

I took a deep breath, as if taking in the profundity of his words. "You're absolutely right. But you see, I need to know more about it, too. Linda was doing beautifully. She was so happy to finally be a mother. I know she was having some difficulties with her marriage, but—"

"Difficulties? What are you talking about? There were no difficulties." Marty looked honestly perplexed.

"Well, you were getting a divorce, right? Wouldn't you call that a difficulty?"

Marty stood up in disbelief. "*Divorce*? There was no divorce." He could tell I was skeptical, so he added, "I swear. I swear on my wonderful wife's soul. There was never any talk of divorce. Not even separation."

I hated to admit it, but I believed him. This made me wonder more than ever what Linda's suicide note might've said, since obviously she'd been lying to the both of us. You could even say she was lying to three different personas, since I was both her psychologist and her occasional fuck. She was even nuttier than I realized, which meant she potentially was even more of a threat to my well-being.

"Marty, I was only going by what Linda told me."

"You mean at like a million bucks an hour she was *lying* to you?"

"So it would seem." We both stared at the comatose Linda, as if wondering what other mysteries were buried in her utter silence.

"Just out of curiosity, how much did the cops talk to you?"

"Oh, once or twice. They figured Linda was kind of—well, you know, not all there in the head. One of them wanted to go through all her things, but this other one, an old guy, said it wasn't necessary." Marty looked ready to cry. "He said it was an open-and-shut case. Right to my face."

Hallelujah, praise Jesus. I could only thank my lucky stars for that shitty old cop. Walking up to Marty, I put my hand on his shoulder. "Look, Marty, I think there's a lot we still need to know. What if Linda wakes up? We have to know exactly how to handle her."

He sighed. "I guess you're right, Dr. Falcon. What do you suggest?"

"Let me look through all her things. I'll see if there's a note or a journal or anything that gives a clue to why she did what did."

"I could do that much for you, Doctor. After all you've been through."

"Thank you, Marty."

I think he was being agreeable because the whole situation utterly perplexed him, and he didn't know where to begin. But whatever was going through his mind—and it couldn't have been much—I was grateful for his cooperation.

Claiming that I would be extremely busy starting the next day, Marty let me follow him to his suburban home that evening. He insisted I meet the sleeping baby, whom I studied as much as I could for a resemblance to either Marty or me. I honestly couldn't tell. Babies all look the same to me. I said, though, that the baby was adorable. I next met Marty's mother, who was smilingly nice in a way I never trusted. I had to insist several times to Granny Goldstein that I wasn't hungry and didn't even want a nice cool glass of water. Marty asked me if I wanted to see the bedroom he shared with Linda. I replied that it was doubtful she'd keep any secrets in there, so instead I was led to the spacious garage.

"Here it is," he said grimly. "Linda's Toyota." Marty went back in the house, as if leaving me to perform an autopsy on a corpse.

Linda's Toyota was a bright yellow on the outside but a dismal chaos of crud on the inside. Empty potato chip bags, old shopping receipts, torn road maps, sweaters, broken flip-flops, plastic super-market bags. It was like a landfill.

I did, however, find her purse. It, too, was extremely disorga-nized. I combed methodically through tons of makeup and things, only to come up empty-handed. No note. I searched through every last greasy Taco Bell wrapper in the car and likewise found nothing.

The other likely place to look was in what Marty called Linda's "craft room," though it might as well have been called her Adult Atten-tion Deficit Disorder room. There were piles of unfinished knitting, three or four unfinished scrapbooks, blank drawing pads, unopened boxes of colored pencils and pastels, a set of glitter tubes (unused), about ten types of glue, dozens of brand new rubber stamps, and a wood carving kit but no wood. The one file cabinet had nothing but chaotic scraps of fabric in either of its two drawers. However, Linda did have a laptop computer in the room, and I anxiously turned it on.

Although no password was required to enter, she had a file on her desktop called "Private." She seemed to think that one word would keep people from opening it, though in fairness to Linda she probably never thought anyone except Marty would have reason to be in this room at all. And dimwitted Marty would've respected her privacy.

Inside the file were some extremely bad attempts at poetry that—to make matters worse—were insipidly upbeat. To give one example: "The things I thought were hardest/Turned out to be the easiest/Once I believed in myself." You read something like that, and it's all you can do to keep from puking. To say the least, Linda was totally out of touch with her true nature. She believed in herself about as much as John Wilkes Booth believed in Abraham Lincoln. If her insecurities were specks of dust, they could've filled the Empire State Building.

I regret to say that there also was a file called "My Jesse." In an annoying schoolgirl tone, Linda documented every last secretion of sweat gland that transpired between us.

"The stallion force of his love, love, love," she redundantly wrote, "filled my love spot with pure rapture."

My online photo from my old professorship was pasted into a creepy pink heart. Fortunately, she seemed to think that the more florid her writing was, the better it was. Oftentimes, the actual facts of a given encounter were obscured.

"I gave him the flower of my love," she wrote on the day she told me she was pregnant. "Our love garden will blossom a thousandfold."

Finally, though, I read an untitled document dated the day of her fall.

Jesse, My True, True Love,

You are the love of my life. You have broken my heart into millions and trillions and zillions of tiny pieces. I carry our love secret in my body. I cannot let a child come into this world of nothing but misery. So with all the joy in the world, I do us all a favor. Someday you will realize how much you love me, which is more than there are clouds in the sky on the cloudiest day of the year. I am nothing more than a cloud now. A rainy, rainy cloud. When you are inside me, I feel nothing but your cruelty. I become your cruelty. Nothing but your cruelty and your great, great love.

I die proclaiming my eternal love,

Your Linda

I could only hope that in her final moments of craziness, she either forgot to print out this suicide note or that the printed copy simply was lost forever. Gone with the wind, as they say. I wondered if I should delete the entire private file. I knew little about computer technology, though I'd heard about deleted files being retrieved by experts.

It was good-natured Marty who solved my dilemma. He knocked on the door—though this was his own house—and asked if I wanted to take the computer with me.

"That might be a good idea," I said. "It will take me a while to go through all the files."

I felt so relieved that I let myself think my problems were over. Once I had the computer, I could always say it was stolen or someone dropped it in my swimming pool.

"Can I interest you in a beer, Doc?" Marty was in a more casual mood, no doubt due to the beer he was drinking himself.

"I never drink and drive."

"Good for you, Doc." He patted my shoulder as I took my leave.

I drove around the corner and immediately opened the laptop to give it a password, in case I decided to hang on to it for a while. The password was a random set of characters that I quickly memorized. I drove to my office and put the computer in my safe. Then I decided the hell with it and got the computer back out. I erased all the files, drove to a town dump, ran over the computer with my car a few times, and buried the broken mess into a big pile of garbage. No one but the scavenger birds would find it.

No sooner had I gotten back home than Marty called me with the joyful news that Linda had come out of her coma.

"Gee, that's great," I managed to say. "What a miracle."

"I didn't know you doctor types believed in miracles," Marty said. It seemed an ill-timed moment for a debate between reason and faith, so I simply ignored him.

"As Linda's psychologist, I'd like to go to the hospital right away to see her."

"That's fine. Mother and I are getting Linnie all gussied up."

"Great, maybe we'll all be there together."

I gave Esther a quick peck on the lips and drove as fast as I could to the hospital. I almost fell on my knees in gratitude to God when I got to Linda's room first. This gave me a chance to try to stop her from saying all kinds of things I didn't want her to say, though admittedly I had no idea how I'd go about it. The doctor told me she was still quite disoriented and weak. I reassured him when I told him I was her shrink.

"Oh, by the way," said the doctor cheerfully, "she has no feeling from the neck down. It may be permanent."

I stopped in my tracks. "She's paralyzed? Why are you smiling?"

"Oh, was I?" the doctor said. "I'm sorry. I haven't slept in forty-eight hours."

I took a deep breath before entering her room. "Hello, Linda," I said quietly, for want of knowing what else to say. She was still connected to a monitor that was keeping her alive. Every beep communicated heart activity.

Linda weakly turned her head to face me; she wore a surprisingly earnest expression. "Why can't anyone . . . let me die? Everyone is . . . awful." Her voice was a raspy whisper. "I want to die . . . more than ever. It's . . . It's not even about . . . you and me. It never . . . was. I know that now. Now that I can't move, I guess I really never could." Failed suicide attempts have a way of sobering people up. Linda obviously still wanted to die, yet she was plainspoken and didn't seem at all delusional.

"You have a baby girl, Linda. Your husband loves you. The paralysis may not be permanent. But even if it is, you can still have a life." Whatever I expected from this conversation, the possibility of being an encouraging therapist never even occurred to me.

"I . . . never had . . . a life. I never will. That's what I wanted from you. A *life*. I know now it's not to be." Her voice got a little stronger and so did the expression in her eyes. "I . . . I apologize, Jesse. I never should have put you through this. Not with a baby I don't want. I told myself . . . I wanted it . . . But I can't give it life. Birth, but not life. I'm . . . I'm too dead. On the inside. Not being able . . . to move my body . . . is not the worst of it. That's not what makes me so . . . dead."

"Linda, you can get better. You won't always feel this way. Get a divorce, if you want. Hell, let Marty raise the kid if you can't. Go to college. Run for president. But *live*, damn it."

With some effort, she took a deep, parched swallow. "Please . . . let me die." With her eyes, she gestured to the monitor. "I don't deserve favors. But please, do this one. You're the only one who can."

I was so unaccustomed to crying that it took me a second or two to realize that's what I was doing. "Linda, I can't do that." I should have gotten a doctor to give her a shot, but I couldn't leave her. The beeping monitor seemed to be mocking me.

Linda was crying, too. "Oh, *please*," she begged. "My daughter . . . is better without me. Everyone is. Especially me. Don't make me have to see my daughter." She was breathing heavily, the tears streaming down her cheeks. "Please," she kept repeating. "You're smart, you can get away with it. Marty will be here any minute."

At first, I emphatically said no, I couldn't do it. Then I'd look at her and look at the monitor. "I don't *think* I can do it," I heard myself say. I found myself reaching out to touch the monitor switch—only to back down again. I did this four times in a row. Then I asked her again to give life another chance.

Now she was really crying hard. "Jesse, if anything between us has ever meant anything, please, please, please, give me my right to die."

Well, what can I say? You weren't me in that moment. It got to where it felt like the only sensible thing to do, like turning on a flashlight in the dark.

I took no chances. With one eye to the glass partition, I wrapped my hand in a Kleenex. I rapidly turned her main monitor off and on and off and on, over and over again, too quickly for a code red to start but jarring her enough to weaken her heartbeat down to nothing. I stared ahead at the monitor, unable to look at Linda, who never made another sound. Finally, with the machine on, there was a loud code red alert. I called out for help, knowing full well it was too late. On my way out of the room, I could hear the doctors pronounce her dead. I went into the men's room, splashed my face with water, and rubbed my red eyes.

"Crybaby," I said to my image in the mirror. I stuck around to answer a few questions and that was that. The machine was on when her heart stopped, and my fingerprints were not on it. The same doctor I talked to before shrugged and told me that coma patients sometimes briefly woke up before dying.

"I'm curious," he said. "Was she lucid?"

"Stick your curiosity up your lucid ass," I replied.

I knew I should stay for Marty and his mother and baby daughter. When they arrived shortly thereafter, the doctor pulled them aside. Marty put his hand to his mouth and called out, "Oh my God," but he did not cry. His mother, holding the baby, turned to look at me. I wasn't sure why she did this. I gave her my most sympathetic expression.

"I wanted to be here when you heard," I said quietly, as Marty approached me.

"Thanks, Doc." He gave me another of his awful hugs. I felt I had to hug him back under the circumstances.

"Let us be alone now," his mother said. "You've done enough."

I wondered what she meant by "enough" and shivered a little. Fortunately, Marty interjected. "He's done more than enough, Ma."

"Call me if there's anything I can do." And with that, I left them alone.

What I did was probably wrong. Yet even if it was, it felt like the one selfless thing I had ever done. Not that I felt good. Far from it. I felt like I was burning up inside from guilt. And obviously I was afraid I might get caught.

Linda was only part of it. I knew perfectly well that what made me do it was not her cries for help but that fucking identity thief. If I couldn't control that asshole, at least I could control Linda. It was a relief to have her secrets rest with her death, and it was cathartic to feel that *something* was completely up to me. Maybe I was rationalizing, but I told myself that the identity thief made me do it, like a child blaming something on the devil.

Even the one selfless thing I ever did was also totally selfish.

Back at my home, Esther immediately asked, "Is everything okay?"

"I suppose." I kissed her hard and held her like I might never let go.

"Well, whatever it was, I wish it happened more often."

"Esther, let's sit down and talk."

She shrugged. "Okay." We walked to the patio table by the swimming pool. It was a lovely night, filled with fragrance from the gardens Esther installed.

"Look, I've been thinking. If we have to change our names, we might as well get something good out of it. So maybe we should start over again someplace else."

"But we just got done doing that."

"Not really, if you think about it. We left because of—well, because of my stupidity. But this time, we'll be in charge. We have to believe that we are or else we'll completely fall apart."

Esther thought about it. "Well, I do have only one job to finish up. And I did always love it more back home where Sabrina is."

I only wanted to get the hell away from anything to do with Linda Goldstein. Yet the more I thought of it, it made good sense to move back where we came from, since the identity thief was almost certainly back there someplace. I'd catch him myself, if I had to move into my bank with a sleeping bag. And if anyone became suspicious about my behavior in light of Linda's death, I'd tell them the truth: we changed our names because my lawyer said to, and we'd moved because my wife wanted to be closer to our beautiful daughter.

"Great. We'll change our names and move by the end of month, back across the country. Back home, where we belong."

The next day—after a sleepless night—I saw my two male patients. The first one was the guy who was full of himself. He told me that he should've won first prize at a karaoke contest the night before but that someone else got more applause because everyone felt sorry for her.

"Can I sing for you, Doc?" he asked. "It would validate me."

"Sure." I smiled encouragingly. I had to endure his thin, mediocre voice as he crooned, "This Guy's in Love with You."

Next came that morbid male patient. I always dreaded seeing him, though of course I couldn't give the slightest indication of this.

"You know what really gets me?" he asked.

"No," I replied pleasantly.

"When people say really nasty things, but afterward they say they didn't mean it."

"Why does that bother you?"

He became agitated, twisting his fingers and breathing hard. "It makes no sense. Why would someone say something cruel and then supposedly not mean it? If you ask me, anger is when people are alive. They're honest and raw. It's the polite bullshit afterward that's the lie. 'I didn't mean it!' Like hell you didn't mean it. You *did* mean it. What you don't mean is your apology."

I didn't like hearing all this, but I had no choice. "Do you ever say things you don't mean?"

He slammed his fist on the table. "Of course I do. It's all the nice bullshit I tell people because I have to. That's what drives me crazy."

"That's very interesting."

He sat in silence before finally saying, apropos of whatever went on in his head, "Is it normal to think about killing people?"

Patients confide all sorts of nutty things, but I couldn't help feeling this was some sort of cosmic retribution. "Why do you ask that?" I replied evenly.

"Sometimes I'm afraid I'm going to end up killing someone. Or it's more like I know I will. The *anger*, you know? It gets to be too much. I stay awake all night, listening to Beethoven's 'Pastoral' and thinking about killing my parents. It feels like the only way out. The only way I'll ever stop being angry."

I shrugged. "I think everyone has at least one moment in life thinking about killing someone. In fact, I wouldn't believe people who told me they never did."

"You're saying I'm normal?"

I thought carefully before speaking. "Let's say I think you should also see a psychiatrist. The right medicine may help you even more. In fact, I'll drive you to the hospital right now."

His face brightened. "You will? Gee, thank you, Dr. Falcon. You're the best."

"It's my job," I replied neutrally.

7 : AKA JESSE FALCON

"I WANT TO MEET BETSY," Sequoia said brightly, as if deciding she was in the mood for a cup of tea.

We were in bed together, which had become like an office for us. While other couples watched TV in bed, we were always shuffling papers and checking our laptops and making major decisions in between another round of going at it. Sex, money, identity theft, divorce, McShrink, the shared secret of Biff's death and Scotty's abuse, take-out food for breakfast, lunch and dinner—it was all part of a singular whole that transpired on the exotic island of black satin sheets that was our bed. Given Sequoia's food fetishes, I had developed a passion for pizza with white sauce and black olives. Yeah, love brings all the pieces of your life together. But sometimes those pieces are better off apart.

At the moment, I was answering my latest batch of McShrink e-mails. One guy wanted to know if his transsexual brother-to-sister should still be best man at his wedding, and a woman wanted to know if she should punish her son for punching her so hard he broke her nose. She said she'd never punished him before but always tried to reason with him as if they were best friends. My mom would've had fun answering that one.

It took me a moment to comprehend what Sequoia said. When I did, I sat up, startled. "Let me get this straight. You want to meet Betsy? It's too bad Attila the Hun is dead, or maybe you could meet him, too."

Sequoia giggled. "Now that's no way to talk about the mother of your son." She put her arm around my shoulder, easing me back into bed. "Seriously, sometimes women can work things out between themselves, without a man around."

"Work out? What is there to work out?"

Sequoia wore a mischievous grin. "Oh, you know, to leave you alone to let us raise Scotty."

"That's Ondine's job."

She rubbed behind my knee with her bare foot; this was a super turn-on spot on my body. "Ondine's very good at what she does, but she's a lawyer. I'd talk to Betsy as one woman to another. Besides, Ondine doesn't know everything, and I do."

It was true. By the time Ondine was back in town, Sequoia had long since convinced me to tell her nothing more. As far as my lawyer was concerned, Biff was still mysteriously missing, I had never stolen anyone's identity or money, and Scotty would be moving in as soon as Sequoia and I found a place for the three of us—assuming the judge agreed, which seemed pretty much a no-brainer. Scotty had met Sequoia twice so far and thought she was "intelligent," which was his nerdy kid's way of saying he liked her. Mom, for her part, shrugged and said that anyone was better than Betsy. I had to explain to Sequoia that my mom was not one for warm fuzzies. Mom, of course, knew nothing about Sequoia being the niece of Jesse Falcon.

I hadn't heard from Betsy since our crazed meeting in the coffee shop. This brought me comfort and alarm at the same time. I enjoyed pretending that she'd simply vanished, like someone I'd only imagined to have existed all those years. Or maybe she was in the Bahamas or Timbuktu searching for Biff. But the same silence could've meant she was up to something. According to her lawyer, she was still fighting for sole custody.

Sequoia put a silencing fingertip to my lips. "Wait, hear me out. I know that if I talk to Betsy, I mean really talk to her, I can convince her to leave us alone. And drop the custody thing with Scotty."

"How?" I sat up on my elbow, stifling a yawn.

"She obviously can't hack into the system by herself. And I'm sure her hundred grand from Biff's parents is ancient history. So we pay her off. She can go on a fancy cruise to meet a billionaire with a bad heart."

I did a little mental arithmetic. "I don't want to keep stealing. And McShrink doesn't do *that* well—I mean, not well enough to satisfy Betsy. Knowing what she knows, seven figures is the least she'd go for."

"But we could put it—I mean I could put it—in investments for her. She can live on the interest of a well-invested quarter mil, especially if we also pay off the mortgage."

"You don't know how she spends money."

Sequoia absently braided her hair, which was so soft that the braid kept falling right out again. "Oh, I think I have an idea. And the thing is, you have serious communication issues with her. You shouldn't be talking to her at all."

"'Serious communication issues.' That's one way of putting it."

"What you don't see, dummy, is that in her mind if you offer her money, she's a whore. But if I, the quote-unquote other woman, do it, it's like she can convince herself she has the upper hand. Everyone needs to feel sometimes like they're in control."

I sighed in resignation. Something told me that there was no stopping Sequoia on this one. "Okay, on the condition that you meet in a public place, and I'm nearby, just in case."

Sequoia laughed. "You mean you'll wear a disguise?"

"Of course not. But I'll . . . I dunno, I'll be in my car right outside the restaurant or whatever it is."

Sequoia snapped her fingers. "Wait, I've got it. Why don't we get one of those wire things? You know, like the cops use to record conversations."

I thought about it. The last conversation I had with Betsy had her confessing to a murder she didn't commit. Her story was absurd, yet she also talked all about Jesse Falcon. But Sequoia had a way of making me trust her, as if I were a fish that after some perfunctory struggle enjoyed getting hooked and reeled in. "I suppose it could be fun. Where do we get one?"

"Oh, there are stores that sell all kinds of junk like that."

I'd never seen such a store, but then I'd never been much of a shopper. "I wonder what such a store would be called. Paranoid Plaza?"

"Leave it to me." She squeezed my small nipples; the gesture took me by surprise. And so the plan went into action.

Sequoia sent Betsy an artsy card asking to meet with her. She explained how she wanted to know her because she was an important part of my life, and it would be good for Scotty, and so forth. Betsy normally hated other women—I guess she pretty much hated everyone—but like many people, she occasionally fell for an innocuous, flowery message.

I would've loved to have been a fly on the wall when they met at a trendy wine bar. But I needn't have been envious. Their conversation only lasted maybe five minutes. Sequoia emerged with flushed cheeks, as though she'd heard a bad word for the first time.

"Well, that's that." Sequoia pulled her car door shut; it didn't quite catch, so she closed it again. "Why are you staring at me?"

"Why do you think?" I revved up the engine. "What the hell happened?"

She cupped her chin in her hand and stared out the window. "I wrote her a check. She's dropping the custody hearing. I didn't even need to record anything."

"And?"

"And what? I told you I'd get her to do it. Well, I did it."

"So in other words, you sat down and said, 'Hi, my name is Sequoia and I fuck your husband and how much would it cost for you to go away forever?'"

Sequoia turned on the car radio. As always, it was important for her to have light pop music on in the car, even though she played it so softly you barely could hear it. "Well, there was a little more to it than that. First, she refused to shake my hand and said how I was probably wearing a wire, and she would frisk me right there in public unless I turned it off. I pretended to have no idea what she was talking about, but I kind of subtly scratched at my chest to turn it off. Then she said how probably I put on a King Kong suit every night and gave it to you up the ass because that's the only way a man could ever want me. I said that even as insults go, that made no sense, and Betsy was like, 'What doesn't make any sense is why any man would want you over me.' I tried to lighten things up by saying, 'Well, whoever understands what a man wants?' But she goes, 'Certainly not you, you frigid, gangrene twat.' So I go, 'It takes one to know one.' Anyway, I guess she got insulting me out of her system, or maybe she realized it wouldn't make me burst into tears, because then she turned all haughty and said how she couldn't possibly see how I could have anything to say to her. I didn't point out the obvious—that she showed up to the meeting voluntarily. Instead, I'm like, 'Well, I have two hundred and fifty thousand reasons why.' She goes, 'Ha!' Just like *that*, you know? 'Ha! What makes you think I can be paid off? Love has no price tag. The love between a mother and her son can never be bought.' I'm thinking, 'Oh, brother,' but of course I don't say that."

"All *that* happened in like two minutes?"

"It was seven minutes. My watch is excellent. But obviously you don't know women nearly as well as you think."

"No, indeed."

"Anyway, instead I ask if a half mil will do the trick, and after batting it around for a while, she settled on two mil."

"Two million bucks? I don't have that much money. I still want to pay back Jesse Falcon, and I feel like hell every time I take more money from him. I can't do it." Some prick in front of me was driving at about two miles an hour. I honked at him and shot him the finger.

"No, but I have a little to throw into the pot. Plus . . . well, you have to promise you won't be mad at me?"

Finally, the idiot in front of me changed lanes. "I promise."

"Well, I've watched how you hack into my Uncle Jesse's account, and I guess I . . . you know, took a little myself. Don't worry, it's in a secret offshore account. I figured he owed me, plus I had to prepare for the worst with Betsy, from what you told me. I mean, this is hardly the first time in history a quarter million turned out to be two million. It happens all the time."

I looked at her angelic face, trying to comprehend what she said. "Sequoia, I trusted you."

"Yes, Your Holiness. And your point is?" She sighed and patted my shoulder. "Seriously, I think you need to stop being in denial about something important. You *know* you have no intention of ever paying my Uncle Jesse back. It's something you tell yourself. It's like someone who will never look for a job who keeps saying that tomorrow he'll start looking for a job, or someone who will never stop drinking saying tomorrow he'll stop drinking, or someone who never plans to diet and exercise saying that tomorrow—"

"Yeah, okay, I get it." I was grateful for a red light to gather my thoughts. "Look, I know you did it for us. And for Scotty. Life is hard enough with Betsy for a mother, especially after—well, you know. But you act like you said you spent too much money on a new pair of shoes. These are serious crimes. I really—I mean, we really need to be careful."

"I don't appreciate that stupid remark. Very sexist. I expect better from you. But you need to admit that you love what you're doing. Wrong, shmong. Even cops break the law. Even presidents. Sometimes people—"

All of a sudden, she grabbed my arm, shoved me over, and put her foot to the gas pedal, flooring it. We barely missed hitting a city bus and caused a cacophony of honking horns.

I quickly regained control of the car. "What the fuck was that? Have you lost your mind? What if Scotty was in the car?"

I'd never known Sequoia to yell at me before or for that matter, to swear unless quoting someone like Betsy. "Shit, it was my Aunt Esther. As in Esther *Falcon*. I haven't seen her in years, but I'm sure of it. She was walking into a realtor's office. Jesse, don't you get it? They're moving back."

It was strange to still be called Jesse under the circumstances. "Well, I guess we always knew this was a possibility."

"Speak for yourself. I was hoping to never have to look at any of them again. I only moved back here when I heard they were on the other side of the country."

It seemed odd that I never knew this before. Somehow I'd assumed that Sequoia had lived in the city for years. "Where did you live between Swiss finishing school and here?"

"What does that have to do with anything? I lived a bunch of places."

"Excuse me for wanting to know about the woman I love." I smiled at her, and I could tell she was resisting the urge to smile back.

"Yes, you're a dear. Now, what are we going to do? Maybe they already know about us. Maybe—"

"If it will make you feel better, Sequoia, we'll move. McShrink can do his work anywhere and so can you." I put my hand on her knee.

She didn't seem to notice. "But what about Scotty? It would be awful for him. To uproot him again to some new school—"

"Scotty will be fine. It's not his nature to make friends or get close to people." I'd never quite said this out loud before, but I knew it was the sad truth. If we were more religious, he probably would've been happy as a monk. Instead, he'd probably grow up to be a professor of something obscure who never cracked a smile.

"It's nice to know his father has such confidence in him. Don't you believe in change? Why do the McShrink stuff if you don't?"

"Ever hear of money?"

"I'm serious. I thought on some level you were proud of yourself for helping people."

I thought about it. "I believe that from time to time we can stand up to the people we're afraid of or the people we silently hate—if there's a difference—and feel satisfied for ten minutes. We think it's a guarantee that we'll never have to stand up to them again. But we will have to, and maybe next time, we'll back down and be back at square one. I believe people can pretend to be happy or hope they'll be happy and maybe even be happy because something special happens. But then all the bullshit takes over again."

"You missed our turn-off street."

I could tell my cynicism disappointed her. Prince Charming was supposed to be happy all the time. "See? It proves my point."

She put her hand on top of mine. "If you really feel that way," she said quietly, "I feel sorry for you. I want to help you get your faith in humanity back."

"Said the extortionist to the identity thief."

"You know what I mean. Anyway, I think Betsy is very nice."

I damn near ran the car off the road again. "Nice? You call a two-million-dollar bribery nice? She's crazy, she's a total nut job bitch, she's—"

"She's the mother of your son. And yes, she has some issues. I treated her like a damaged child."

"Do women take some secret oath to defend the most fucked-up people in the world? That 'damaged child,' as you call her, could drive us to the poor house. Or jail."

"Oh, stop worrying so much."

I slid the car into a parking space about a half block from where we lived. We walked thoughtfully to our building.

Sequoia stopped as she let us into the main lobby. "And people do make sense. I know I do." She kissed me and put her hand inside my crotch, massaging my hardness. I didn't love her any less, but I realized in that moment that Sequoia was *limited* by her optimistic nature. Except for having money, which she didn't particularly seem to enjoy, her entire life had been one fucked-up thing after another, yet she had to believe that everything was wonderful.

As we settled in and made love, I told her I would call my mom to get Scotty as soon as Betsy dropped her case and I was awarded full custody. Sequoia said we should invite Mom to move across country with us to help Scotty make the adjustment. I didn't want to live with my mother, and I put up some resistance, but by the time we both came and moaned with ecstasy, I agreed that she was right. Besides, I was sure Mom would never want to move that far away.

We usually were too busy to watch much TV, but at the end of a long day, sometimes we relaxed in bed by turning on the boob tube and numbing out to something mindless—the sillier the better. So as we nuzzled close under the sheets, I turned on the remote.

"Please don't spend the next hour channel surfing," Sequoia said. "You know it drives me up the wall."

It was true. I had a short attention span for most programs and was happy to catch two minutes of this and five minutes of that. Sequoia, though, had this thing about watching a show from beginning to end. Once she went so far as to say that my channel surfing spoke to my nature—my inability to commit on a deep level. I did not have the heart to respond that by the same dime-store analysis, her insistence on watching a program from beginning to end spoke volumes about her abandonment issues. In truth, it irritated me when she said things like this about me, but I loved her and kept my negativity to myself.

"Yes, Your Majesty," I joked.

She gave my arm a playful punch. We were watching some reality show about cowboys trying to go vegan when there was a sudden news bulletin.

The chief of police had called a press conference to say there was a person of interest in the disappearance of Biff, the only child of his prominent—meaning filthy rich—parents. For a second or two, my stomach flooded with burning liquid fear. But my fear turned to relief when the chief went on to say that this person, though unnamed, was a known local racketeer whom Biff owed money for his gambling debts.

"Let it go," Sequoia whispered, reading my thoughts. "This guy's probably been bumping people off for years. He's only getting what's coming to him."

I looked at her meaningfully. "I want you to know that if I killed Biff myself, I'd turn myself in. But Scotty . . ."

Sequoia considered my declaration. "Hmm, I disagree. It would destroy Scotty to have you in prison."

"Yeah, I guess you're right."

I, of course, did not know where things stood with Biff's parents on all this, but between the intimations of his being a child molester—which might now surface—and the fact that they already knew what a fuck-up he was, I imagined it caused them embarrassment more than relief. Not surprisingly, the reporters lined up around Biff's mansion had received comments of little value from his parents as they entered their home.

His mother said, "Please, go report some nice news. There's an orchid show at the Expo Center."

And his father said, "We raised our boy to believe in America and do the right thing."

As much as I hated to admit it, I understood for the first time what Biff had been up against all his life. Not that this excused molesting children. But when you're dealing with rich people who think they own the world, maybe you find passive-aggressive ways of getting back at them. Or who knows, maybe it was a sick way of trying to re-parent himself. I still hated his guts for what he did to my son, but a tiny trickle of pity made its way into my consciousness. As for his stealing Betsy or always having Betsy's love or whatever the fuck it was, I'd long since come to see that as a blessing in disguise.

But such philosophizing was short-lived. My cell phone rang, and I saw that it was Mom calling. She rarely called ever since finding out about Jesse Falcon. She took it for granted "they"—whoever "they" were—tapped our phones. I had a sinking feeling about what she was going to say and figured I might as well get it over with.

"Hi, Mom," I said cheerfully.

"Hello, my darling son," she replied with equal approbation. "Why don't you come over for a visit? I'm sure Scotty would love to see you."

I was certain that she'd seen the same news report on Biff and that she assumed I killed him.

"Great, Mom, I'll be right over." I was careful never to mention Sequoia to her over the phone.

As soon as Sequoia and I arrived at the condo, Mom pulled me aside and said she and I were going to a restaurant to talk. Scotty was already in bed, and Miss Vargas—as she always called Sequoia—could babysit. She said it would be good for her.

"If the kid wakes up," Mom instructed, "ask him to tell you about the shit he's learning in school."

Mom liked chain restaurants that served a dozen kinds of burgers and an assortment of pies for dessert. We pulled up into the nearest place, waited to be seated, and pointed to a pink booth in an area where no one was sitting close by. Of course, it was possible we were still being watched or recorded, but you have to draw the line somewhere and go about your life.

The table server wore a nametag that read, "Leonardo." He also wore a button that stated, "Ask me about our breakfast two-for-ones." I told Leonardo I'd have a small dinner salad and water. After ordering something called a triple fiesta burger with onion rings, extra fries, hot sauce, a slice of peach pie with peach ice cream topped with peach syrup, and an extra-large cherry cola, Mom got right to the point.

"Biff?" she sneered. "*Biff?*"

"What about him? He's been missing for a while. They have some gangster as a person of interest."

"You said he was afraid of Betsy, and I believed you. What spineless fuck of a man wouldn't be?"

The smiling table server refilled our ice water; we smiled and nodded our thanks as he departed. "Mom, I said *probably* that was what happened. Maybe it still was."

She shook her head at me sadly, as if to say, *Where did I go wrong?* "Look, where's the body? Knowing you, you probably delivered it to the police station with your name and address and photo ID."

I had to decide whether to keep denying everything or come clean. I chose to come clean.

"It was Scotty. Biff molested him." I then proceeded to recount the awful events of the morning I had left Betsy.

As Mom took a generous bite of her four-inch-high burger, she thought while she chewed. After swallowing a swig of cherry cola, she said, "Okay, that was a pretty good one. Now tell me what really happened."

The look on my face must've told her all she needed to know.

"Oh, God. You let that happen to my grandson?"

"I didn't know, Mom. Not until Scotty told me that morning. I knew Biff was flaky, but I didn't think—"

"Shut up, shut up, shut up." She opened her purse, plunked down some cash, and stormed out of the restaurant, leaving her mountain of food unfinished. I hurried after her. She ignored me. After we were buckled into the car, she slapped me so hard across the face I literally saw stars.

"How can you be my son?" She pointed to her head with her finger. "Don't you have *anything* going on up here? Out of all the people who could've been your lifelong best friend, you picked a child molester. A whore wife? Okay, men are idiots. But Biff. And to leave him alone with your own son? And don't even think about saying you were always at the office. Men and their goddamn offices. They should all be locked up inside them, and let their wives throw away the key."

As I rubbed the side of my face to massage away the sting, I realized that Mom was at least in part angry over something my dad did that I never knew about. But I didn't think it politic to inquire further.

"When we were eight years old, Biff was just an eight-year-old kid." I was yelling without realizing I was going to. "If you know people so well, why did you let me play with him? Don't put this on me. Don't you get it? Everything I've done—Jesse Falcon and everything else—has been to protect Scotty."

"Keep telling yourself that." She fiddled absently through her purse. "And you should never yell at your mother."

"I'm not telling you about the body. It'll only get you in more trouble."

"Thank you so much for considering my well-being." She took out a roll of hard candies and snapped her purse shut. "Thanks to you, I had no dinner tonight."

I rolled down my window to let in the cool night wind as we drove. "Do you love me, Mom?"

"What the hell kind of question is that? I'm your *mother*."

I wanted to say that sometimes I wished I'd been adopted, but didn't. Instead, I told her about Jesse Falcon's probably having moved back to town and that after the custody hearing, Sequoia, Scotty, and I would move across the country. I invited Mom to join us for Scotty's sake. At first she said she'd lived in the same town all her life and was too old to move, but upon brooding for a few minutes, she agreed to join us.

Following a few uneventful days, Ondine called me to say she had the signed papers from Betsy granting me full custody. Our family court judge had a cancellation, so the following afternoon, we were able to make it final. Betsy did not show up in court, but the judge mused that perhaps it was an omen. After a short and highly anticlimactic hearing, Scotty was all mine.

"Thanks so much for everything, Ondine." I offered my hand.

She took a step back, as if studying me. "Next time you need a lawyer, get someone else." And with that, she walked away. I wondered if she knew or at least suspected all kinds of things but knew there was nothing she would tell anyone.

On the Internet, Sequoia arranged to rent an unobtrusive four-bedroom house in the suburbs, three thousand miles away. From the online pictures, it seemed to be in good shape, and we looked up the school district, which was supposedly one of the best in the state.

Mom pointed out that they always say that. "*You* supposedly went to good schools," she said, glaring at me. "And look what happened."

Sequoia thought it was a cute joke and laughed.

After considering plane, bus, and train, it was decided that the four of us would drive across country with Sequoia at the wheel at all times. She was the safest driver and least likely to get us stopped by the cops. She was also the least likely person that the cops would be looking for. Sequoia decided to leave her apartment unoccupied, but Mom found a friend of some elderly woman to rent her condo. We all packed light. Porky the Hamster had died, though I wondered if Mom poisoned him. We were able to fit ourselves and our belongings into Sequoia's four-door sedan for the big day of the move.

"I want to say good-bye to Mom," Scotty said, as soon as we hit the interstate.

My mom gave a mean laugh, as though she relished every new complication I had to deal with. "Tell him Betsy has the clap," she said to me.

"What's the clap?" Scotty asked. "Is it like when you clap your hands too much?"

Mom laughed some more. "Sort of."

As she drove the exact speed limit, Sequoia said to me, "What do you think? Would it really do any harm? Maybe she's not even home or doesn't—"

"Mom is *always* home," Scotty said. "And she'll *want* to see me."

There reaches a point where one more possible misstep doesn't seem to make any difference. "Fine," I decided. "Let's turn around and see Betsy. Or let Scotty see her. Just for a few minutes."

Betsy uncharacteristically was sitting on the front steps of what was now her house, seeming to contemplate the meaning of life as she drank her Diet Pepsi. I got out of the car first. It was one of those days in which it went from sunny to cloudy and back in a matter of minutes. I never liked that kind of weather.

"Have you come to gloat?" Betsy asked me, presumably forgetting about the two million dollars and paid-off mortgage she now possessed.

"Scotty wants to say good-bye for now. We're moving away."

"Where to?" she asked distractedly. Her usual high energy had been drained out of her, like a fire hydrant that ran out of water.

"I don't have to tell you. You gave up all visitation rights."

"Isn't there anybody in the world who wants my love?"

It occurred to me she may have taken an anti-depressant, but if so, it zonked her out more than anything else.

"Cut the crap, Betsy. Look, we need to get going. I'll go get Scotty and you can say good-bye."

I stood by the car, maybe twenty feet away, as Scotty gave his mother a hug. She did not hug him back but made a cruel face. "My son. What a joke. He hates me. He hates his own mother."

Scotty started crying. As I approached them, I heard him say, "Mom, please speak to me. Is it because of Biff? Did you find out? I'm sorry, but I had to do it."

Betsy's nastiness turned to a lewd grin. "Biff? What about Biff?"

"Scotty had an argument with Biff. It was nothing. But he thinks that's why Biff ran away." I glared at Scotty and grabbed his hand to lead him back to the car.

Betsy stood up. "Oh my God. You know what happened to Biff, don't you?"

"According to you, you killed him yourself."

"I had no choice. I mean, I had to say that I did. I couldn't let you win. But you really know about him, don't you? Is he alive? Is he dead? Did you—?"

Scotty broke free of my hand and gave her a shove. He was only a small boy, but Betsy was pretty unsteady on her feet. Losing her balance, she hit her head against the porch support beam and fell down, unconscious.

"Is Mom dead?" Scotty asked, considerably more concerned than when he'd asked the same thing about Biff.

"No. Don't worry. Go back to the car." He scurried back to Mom and Sequoia with his little-boy high energy.

After a moment, Betsy came to and sat up on the porch step, rubbing her head. "That's it. I'm calling the cops."

"And telling them *what*?"

"I'll think of something. Maybe Dr. Jesse Falcon, for starters."

I stood over her, trembling with rage. "I swear, Betsy, I should've killed you. That last night together, with my hands around your neck, I should've kept going and going until all that ugliness inside you was gone. Your precious Biff molested our son. Did you know that? Your one great true love liked to diddle with little boys."

"No, it was nothing." She started to cry a little.

I could feel myself turn pale. "What do you mean, nothing?"

She would not look at me. "I—I saw them once. Like I said, it was nothing. Biff sort of played with him a little. It was like tickling. He barely touched Scotty's you-know. I swear. It was probably just an accident. Biff was drunk."

"You knew?" Now I was convinced I really would kill her.

"I . . . Look, Biff had a lot of money. He could give me—I mean, he could give Scotty things you couldn't. I was doing what was best."

I pushed Betsy from the side. She fell onto the lawn and reached for a garden stone. She hit me in the stomach with the rock, right where my scar was from the shooting. It hurt like hell. Then she scratched my cheeks with her fingernails. I tried to hold her down, but she bit my hand. In the chaos of the fight, I caught a glimpse of Sequoia getting out of the car, presumably to break us up.

As if Betsy had magical powers to conjure up her wishes, seemingly out of nowhere a police car with a glaring, spinning, red siren drove up to the house. It was too soon for the cops to have responded to some nosy neighbor reporting a domestic disturbance; I hoped against hope that Betsy had done something, and they were there for her.

Two officers got out of the car and walked to the porch. I could see my mom ducking her head down in Sequoia's car.

"You!" One of the officers pointed his finger at me. "Come with us. Right now."

"She started it, officer," Sequoia said loyally. "He was only trying to defend himself."

"You fuck!" Betsy lunged at Sequoia, but the other officer held her back.

"We're not here for your dumb-ass domestic squabble," the first officer said. "This is something else." He looked at me like I knew exactly what he meant, though I tried to play dumb.

"Like what? Am I under arrest?"

"I'll call a lawyer," Sequoia said.

"Sir," said the officer calmly, "I promise you it is in your best interests to cooperate."

As I drove off with the two officers, I could see my mother's middle finger subtly extended above the car seat she was hiding under.

8: DR. JESSE FALCON

WE WERE BACK IN MY HOME CITY, to make yet another fresh start, with new names intended to keep me from further identity theft. We did not formally petition to change our names, as that would've left a paper trail. But one of the FBI agents I'd been dealing with said, "Abracadabra," and there we were with passports and driver's licenses that had our new names: Randall and Valerie Van Sant. We also had new social security numbers, though I couldn't remember the last time I had to use my old one. Sabrina refused to change her name. The idea frightened her for some reason, and she started to cry. We never mentioned it again.

Of course what I knew that nobody else knew was that I needed to move like a bat out of hell for technically killing Linda Goldstein. Dr. Jesse Falcon had to more or less die as well.

I took out a license to become a private investigator. This was surprisingly easy to do. I had no interest in finding someone's second cousin twice removed, I only wanted to find my identity thief. I knew this was the only way to go about it, since law enforcement had been no help. There was strong reason to believe the thief was right there in my hometown, or at least had been, given that stupid bank robbery. So there I was, Randall Van Sant, PI. I decided to stop contacting the cops or the FBI. Nothing came of it except more psychic damage to me. I also closed all of my accounts under the name of Jesse Falcon.

In order for no one to take me for Dr. Jesse Falcon, I dyed my hair, got it cut differently, and wore tinted contacts. I should also mention that I got a little plastic surgery. I was pleased with how I'd been aging, thanks very much, but I figured it would never hurt to look younger if I didn't want to be recognized. So I got a facelift.

(While they were at it, I had them throw in a tummy tuck.) Esther and Sabrina insisted I looked the same, though I knew perfectly well that I looked quite different.

With Esther's help, I bought all new clothes that signaled a different style of dressing and a different kind of person. I even changed my cologne. If anyone from my old university thought they recognized me, I easily could deny it.

Esther could've kept working as an interior designer. Instead she decided to go back to school and study French. Like a good Girl Scout, she kept trying to call me by my new name—even with a French accent. But finally she gave in to my protests and called me by my real name unless other people besides Sabrina were around. The truth was, we'd never made a lot of friends, and despite our plans to start doing so, day by day it never happened.

Besides, it's hard to make boring small talk when all you can think about is your fucking identity thief.

We settled on a narrow tri-story in an upscale neighborhood. As proof that she was done with interior design, Esther proclaimed that she would hire someone else to decorate our new home. Needless to say, the poor designer ended up being more like her assistant.

Before moving away, I had to tell my patients I was retiring. Most of them took it well. In fact, that super-obnoxious male patient waxed poetic for the full fifty minutes about how much we had done what he considered "connecting." I realized that underneath all his posturing, I probably was the only person who talked to him. Contrarily, the sad and nutty male patient I saw right after him claimed that I was abandoning him like everyone else had always done, especially now when we were making what he considered to be progress. I supposed that meant there was a minute a day in which he didn't think about destroying the world.

Thus did I bid adieu to the world of Shrinkdom. No more Linda Goldsteins, no more inferiority complexes, no more superiority complexes, no more boring life stories, no more bitchy mothers and clueless fathers, no more obnoxious conference speakers who began their speeches by bragging, "I don't need a mic."

Truthfully, I don't even remember why I decided to become a psychologist. Probably I heard it paid well. I can't recall ever having a strong motivation to want to help people solve their problems. Which, by the way, seldom, if ever, happened in my experience. Most people loved their problems more than anything. There was this website I heard about called McShrink, in which people got the kind of straightforward advice I would've wanted to give people: get off your ass and do something about it. But that's not what I got trained to do. I got trained to *listen*. The only problem was, most people didn't say much worth listening to.

Esther cried with joy at seeing Sabrina again as she realized she could see her all the time. Sabrina wasn't angry with me anymore, but her evasiveness kept me wondering what she was hiding. She said she was on a sabbatical from her teaching job but wouldn't get specific about what she was doing.

"It wouldn't mean anything to you, Dad," she told me.

Yet she apparently didn't tell Esther, either. "Give her some space," Esther told me. "She's been through a lot."

I assume this meant the bank robbery, unless it meant the elusive ex-boyfriend Cole Colton.

As soon as we were reasonably settled in and the bandages were removed from my face, I was off to the bank that had been robbed. Or should I say that Randall Van Sant, PI, was off to the bank.

"I've been hired to locate a missing person," I explained to the bank officer, a woman who bore an uncomfortable resemblance to

Linda Goldstein. It was as though I was now in the *Twilight Zone* and would be haunted by her everywhere I went.

"Who are you looking for?" asked the bank officer, offering me a seat in her cubicle.

"His name is Dr. Jesse Falcon."

The bank officer did a double take, scrutinizing me carefully from her desk. "The police have been here many times on Dr. Falcon's behalf. There seems to have been—"

"I know," I interrupted. "Identity theft. Now it appears he's missing. The real Dr. Falcon, that is. And let's say some people are concerned it might all be connected."

"Then why aren't the police involved?"

I winked at her. "The police? Give me a break."

She winked back, which I found faintly revolting. "Between you and me, I feel the same way. Unfortunately, the teller who waited on the man who said he was Dr. Falcon was killed during the robbery."

"How tragic." I thought, *I hit the jackpot; he really was here.*

The bank officer sighed. "Oh, you don't know the half of it. We still haven't recovered. But another teller did see him up close. Let me get Luanna for you."

I saw the bank officer and Luanna exchange a few urgent words, then they both came back over to me.

"My name is Luanna." She smiled efficiently. "How may I help you?" The bank officer seated us both and took her place behind her desk, as if a chaperone on a blind date.

"Well, Luanna, it would appear that Dr. Jesse Falcon is missing."

"You mean that nice man who got shot in the bank robbery?"

I quickly exchanged meaningful glances with the bank officer; obviously Luanna knew nothing about the identity theft.

"Yes, that's the man." I nodded sadly before adding, "However, we need to make sure. Please, describe him for me, Luanna."

"Oh, absolutely. Every last detail of that day is burned into my memory. How could I ever forget it?"

I took out a pad and pencil from my jacket pocket. "Tragedy does that, I'm afraid. Now, what did he look like? About how old was he? Was he tall, short? What color hair?"

"Oh, he wasn't really *that* tall or short. You know, in between. Kind of regular hair. I can't think of the exact color. He was probably like thirty or so. But cute, you know? An expensive blue suit. Like you'd feel safe taking him home to meet your parents."

"Thank you, I see. Anything else?" Oh, please, please, let her remember something else.

Luanna shrugged. "Not that I can think of."

Just my luck to get help from an airhead. Gee, when had this happened to me before? How about for my entire life?

"Thank you for all your help." I stood up to take my leave. "Here's my card if you think of anything else." My new PO Box and cell phone number were on the card.

"Oh, wait," Luanna said suddenly. "I thought of something else."

My heart practically burst into song. "What's that?"

"There was this woman. Very pretty. With beautiful long hair. They were flirting, even during the robbery. I could tell. I mean, you know when people are flirting. They kept looking at each other in, you know, that kind of way." She scrunched her nose.

I took out a picture of Sabrina from my wallet. "Was this the woman?"

Luanna studied it carefully. "Maybe," she decided. "It *kind of* looks like her. The woman in the bank was prettier. Maybe this is a bad picture of her."

I almost blurted out that no one was prettier than my Sabrina but kept my emotions in check, piling on the thanks some more before leaving. "Thank you again. You've been a lot of help." As I thought about it, Luanna had done me some good. The flirty girl might well have been Sabrina, and the guy claiming to be me would've been exactly Sabrina's type. A nothing.

All I had to do was find out who this guy was and probably my own daughter could tell me at least something about him, if not everything. When you're a parent *and* a shrink, it doesn't take much to add two and two. My daughter had a crush on my identity thief. There was an obvious down side, but the upside was she could lead him right into Papa's hand.

I made sure I met with Sabrina without Esther around to tell me to go easy on our precious baby. She had an art studio in an old factory district, so I met her there that very same day.

The studio was creaky and messy, as I imagined most artist studios were. It was near an elevated freeway exit, and there was a constant roar of cars in the background, which I would have found distracting. Still, it was quite spacious, with high ceilings. Jeremy, my ex-bulldog, lay restfully on a dog cushion in the corner. He barked a little when I came in and quickly fell asleep. He didn't seem to remember me. Or maybe he didn't care.

Sabrina was high atop a ladder and endearingly attired in overalls, which, like her face, featured messy dots of paint. She protected her hair by stuffing it inside a baseball cap. Sabrina was working on this enormous, wall-sized canvas that reminded me of why I had so little feeling for art. The canvas had a solid black background with these splatters of white on top. Climbing down the ladder, she explained to me that she would keep splattering on the white until the painting was fifty/fifty black and white. It would be given the ingenious title, *Composition #11*. For my benefit, she slid out several earlier wall-sized pieces, all of which looked the same to me.

As if reading my mind, she said, "They're not all the same, you know. The splatter patterns vary. That's the whole point. Nothing is ever the same as something else, even when you think it is."

I thought about how much I disagreed with this. As far as I was concerned, everyone and everything was one great big blah. Okay, with a few exceptions, but that was the general idea. I supposed that was what art was for—to try to make everything seem nicer or more interesting than it was. Assuming you could relate to it.

"Huh. I never thought of it that way before, princess." I stood back and squinted in mock fascination for the piece. "Is this what your sabbatical is for?" Lord help the patrons of her university if it was.

"Sort of." She critically studied a tiny section of the painting and splattered more white on it. "It's hard to explain." She quickly added, "If you don't know much about art." She climbed back up her ladder, paintbrush in hand.

"Sabrina, I'm here to talk about that bank robbery."

"Uh, huh. I'm listening."

"It doesn't seem to upset you anymore."

"When I'm painting, Dad, nothing upsets me." Deftly balanced on the ladder, she dunked her brush into her can of paint and struck it at the canvas with a firm determination in her wrist, as one might swat a fly.

"I remember you mentioned some guy. You thought he was handsome." I hoped to go to my grave without ever saying the word "cute."

"Did I?"

"*Yes.* Even though you were scared out of your mind, you said you noticed some guy."

She set her paintbrush in the can of paint. "Yes, I think I'm remembering now. The thing is, I've blotted out a lot that happened."

"Sabrina, are you involved with this young man?"

She looked down at me, grinning; there was a spot of white paint on her nose. "Dad, I don't get it. What if I was? I'm not. But what if I was? Do I have to tell you about every guy I date? Really, your Sabrina is all grown up now. Daddy's little girl has known a number of men in the good old-fashioned Biblical sense, and it didn't exactly start happening the day before yesterday."

"Believe it or not, young lady, at your age I did not spend my evenings eating cookies and milk, though, of course, the dinosaurs made for some bad times. I *know* that people have sex. I was a shrink, remember? When you said that Cole Colton person was the love of your life, I didn't think you were doing pinkie hugs."

It made me quite uncomfortable to think that my daughter fucked around like a whore. If I'd had a patient who was a virgin—if anyone over eighteen *was* still a virgin—I would tell her to go out and get laid. Hell, I might've even done her myself. But I could barely stomach the thought of my daughter having sex, let alone casual sex. I wanted to beat up any man who so much as touched her. If she got married and wanted a kid, I'd encourage her to consider artificial insemination.

"'Cole Colton?' You don't even remember his name. It was Colton Cole."

"I know that." I said quickly. "I was making light of it all. You know, as if I'd said, 'Doe, John.'"

"There was nothing funny about our relationship. Colton called me the other day. He wanted to get back together. It took everything I had to tell him no. It was the hardest thing I ever had to do."

Something in me had changed because I had to resist the urge to reply, *Yes, I can tell you're devastated.* Or maybe, *How the fuck was I supposed to know how you felt about anything when you never say what's happening to you?*

"Do you want to talk about it, Princess?" I properly furrowed my brow in concern.

"No, I'm fine now." She made rapid brush strokes with her white paint.

"Anyway, I *know* you're all grown up, sweetheart. That's why I don't pay your bills anymore. I want to know about that one guy from the bank."

She climbed down the ladder. "Why? Is he really my long lost brother?"

"That's not funny."

"When you're adopted, you wonder about these things. I saw this old movie once where this guy was jealous of his twin sister's boyfriend, and then it turned out that they were both adopted, and—"

"I hate it when you talk about being adopted. Don't you know your mother and I never think of you that way?"

She sat herself on the ladder and cupped her hand to her chin. "A friend of mine in college said that I was lucky. Because non-adopted kids wish they *were* adopted. That there's these nicer, real parents waiting for them someplace. The same friend used to say she was raised by nuns in a French orphanage. Instead, she was from Milton, Ohio. I remember her father collected hubcaps."

"Look, stop changing the subject. Do you know the man you saw at the bank robbery or not?"

She made a point of staring at me dead-on. There was not even the slightest flicker in her eyes. "No. I never saw him again."

"You're acting like you have something to hide."

"So are you, Dad. Why do you care about this guy? You even asked me about him when I came to visit that time." She leaned toward me. "Don't worry, I know I'm covered in paint. I won't touch you. But really, Dad. Whatever it is, I can handle it."

I thought for a moment, took a deep breath, and told Sabrina about the identity thief. At one point I got carried away and touched her shoulders, getting some paint on my hands. "Promise me," I concluded, "that you won't tell anyone I was here." I washed my hands in her industrial sink.

"Not even Mom?"

I reached for a paper towel to dry my hands. "Especially not Mom. All she'll do is worry that you're worried."

"It must be awful. Knowing that some total stranger is stealing who you are. If it was at least someone you knew, they might have a reason for doing it. You know, like if they hated you." She stood back to observe her painting, her hands on her hips.

"I want my money back."

She walked to the other side of the studio to study the painting from a different angle. I couldn't imagine what could be right or wrong with it from any angle. "Really, Dad, he was a guy kind of guy. He wore a blue suit, if that's any help. He had a bank check, and the bank robbers wanted cash. In fact, they shot him. He might be dead, for all I know."

Gee, that definitely narrowed it down. If I went through the clothes closet of every thirty-something man in the city, I could eliminate the ones who didn't own a blue suit. "I doubt that he's dead, unless people can keep stealing from the grave. I wish the bank robbers killed him."

"I know you don't really mean that. It's only money. A human life is worth much more."

I wondered where she learned such bullshit. Probably her mother. I certainly never thought for one second that I would rather this guy be alive than dead. Unless his death made it more complicated for me to get my money back. Still, if he was shot, there probably were hospital records.

"I should get going. Good luck with your painting."

She laughed. "*Good luck*? It's not like it's a NASA rocket."

"Oh really? That's what I thought it was. But I guess I was looking at it from the wrong angle. It's really a bullfrog."

She sighed with mock exasperation. "Good-bye, Dad."

"If that Colton Cole whatever calls you again, tell him to fuck off."

Sabrina laughed. "I already did."

"That's Daddy's good little girl."

Her cell phone was beeping, and she took it out of one of her overall pockets to shut it off. She scurried over to the industrial sink and started to open a cupboard door. Then she stopped and looked over at me. "I thought you were leaving."

"I was. I mean, I am. Sabrina, honey, are you all right?"

"*Yes.* I'm getting a glass of water, if it's okay with you." She opened the cupboard door to show that it was full of glasses. "I don't like feeling spied on."

I could relate to that myself but thought it best not to admit it. "Okay, okay, I'm going."

I knew from past experience which hospital emergency patients were taken to. Driving over there, though, I couldn't escape the fear that this fucked-up thief was involved with my beautiful daughter. Was he corrupting her? Was he using her to get closer to my money?

The hospital indeed confirmed that a Dr. Jesse Falcon was admitted for gunshot wounds on the day of the bank robbery. I saw his signature on some triplicate copy of a form, and it looked chillingly like my own.

For the first time, it occurred to me that the person I was dealing with was a highly skilled and experienced criminal. Which, of course, meant I might be in danger if I did find him. I didn't care. I'd rather get shot to death if I at least knew who he was.

I talked to a doctor and a couple of nurses. They revealed little more capacity for observation than Luanna from the bank. He was nice, he was thirty-something.

I was still on my meds for stress, and to please Esther, I was trying not to drink at all. But I thought I'd earned the right to a scotch—and make it a double, if you please. I don't like chi-chi bars, so I stopped inside the first dimly lit, liquor-smelling tavern I found. Midway through my drink, my cell phone rang. I almost didn't bother to answer the unfamiliar number but figured I had nothing to lose.

"Yeah, what's up?" I figured that was how a good PI would answer the phone.

"That depends," said the female voice. "Is this Randall Van Sant, Private Investigator?"

"Speaking."

"I need to see you about an urgent matter. How soon could I stop by your office?"

Office? What office? "How did you find out about me?"

"I looked you up on the motherfucking computer," she replied, which made me sort of like her in advance. "You were the last private eye alphabetically; I figured I'd start with you."

"Do you mind meeting in a bar? That's where I am now."

"I suppose I could use some liquid refreshment."

I told her the name of the pub, and before I gave her the address, she said she remembered it as a dump she used to go to with her college friends to try to be sleazy.

I was on my second double when this blonde walked in. I felt like I was in an old movie. She wasn't pretty exactly, but she gave off a constant aroma of sex, as if she were ready, willing, and able to fuck 24/7. But she wasn't hard-edged. Not that she seemed soft, either. She was like some pleasant, forgettable, one-night stand who probably wondered why she didn't do better with men than she did.

"Call me Betsy." She extended her hand, which I shook.

"I'm having a double scotch," I told her.

"In that case, I'll have a triple." Betsy smiled at me.

As she coyly sipped her large drink through a cocktail straw, Betsy told me her story. "The love of my life is gone. He disappeared, the day we were supposed to move in together. His name was Biff. Maybe you heard about him in the news?"

"Maybe," I answered in an uncommitted tone. I didn't want to tell her that I'd only recently moved back to the area. "Do you have a picture of him?"

"Do I ever," she replied, as though I needed a great deal of convincing that this Biff person even existed. She handed me a photo of a man in bathing trunks, smiling as he had his arm around Betsy, who wore a skimpy bikini. A pair of tall drinks stood on a table beside them. I saw a swimming pool in the background, but since no one else was in the picture, I imagined it was someone's house and not a resort.

"Oh, this is the guy that's been murdered," I said. "No wonder you can't find him. Just this morning, I think, I heard that some local mob guy and his hit man finally were arrested."

Betsy shrugged haughtily. "No body. Big deal. They're building some circumstantial case to pin something on a gangster. His own attorney said so."

I could scarcely believe what a dingbat she was. "Of course his attorney said so. Did you think he'd say, 'My client is guilty?' There've been many murder convictions without the body ever being found."

"I'm telling you, Biff is alive. His parents *always* paid his gambling debts. Or for abortions and whatnot. They can't say it, but it's true. Biff never would've hooked up with mobsters. He didn't *have* to."

Probably this Betsy person was in denial, and I felt a little sorry for her. "Tell me more."

"Biff comes from a very good family," Betsy explained, going on about his pedigreed but uninteresting genealogy before finally getting to the point. "Anyway, he e-mailed me that he was going to meet his parents in the Bahamas to get more money before moving in. And that's the last I heard from him. His parents said he e-mailed them at the same time to say he was scared of me and didn't know how to tell me to get lost, so he was going away."

I thought about it for a moment. "Do you believe he was scared of you?"

She laughed. "Biff scared of *me*? I mean, come on. He was a man's man. Besides, why would any man be afraid of me? I'm a very feminine woman."

I figured I'd humor her. "Take it from me, those are the worst kind."

She reached across the table to give my face a light, playful slap. "You men! You're all such jokers. But seriously, I've been devastated ever since. Devastated and . . . all alone."

"I can see that." Yeah, she seemed about as devastated as a floor lamp.

Betsy looked at me hopefully. "Can you really? You're the first person who has. Biff's family treats me like dirt. Even though he's the father of my son. They like filed a missing person's report. If you ask me, they don't give a rat's ass about him."

"Son? You mean you have a child?"

"Oh, didn't I mention that? Scotty's nine. I *think*." She took the straw from her drink and licked off the scotch.

I was trying to get the story right. "You and Biff had a child, but you never lived together?"

Betsy seemed annoyed for my slowing down her story. "Biff didn't know he was the father. I mean, he *knew*, but he didn't know-know."

"In other words, you never told him?"

"No, not like, 'Biff you're the kid's father.'"

As if there was some other way to tell him—maybe by playing Pictionary? But I let it pass. "I'm a little confused."

She gave a heavy sigh, as if exhausted for having to go over it all. "Biff knocked me up in college. We were in love, but I married this other prick instead. Don't ask. Anyway, I finally got rid of that asshole, and Biff was going to move in. Instead he suddenly decides he's scared of me. Supposedly. After we fucked for like our whole lives." She meditatively stirred the ice in her drink.

"And when was this?"

Betsy told me the date. When I realized it was the same day as the bank robbery, I just about shit in my pants.

"Did Biff have a job? Did he have any enemies? Did he do drugs? Did he gamble?"

"No and no, yes and yes. His parents supported him. They could throw money out the window all day long and never go broke. They were always bailing him out of money jams. His father owns like a million banks."

"Oh really? Which ones?"

Lo and behold, she mentioned the name of the bank that was robbed. Biff was getting more interesting by the moment.

"My ex-husband was Biff's only friend," Betsy continued. "Most guys were jealous of Biff because he had so much going on. You know, everyone always says women get catty with each other. But if you ask me, men are just as bad."

"Very true, Betsy."

"I could write a book about men," she agreed. "Like my ex. I think he was cheating on me all along because like five minutes after we broke up, he found a new girlfriend. They even stole my son away.

They have custody of *my* baby."

"That must be awful," I empathized. "No one likes to be cheated on." But I was thinking, *Biff had a lot of debts. What if his family got tired of helping him?*

"Tell me about it." She signaled for another triple. "It's the nice guys who really know how to break a woman's heart."

From under the table, her foot rubbed against my leg, possibly by accident. "Do you have a picture of Scotty? He sounds like a fine boy."

"Uh, let me think . . . not in my wallet. Maybe I have some at home. Oh, sure I do. You know, school pictures and things. Can you really find Biff for me?"

I wore my best serious frown. "I can try. I'll need to know more about him. Where might he go if he wanted to get away from it all?"

"Beats me. He was such a homebody. Not that he spent time with his parents. Who would? But you know, he kind of hung around the house and watched TV and drank and smoked weed and snorted coke and did X and stuff. He played online poker, and it was weird because he always lost. I figured the guys he played with were cheating. He traveled when his parents made him. Otherwise, he spent time with me. In the bedroom, if you get my drift."

"Oh, I do indeed."

She rubbed my leg again with her foot so I knew it was no accident. "Or he'd pal around with my ex. They'd play golf."

"Did your ex also gamble and take drugs?"

Betsy made a dismissive gesture with bent wrist. "*Him?* Are you kidding? I mean, his favorite flavor of ice cream was vanilla. Do you have any idea how annoying it is to live with someone like that? If someone chased him with a gun, he'd stop if the traffic sign said *Don't Walk*. He was always trying to straighten Biff out. To make Biff as boring as he was. To take the man out of him."

"And you can't think of anyplace else Biff might be?"

"I already told you, Biff hated to go anywhere. That's what's weird."

I rubbed her leg in return—subtly, but enough so she'd notice. "Do you think there might have been . . . that is . . ."

"You mean do I think someone offed him? No way. For a while, I was saying that I killed him, and—"

"You said *what*?" I withdrew my foot from under the table.

"I had my pride to think about. Better to say I killed him than to have everyone think he abandoned me. I couldn't hurt a fly. Honest. Well, I *do* swat flies, like if one comes in the house or something. Don't worry, I straightened it all out."

"I'm sure you did." She was a total numbskull, but who wasn't?

"I mean, why would I pay you to find him if I killed him? It makes no sense."

Sometimes people say such dumb things you can't help but correct them. "Unless you were trying to make it look good. You know, 'Gee, where is he?' When all along you murdered the son of a bitch."

She threw the dregs of her drink in my face. "You can't talk that way about Biff. The son of God would be more like it. He was, I mean, he is so wonderful." She took out a Kleenex and perhaps really sniffled a little, though probably it was an act. But I didn't think she killed him. She wasn't smart enough to murder someone. Yet, it wasn't hard to imagine why this Biff person wanted to get away from her. I suspected that his parents knew perfectly well where he was, but they weren't saying. Rich families often closed ranks in this way. In fact, if he was stealing my money—or who could say, even other people's money—they'd close ranks all the more.

Blame it on the scotch, but next thing I knew we were in a hotel room together.

Contrary to the impression she tried hard to create, Betsy was hardly a tiger in bed. She was one of those women who simply sprawled out horizontally and expected the man to do everything. She made little mewing sounds throughout, which were annoying as hell. Still, I had this image of Biff as my identity thief, living on a yacht in the Caribbean or someplace, thanks to my money.

"I'll take your case," I said quietly, nuzzling my face to her stiff blond hair.

"I thought you already were taking on the case." Betsy registered hurt. "Why else are we here?"

"What do you mean? Are you paying me with sex?"

She shoved me away. "Of course not. What do you take me for? I have *cash*. And lots of it."

"Divorce settlement?" I rubbed some watered down scotch on my face.

"Yeah, you could say that. I made a trade. I gave up all visitation rights to my son."

"I'm sorry to hear that." I touched her shoulder.

Ignoring my gesture, Betsy sat up in bed with a look of utter determination. She demurely covered herself with the hotel bedsheet, as if to signify she meant nothing but business. "So what are you going to do first? About finding Biff."

"I'll want that photo you have of him. And what about your ex-husband? You said he was Biff's only friend. Maybe they confided in each other."

Betsy looked down and away. "I don't think you should talk to him. He's . . . he's hard to talk to."

I had a strong sense she was hiding something but that it was something that would matter to no one except herself. Betsy, I could tell, was one of those people who made everything much more complicated than it needed to be.

"Maybe I could meet him by accident."

"Right. Like, 'Here's this private detective I hired to find Biff?'"

"Certainly not. But we could pretend to be on a date. You could invite him and his girlfriend. Or are they married now? And to show there's no hard feelings, we could all go out."

"You've gotta be kidding. *No hard feelings?* I hate that prick, and I hate that whore." She grabbed one of the pillows, and I thought she'd rip it in half.

"I thought you wanted to find Biff no matter what."

She threw the pillow at me, as if in punishment for forcing her to be logical. "I will never socialize with the two of them. I don't care if I was married to the King of Fuckville."

"I don't think there is such a place or person. The main thing is that I connect with your ex. Gain his trust. To learn about Biff."

"Fine. I'll give you his address. But promise me one thing. Never talk about money. It's a really sore spot between us. You know, the divorce and everything."

"You took him to the cleaners?" I feigned a smile, but I hated when this happened to men.

"Ha! That's a good one. That whore he lives with is filthy rich. He never has to work another day in his life. They gave me money to keep me away from own child. More money than he wanted to part with, the cheap fuck."

Betsy seemed to truly believe that she got screwed by giving up rights to her son in exchange for what was probably a hefty settlement. Lord only knew what happened to make her such a confused, vindictive mess. However, I had no interest in discovering it, thanks just the same.

Driving back home, I started thinking. Sometimes when you're face to face with someone, it's totally different from when you think about that person afterward. And usually, it feels worse than when you saw them. I supposed that's a sign that someone was not to be trusted. But whatever it meant, I knew I didn't trust Betsy. Who could? She wasn't really pretty or much of a lay, she had all the intelligence of a petrified rock, and she was incapable of thinking of anyone but herself. Yet somehow she got what she wanted.

I got home looking no worse for the wear. Esther turned off her French/English lesson to run to the door to kiss me. I didn't feel guilty; having sex with Betsy was like having sex with nothing. And anyway, a strong case could be made that Betsy took advantage of me.

I told Esther about my little adventure in finding a client—leaving out the part about the hotel room, of course. I obviously didn't mention Sabrina. I also didn't say that I may have learned who my identity thief was. I didn't want to jinx it. Besides, Esther might try to talk me out of tracking him down by myself.

"I don't know, Esther. I have a bad feeling about this client."

"Oh, go for it," she replied merrily. "It sounds like fun. Didn't you always want to be a detective when you were a kid?"

I tried to remember back that far. "Not at all. I wanted to be . . . I don't know, really. But it wasn't a detective. I wanted something more. I can't explain it."

"Are you saying you wanted to be a fireman?"

I laughed. "Sure, why not?"

That very evening, I rang the buzzer at the apartment of Betsy's ex. I figured it was better to show up than to call him; he was more likely to talk to me if I was right there. A man's voice came on the speaker and asked who I was. I said I was Randall Van Sant, PI, and that I was looking for a missing person who apparently had been the best friend of Betsy's ex-husband.

After a long pause, he buzzed me in.

9: AKA Jesse Falcon

"**A**RE YOU DR. JESSE FALCON?"
Having bid farewell to my bewildered family at Betsy's house, and then enduring a silent ride to the police station, I was roughly dragged inside. Though I was not handcuffed, they treated me like I was. They led me through a corridor in which many busy, noisy people utterly ignored me. I guess they figured I was just another scumbag, like they saw every day. Finally, I was deposited in a private room with no windows. I assumed I was being taped or watched through a one-way window. It was hard to sit there as if nothing was wrong. But finally a bald detective wearing rolled up shirtsleeves and a bow tie slammed the door and shouted at me. "Are you Dr. Jesse Falcon?"

After mulling it over in my mind, I finally answered, "I want to talk to my lawyer."

The detective opened his mouth in shock, as if he could not believe I would say this, that his interrogation of me could not possibly be over, given all the plans he had.

"What a big baby," the detective finally said, getting his revenge on me. "Okay, I'll get the little boy his little lawyer."

"I'm sure she's already on her way." But he slammed the door shut on his way out and didn't seem to hear me.

I pretended to be very calm and made a point of avoiding eye contact with the wall where the one-way window would've been. I still did not know what I was doing here, though obviously I kept hoping it wasn't about the identity theft. Still, I wasn't stupid enough to think it could be about anything else. Fortunately, my problem-solving skills had been getting a lot of exercise as of late, and I was already making plans: Ondine could fashion a plea bargain if I returned the money, which I could if I absolutely had to. If I didn't have enough, I could work out a payment plan. I could offer to show how I broke into Jesse Falcon's accounts to help them catch some other crook. Or if I did go to jail, my mom could have custody of Scotty, and Sequoia could take him to visit me.

Finally, Ondine arrived. The look on her face told me it was bad news. Despite all my cool, detached planning, the reality of the trouble I was in made me shudder. So much had happened so quickly that only now did I know true fear.

"I told you to call someone else next time," Ondine scolded.

"I forgot," I answered. It was the truth, and I hoped she'd see the humor in it.

She did not. She roughly threw down her briefcase and matter-of-factly sat down across from me. "They think you murdered someone."

Oh my God! They must've found Biff's body. I was so careful. But there had to have been a trace of my DNA on him. And they linked it to me, instead of those mob guys. Only they thought I was Dr. Jesse Falcon. Between the bank robbery and the hospital records, my own bank transactions—plus the fact that the real Jesse Falcon now lived in my city—it wasn't hard to see why they'd confuse us.

I laughed, not knowing what else to do. "Murder? Who would I have murdered?"

"Someone named Linda Goldstein. She lives—I mean, she lived—across the country. Don't worry, they turned off the microphones. It's the law."

It took me a few seconds to gather my thoughts. "I never even heard of Linda Goldstein. And I've never even been out that way."

"Well, she'd been in a coma, and as soon as she snapped out of it, someone turned off her monitor. The autopsy showed why her heart stopped beating. They did a little digging and found out that this baby she had wasn't fathered by her husband, but by the guy they think killed her. Who, incidentally, has a wife. That's Dr. Jesse Falcon."

"Oh." I didn't know what else to say.

"Now, would you be so kind as to explain to me why they think you are said Dr. Falcon?"

I could tell Ondine was really pissed off at me. Her worst suspicions about what I might really have been doing all this time were about to be confirmed. I didn't like the thought of Ondine being mad at me. She had this way about her that made you not want to disappoint her. Rationally, I knew she could not harm me, yet I was afraid of her moodiness.

At least I knew this Jesse Falcon guy was a total creep. But now I would have to explain everything to Ondine. I knew about privileged information between lawyer and client, but I also knew lawyers were sworn servants of the court and supposedly were obligated to report any known wrongdoing.

In the end, I told her about the identity theft, but not about what happened to Biff, in order to protect Scotty. I said that Sequoia knew nothing about anything.

Ondine tapped her fingers on the scratched tabletop for a minute, deep in thought. Then she stood up, grabbed her briefcase, and said, "I'm going to go have a talk with the DA. I may be a while. Say *nothing* to anyone. Even if they offer to get you a Coke." She paused to look at me. "You stupid son of a bitch."

Her ire gave me pins and needles down my shoulders. But if that was the worst of it, I'd survived.

As I waited for Ondine to return, I amused myself by making mental lists, thinking about old TV shows, one dumb thing after another. At one point, I said to myself, *This is how it must feel to be Scotty.* I wondered how he managed at all, especially after everything he'd been through. It was strange, but though I did what I did to protect him, I'd never really stopped to feel unhappy for him. Not until I was sitting alone at a police station, wondering if I would go to jail or what.

I held back the urge to bawl like a baby, in case people were still watching me.

It was a good two hours before Ondine came back into the room with the same detective who tried to grill me before, plus this surprisingly friendly man who was an assistant district attorney. He smiled cordially as he shook my hand and sat down.

"My client," Ondine began, "is willing to plead guilty to grand larceny. Two years' incarceration and five years' probation. In exchange for helping you find the real Jesse Falcon."

"You see, *Dr. Falcon,*" joked the DA with a nudge of his elbow, "we think he may be responsible for more than one murder. In the past eighteen months, there's been four patients in that same hospital who died by someone turning off their monitors. In each case, the patient had awoken from a coma. We also think he may have pushed Mrs. Goldstein off a building, which caused her coma in the first place. This was while she was pregnant with his child. His former receptionist confirmed they were having an affair. Taking his money—so what? It's the least the bastard deserves. I'm guessing you're new to identity theft, am I right? Maybe no job, no money?"

I wanted to know how he would know this much about me without knowing anything about me, but I guessed that's why he was a detective. "Yeah," I admitted. "I mean, yes, sir."

"Our deal's only good if you bring him to us," added the detective. "Obviously, you're clever on the keyboard, so we're sure you can locate him. Our own expert hackers have come up empty-handed. We're guessing he's changed his name and gone underground. We've tried talking to his daughter. She claims she hasn't heard from him, even though we didn't say what we wanted him for. And he used to call another precinct about someone stealing his identity, but then the calls stopped. Now even his bank accounts are gone."

I hadn't been able to get into Jesse Falcon's accounts recently, and I almost blurted out loud, *Oh, that explains it.* Fortunately, I caught myself in time.

"I . . . I only did what I did because I couldn't find a job. Honest." I felt I had to say that.

"Not another word," warned Ondine. "You're not going to get a better deal than this. Two years up the river—that's like nothing. Take it. And thank the Good Lord that you stole from a serial killer."

Two years in prison didn't sound like nothing to me. I knew it was better than twenty years or two hundred years. And I always knew I might get caught. But Sequoia, Scotty, and I were finally about to have a normal life together. Thinking about Scotty visiting me in jail was different from the reality of it happening. It seemed to me it would be the final blow to what had to be an extremely fragile state of being. No, I wanted us all settled and living together. Scotty would get therapy, and he would form a positive bond with Sequoia and finally have a real mother.

"When you say 'bring him to you,' you mean give you his address?"

The DA laughed. "His head on a silver platter with a side of parsley would be even better, but we'll settle for an address. Don't worry, you'll have access to state-of-the-art equipment to track him down from prison. Or should I say *hack* him down. Get it?" He laughed some more.

I would never involve Sequoia in this in a million years. But I did know he was living here in town, so I didn't think it would be that hard to find him. "How's this sound? I bring him to you in person, no jail time at all. A suspended sentence."

Ondine said, "You'll have to excuse my client. He's kind of a dope." She turned to me. "This is a *serial killer*. Now how are you going to protect yourself? I've got news for you. You ain't no cop."

"You don't know for certain if he's a serial killer. And anyway, the other victims—am I right in guessing they were all women?"

"Right you are," said the DA. "And to answer the question I'll bet you're going to ask, all fit the same profile as Mrs. Goldstein. Say, you're pretty good. Too bad you didn't become a shrink or something instead of a crook."

I got the impression that the DA had a certain begrudging respect for criminals, as long as they didn't physically harm anyone. Jewel thieves and people like that. He seemed to think I was some sort of identity theft mastermind, capable of ruling the world from my keyboard.

"We'll give him protection," said the detective, which surprised me, and made the heaviness inside me dissipate. Was he overruling Ondine and agreeing with me? "If he meets the guy, we'll set up a wire. We'll also give him a hotline he can call anytime. Serial killers usually stick to one MO. Ex-comatose women are Jesse Falcon's cup of tea. Lord only knows why."

"And if something happens to him anyway?" asked Ondine, trying not to show how shocked she was.

The detective shrugged. "It's a chance he seems willing to take." Then he smiled at me. "Tell me something. Who is she?"

It took me a second or two to catch on. "Never mind who she is. But she's worth it. And so is—" I was about to say my son, but I obviously didn't want to mention him, either. "And so is staying out of jail. I'd rather be dead." And I realized this was true.

"So two years' suspended sentence, five years' probation?" Ondine asked.

"Seven years' probation," replied the DA. "Take it or leave it."

Ondine quickly looked at me. "We'll take it."

"I'm really not a bad guy," I said. "I made a mistake. If this Jesse Falcon is a serial killer, I can redeem myself by catching him."

"Our sentiments exactly," said the DA, offering his handshake.

"Handshakes are sweet," said Ondine. "I want an iron-clad agreement in writing."

I called Sequoia to come and get me and told her that I wasn't in any trouble after all. The cops had mistaken me for someone else. I didn't like lying to her, but it felt better than telling her that her estranged uncle was possibly or probably a serial killer.

Sequoia kissed me with relief, and with arms linked, we walked to her car.

"I assume the move is still on?" she asked casually, as if to make sure about what she already knew.

"Uh, no. I've decided we need to stay here."

Sequoia pulled the car over so fast that the brakes squealed. For her, this was a very big deal because she normally drove as if the slightest error would mean certain death.

"You decided? What about me?" She hit the horn with her fist.

I think a lot of men go through this with women. You see how far you can push the old-fashioned bit about men being in charge. Because the thing is, sometimes women do acquiesce, even though they don't like to admit it. Unfortunately for me, this was not one of those times.

"I guess that came out wrong. I meant to say that you were right in the first place. That Scotty needs stability."

Her anger melted about halfway back to pleasantness. "Well, that's a little better, I suppose. But we still need to discuss this. As partners. As equals."

"Oh, absolutely. But think about it. We can get back most of the rent deposit. We all have our lives right here. Why move to the other side of the country?"

She put her head on the steering wheel. I could tell I was exasperating her or maybe was giving her a headache. "Do you perchance recall the identity thief stuff? My Aunt Esther and Uncle Jesse are living here now. You were the one who said we had to get away."

"We only think they're living here. And even if they are, so what? You don't speak to them, and they don't know who I really am. If the cops are going to catch me, they're going to catch me. And as long as we don't steal anymore, that might never happen."

Sequoia grinned shrewdly. "I notice you stopped talking about paying him back. How long do you think you really will go without stealing again?"

"I'm done with all that. I can't explain it, but I know it's true."

She arched an eyebrow. "If you say so."

"I don't get it. Do you *want* me to stay a criminal?"

"No, but you do. And you know I'm right, so don't even try. It's like . . . it's like you feel you're making a sacrifice by giving it up. That means your heart is really still in it."

"No, it isn't." I looked out the window. "Anyway, what I meant to say was that you were right all along, and I was wrong all along. I mean about moving and Scotty and all that. Being in the police station . . . I realized how frail what we have is. Let's stay put. Let's not tempt fate anymore." I took her hand, and she tilted her head in a sigh.

"Okay. I guess we can unpack. What about your mom?"

"We'll all squeeze into the apartment for now. Until we find a place here in town."

Mom and Scotty were quite relieved to not have to move. Though Mom claimed to hate living in the city, she found all kinds of stores and activities to keep herself busy. I kept up with my McShrink e-mails and made a few more anonymous TV appearances to great acclaim, while Sequoia looked for what she called the ideal home. She took Scotty with her sometimes when she did her volunteer art projects with needy children, thinking it would help him to see kids that had it much worse than he did. Presumably, none of these kids had shot anyone to death yet, but in a strange way that seemed beside the point. Scotty was doing well in school, as always, and we found an understanding therapist who specialized in sexually abused children. As if reading my thoughts, Scotty told me of his own accord that he'd never tell her specifically about Biff but instead say that some stranger did it to him. This, of course, put a serious damper on the therapy process. It was the best we could all do for now.

Jesse Falcon's accounts may have vanished, but I was kept plenty busy dealing with the money I'd put into the phony offshore accounts I created in Biff's name. I next created more fake accounts to launder the money from the Biff accounts that I wanted to put to good use. Scotty's college fund got a major boost, and I bought

Sequoia an expensive necklace. I knew I shouldn't be doing this, yet I had a strong sense the cops didn't care what I did as long as I caught Jesse Falcon. It was like when you're a little kid, and you know you'll get away with stealing from the cookie jar.

Still, it was strange how difficult life made it to ever tell anyone the truth. Even when you really wanted to or needed to or loved someone with every cell of your being, there were at the very least some lies scattered about. And even more likely, there were major whoppers that you told to keep things moving along. In this philosophy class back in college, I read books by all those guys who'd been dead for thousands of years about what is truth. At the time, it seemed mind-boggling. Now it seemed to me that the answer was simple: truth didn't matter because it's never given a chance to exist. I lie, therefore I am. The real identity thief is life itself. Maybe death was the only time there really can be truth—but if so, what difference did the truth make? There's that famous poem in which the author explored the shortcomings of all these different ways of killing yourself and concluded: "You might as well live." Lately, it seemed to me that the better conclusion was, "You might as well lie."

Actually, neither lying nor telling the truth was helping me to find the real Jesse Falcon. Supposedly, he was right under my nose, but I couldn't find any current information about him, even when I tried breaking through court, FBI, and U.S. Marshall databases for name changes. The cops were starting to lose patience, but Ondine kept them at bay. Difficult as it was to do, I even asked Sequoia if there were places that her Aunt Esther and Uncle Jesse used to like to go.

"To Hell," she replied. "Why would you want to know?"

"Just trying to get a sense of them," I replied.

Then came a strange weekend. I was alone. Mom wanted to take Scotty to visit some relative who, according to Mom, shouldn't be exposed to someone like me anymore. And Sequoia said she had to go to this art museum in a nearby city to do some research. The sheer, unfamiliar silence of being only with myself caught me off guard. After a lifetime of doing what I was supposed to do or doing what I was not supposed to do but in any case doing things because I thought I had to do them, I was surrounded by nothing but silence. I'd looked forward to it. "Peace at last," I told myself. I had visions of eating pizza in bed and taking long naps and catching up on the home team games.

I had no idea why I felt so bad. I felt worse than when I'd worry about getting caught for the identity theft or for what happened to Biff. I felt worse than I did when the cops first apprehended me at Betsy's, and I had no idea what was even happening. I felt worse than I did when Betsy told me Biff was Scotty's father, or when I lost my job after years of hard work. I felt worse than when I got shot. As much as I hated to admit it, I even felt worse than when Scotty told me about Biff, or for that matter when Scotty shot and killed Biff, or when I was burying the body.

I kept telling myself nothing bad was happening. If anything, I should be grateful for all the trouble I was *not* in and look at the great future I had to look forward to. Yet it seemed like my entire life was caving in, and I would never feel better again. I'd always taken great pleasure in writing my ballsy answers as McShrink, but suddenly I thought I'd been belittling all those people who wrote me. Their problems were real; they *hurt*. And they probably still hurt after they got even with their tormentors.

I crashed and burned so rapidly. By Saturday afternoon, I found myself deciding that now was as good a time as any to get out of everyone's way. Scotty had a support system. Sequoia and Mom would not have to deal with any more of my messes. The cops would have to solve their case without me. For what it was worth, I wasn't able to find Jesse Falcon, anyway.

I thought some more about that poem about different methods of suicide. How did it go again? I knew that cutting your wrists was supposed to be a female way to die, so I didn't want to do that. I didn't have a gun. The oven was electric and that also seemed more of a woman's way of doing things. I didn't have a private garage, unless I went to my mom's place, but that seemed a bad idea for any number of reasons. Carbon monoxide was out, too. I could hang myself, but what if Scotty saw me that way? I could drown myself in the nearest body of water, only it might take days to find me, and I couldn't put Scotty through that, either.

Setting myself on fire seemed too gross. Ditto jumping off a high building.

Finally, in a detached, why-didn't-I-think-of-this-before way, I figured it out. Sleeping pills! Talk about the answer staring you right in the face.

There was nothing dramatic about it. I didn't take one last hard look at myself in the mirror. I got out my sleeping pills and Mom's sleeping pills, which were different from mine. And a bottle of vodka for good measure. I figured I'd do it lying in bed. It might look like I'd simply fallen asleep.

At the last minute, I wrote a quick note to Mom and Sequoia, asking that they not tell Scotty the truth about what I did. But that was all it said.

I took three of Mom's pills—which I knew were weaker—and two of mine, and a swig of vodka. I quickly repeated the process.

Out of nowhere, the buzzer rang.

I told myself it was Fate intervening and that there really was a God. But maybe I was relieved that I had some excuse to stop what I was doing. Maybe I was more afraid of death than I wanted to die. It's weird the way you can be certain you want something, only to realize you want the exact opposite.

Whatever it was, I hurried to the intercom. I wasn't feeling at all woozy. Some guy named Randall Van Sant was a PI looking for Biff.

"He's dead," I said. "They arrested somebody. Two people, I think."

"That's nice. My client thinks he may still be alive. May I come in?"

If nothing else, it sounded interesting, and anyway I obviously should be aware of any efforts to find Biff. My purpose for living renewed for having more dishonesty to engage in, I experienced a sudden rush of adrenaline. I ran to the bathroom and stuck a couple of fingers down my throat to puke up the pills. Though I tried and tried, only one of the pills came back up. Oh well, I could put on some coffee and everything would be fine. I often had to take more than one pill to sleep, anyway.

I hit the button to buzz in Randall Van Sant. To be on the safe side, I murmured, "Thank you, God."

By the time we shook hands and introduced ourselves—he said to call him Randy and gave me his card—I was feeling light-headed. Randy looked vaguely familiar to me, but I didn't know what to make of it. I showed him to our black-and-white living room and quickly nuked some water for instant lattes. I drank one down in the kitchen in a single gulp and brought out two to the living room, one for each of us.

Never did I feel more grateful for Sequoia's phobia about

photos of us on display. This would give me free rein to say all kinds of things. Though Randy said he couldn't tell me who his client was, I was reasonably certain it was Betsy. Who else could it be? Certainly not Biff's parents.

"You're Biff's best friend, is that correct?" Randy blew on the steam of his latte.

"You mean am I Biff's BFF?" I joked. It's strange the way humor had nothing to do with how you otherwise were doing. We both chuckled. "It was by default. Even in grade school, the other kids didn't like him. You know someone is pretty screwed up when he's the richest kid in town, and you still feel sorry for him."

"Do you believe he's dead?"

"I have no idea."

"When was the last time you saw him?"

I put a couple of fingers to my chin in mock thought. "I guess it was . . . I dunno, maybe a week before he disappeared?" I shrugged. "I knew him all my life. It's not like I kept track of when I saw him."

Randy nodded in agreement. "That makes sense. You know, I always think it's weird on TV shows, when they make a big deal about how someone can't remember what they were doing at some precise moment a year ago."

"A year ago, nothing. I have trouble remembering what I did yesterday." Maybe I was feeling wobbly, but I kind of liked Randy. He seemed like one of those rare sympathetic souls. "Though as I think of it, Biff came to see me at my mother's condo. I remember because she asked him to go get her mail, and afterward he made some really bad joke about this sexy lingerie catalog."

"And your mother's name is . . .?"

I told Randy her name. He smiled broadly and said, "Oh. That's a nice name. A common name to be sure, but a very nice name."

"She'd agree with you."

Randy shook his head in empathy. "Mothers. What can you do with them? Now, I have to ask this, even if it makes you uncomfortable. Was it your impression that Biff was having an affair with your ex-wife?"

I laughed out loud. "Best thing that ever happened to me. She—I mean, Betsy—thought I didn't know about it, but Biff told me years ago. I didn't care. My only reason for keeping the marriage together was my son."

"Is he here now?"

"No, he and his stepmother have gone on a trip. They get along great." I made a point of smiling.

"Now, you say Biff was rich. But did he have any debts?"

I leaned back in my chair and yawned. Though I was getting drowsy, I realized I had a perfect opportunity to get back at Biff. "Always. His parents got sick of bailing him out. I have a background in computers. Biff even asked me if I could help him to hack into someone's account to steal money. Naturally, I refused. I told him if he mentioned it again, I'd call the police." I couldn't have been happier that I'd already set up a computer trail of Biff supposedly stealing from Jesse Falcon, the murderer.

Randy narrowed his eyes. "So if he did hack into someone's accounts, he couldn't have done it alone?"

I yawned again. "He could've paid some computer crook to do it for him. And probably he'd hire someone to do his in-person transactions. So that Biff himself wouldn't be seen on tape and could deny everything. You might want to check out those offshore island banks. Biff was always . . ." I fought to keep my eyes open. "He was always saying how he wanted one of those offshore accounts. He planned to do all sorts of illegal things. He . . . he wanted to open a gambling house. He wanted to pimp whores. He was setting up Betsy . . . to become . . . a whore."

"Hey, man, are you okay?" I dimly saw Randy walking toward me.

I was confused because there seemed to be two worlds at once, and I was trying to figure out which was real and which was . . . it was hard to tell, maybe a dream? There was someone shaking me in the one world. In the other world—the more vivid one—I was with Biff. We were twelve years old and sneaking off to smoke cigarettes. Or pretending to. We bragged about which girls in school we'd fucked, though of course neither of us had even kissed a girl yet. Some other part of me, the grown man, was thinking, *I remember this day, this really happened.*

Next thing I knew, there was an angry deluge of cold water on my face. Someone's fingers were in my mouth. I saw some puke go down the shower drain. I realized it was Randy who was helping me, saving my life, literally. We were both fully clothed and sopping wet under the shower. The black shower tiles seemed to give off colors, sort of like when you wear those 3-D glasses.

I coughed for a while, then stepped out onto the black bathroom tiles on my own. Feeling fully conscious again, I felt a little crowded. I'm one of those people who, when I don't feel well, prefer to be left alone.

"Easy now." Randy grabbed my shoulders and sat me down on the toilet seat lid. "You'll be okay now. What the hell did you do?"

"I don't like being in wet clothes. Could you hand me my bathrobe? There, on the door hanger. I have an extra one, if you want."

"Sure." He tossed me my bathrobe and took the extra one underneath it. Then he grabbed a towel and stepped outside to dry off and change, keeping the door ajar.

"What's up?" I heard him ask from the other side of the door. "What did you do? Why?"

"I only took a few sleeping pills. It was a mixture. Oh, and vodka. I swear, it was literally moments before you got here. You saved my life." Drying off, I rubbed the towel so hard on my skin it turned red. But it was good—the sense of touch, the sense of being alive.

"When you've been a PI for as long as I have, you learn to do all kinds of things. But you still haven't told me why."

Michelangelo once said that the sculpture was already in the marble slab, and all he had to do was chisel it out. Likewise, a perfectly plausible explanation was right there waiting for me, I only had to catch it. I realized that I'd always been this way. Even back in college, I never wrote outlines for term papers or oral presentations. I improvised as I went along and always got an "A."

"It was Biff," I said quietly. "He's been blackmailing me. He's threatening to tell my son that he's his actual birth father. I couldn't let that happen."

Randy opened the door. I noticed he had tied a double knot in his bathrobe. "I still don't see why you tried to kill yourself. He could tell your son, anyway."

"You don't know Biff. He doesn't want to be Scotty's father at all. In fact, he'd deny it if there wasn't a chance to make money. I figured if I were dead, the secret would be safe. Betsy might tell Scotty about it, but I have no control over that, and anyway, even Scotty knows his mother is liar."

"You were willing to die to spare your son?"

"Yes. But there was—there was a little more to it. You know how I said Biff would have to pay someone to hack into somebody's bank account? That was the blackmail. He didn't want cash from me. He wanted me to commit all these serious felonies and show him how to hack into other people's money. He didn't tell me who'd been helping him, but he said that whoever it was could no longer be reached. He also said something about how he'd been shot at himself, though he didn't get specific. Who knows, maybe the computer hack got bumped off. Biff really needed my help. Maybe it sounds corny, but death seemed better than getting involved with him. I mean, what good would I be to my son if I went to jail? So again, I figured, 'Okay, Biff, here's my answer.'"

"Biff's been missing. How's he been communicating with you?"

"He hasn't been. Not until the other day. He sent me a long text message. I was so freaked out by it that I threw my phone away. Down a sewer." I scooped up our wet clothes and walked over to the laundry room. Randy followed behind as I threw our clothes into the dryer. "I'm one of those sensitive new-age guys," I joked. "I know how to turn on the dryer."

"Just as long as your wife doesn't know," Randy shot back. "Or is she your wife? Have you gotten married?"

"That's set for next month." I rolled my eyes. "My mom wants to put what she calls a little something together for us. Naturally, she's complaining every step of the way."

"Naturally," Randy agreed. "By the way, did Biff mention having a new girlfriend?"

"I don't think anyone except Betsy would be dumb enough to get involved with him." Realizing what I'd said, I amended, "But I guess that doesn't say much about me, either."

Randy laughed again, but then heaved a heavy sigh. "Let's sit down for a moment. There's something you need to know."

"Uh, sure." I acted like I had no idea what it might be.

Randy clasped his hands together in thought. He leaned forward in his chair, almost like a doctor telling a patient a serious diagnosis. "This is what I think happened. Biff disappeared after his visit to your mother's, am I right? This was because he started stealing money online. Identity theft. I believe there was something in your mother's mail that he used to get going."

"That makes sense. Say, you're pretty good." I had to admit, I was genuinely impressed by how quickly Randy was putting it all together, albeit in a totally wrong way.

"I think he stole from the condo's previous owner. Classic identity theft. Then he figured he had to lay low. He might even be off in the islands as we speak. And if he's a gambler and a shitty one, he probably lost everything he stole. No wonder he's trying to blackmail you."

I mulled it over. "Wow, that's an awful lot you're hitting me with at once. But it sounds reasonable. Yes. I'll bet you're exactly right, Randy. What should I do?"

Randy looked at me with dead seriousness. "Nothing. Do absolutely nothing. Wait for Biff to contact you. Tell him you've agreed. Ask how to contact him. Then contact me."

"Sounds good." I lowered my head in embarrassment. "A hell of a lot better than taking my own life."

He stood up and touched my shoulder. "You can't help it if you're a good man. Unlike the Biffs of this world, you have a conscience."

"If I'm such a good man, why did I try to do the worst possible thing?"

"Because . . . because shit if I know."

We laughed in a guy sort of way. I really did like Randy and hoped we could be friends. If, of course, a million different lies never came to the surface. Still, he and I clicked in a big way. I know it sounds dumb, but it was like we'd known each other all our lives. Like we both understood something about life that other people didn't, and we didn't even have to say what it was. He was older than me, not that it mattered. I'd forgotten the pleasant sensation of having a friend and being liked. Yet, at one time I was popular. Did I mention I was vice-president of my senior class in high school and at college three different fraternities invited me to pledge? What happened to that guy, who liked parties and being around people? How did I let Betsy become my universe?

Still, it was a strange feeling to genuinely want to connect to someone while at the same time wanting him to know nothing about me. It made me nervous in a new kind of way, like maybe mixing gin with bourbon. I felt better and better about meeting him while at the same time I felt worse and worse.

"I should see a shrink," I said. "What I did—it's not normal." For all the lies I told him, I genuinely reached out to Randy for answers. I trusted him, the way you might trust a bartender or cab driver. I sometimes trusted people I had no real reason to trust, as if my vulnerability would conquer all my apprehensions. Of course, it never did. Despite all the things I'd done, I was like a little boy wanting to be taken care of. Usually, the closest I came to achieving this was by taking care of other people instead. But Randy genuinely cared. I knew it somehow.

"Normal shmormal," Randy replied. "Have you seen this website called McShrink.com? Write to him. He gives people the best advice I've ever read."

I was flattered. Too bad I couldn't say thank you. "What if Biff doesn't contact me?"

"Oh, he will. I know his type, believe me. After all, I've—"

"I know, you've been a PI for years."

"That's right." As he walked to the door to leave, he added. "And under no circumstances, not a word to the cops. All they do is get in the way."

"I agree. Not a word to the cops."

10: DR. JESSE FALCON

MY FIRST IMPULSE WAS TO IMMEDIATELY CALL THE COPS and tell them I'd found my identity thief. But I quickly realized that the less I had to do with cops, the better. And anyway, proof could be staring them in the face and they still wouldn't do anything. Maybe it was incompetence or indifference. But it also occurred to me that Biff's parents had been using their influence all along to keep the case on the back burner.

I continued to worry about Sabrina when she wasn't exasperating me. The guy who said he was me in the bank robbery clearly worked for Biff. And if she was dating this guy—despite her blithe protests to the contrary—it could mean big trouble for her. Biff was no one to mess with. And I knew Biff was still alive because not long ago, he deposited and later withdrew another ten grand from one of my accounts. Not that he used his real name, but who else would it be? And the mobster guys accused of his murder were sitting safely in jail when this happened.

It enraged me that I was so close to finding Biff, yet still so far away. I'd gotten to know Betsy's ex—a nice but schmucky guy—but I didn't want to come across as foaming at the mouth to catch Biff. It might raise suspicions, even with such a trusting soul as this guy was. I had to kind of hang back a little and wait for the right time to ask for more information. But it drove me crazy, keeping it all to myself. I figured it would only make Esther upset to know that I was getting ever more dirt on my fingers.

"I've never seen you more at peace," Esther said, whose rose-colored glasses mistook my resigned cynicism for contentment. To outsiders, it can be a thin line between happiness and bitterness, especially when you are incapable of thinking anything bad or don't care about the person in question. "Really, Jesse, the cloud finally has a silver lining. You're a better human being."

If anything had a humbling effect on me, it was pulling the plug on the desperate Linda Goldstein. Also in the back of my mind, I wondered if I'd be arrested for murder. But I couldn't say any of this. Yet in a completely illogical way, it pissed me off that Esther didn't know what I didn't tell her. Something about niceness stemming from ignorance always got on my nerves. There's something so smarmy about it.

As for Sabrina, she would blithely ask if there were any new developments with what she called the identity theft "thing," like she was asking if we'd finished remodeling the kitchen yet. My unhappiness seemed barely to register with her, which I found deeply annoying. Once I even blurted out that she was a spoiled brat, though afterward I assured her I was only kidding.

Life is waiting for something to happen until you get so pissed off you make it happen yourself. Just as I had to figure out about Biff without any help from the cops, so did I realize I'd have to bring him to justice myself. I'd have to find him, entrap him, and *then* turn him over to law enforcement. My accountant brother and I were no longer on speaking terms. That's where my new friend came in or should I say my only friend?

It felt strange even to say I had a friend because I'd never really made close friends with anyone. Sex with women was how I bonded with people, if you don't count students I mentored or my patients. I suppose you'd also have to count the ones from either group I had sex with. From the time I hit puberty, I didn't care about hanging out with other guys. And I especially did not care about people who were more naïve than their years should have made them. I supposed I was using him, but in other ways I found myself enjoying his company. He'd been screwed in some of the same ways I'd been, and despite his tepid, hesitant manner, this gave us a bond. Still, there were times I wanted to shake him and say, "Damn it, you're alive, start acting like it." The dope tried to kill himself, but even that seemed more an act of inertia than anything else. When in doubt, kill yourself. He was like a declawed cat that was never allowed to leave the house.

I certainly didn't tell my new pal about Linda Goldstein, though I was able to share my rage about Biff without being judged. He had plenty reason to hate Biff, too. For once, someone really listened to me. Not the way a shrink does, always calculating what it all means to ask some amazingly insightful question, but listening because, well, he *listened.*

We'd drink—or rather, I'd drink and he'd watch—play handball, go to basketball games, or see movies that Esther had no interest in (i.e., anything with violence). Oddly, she also had no interest in my new friend. Esther barely met him for a minute and said she'd rather not have him over to the house. When I asked her why, she said he seemed needy, which she found unappealing in a man. In her universe, only women were allowed to have needs. And anyway, why did he have to "appeal" to her? It wasn't like they were going to have an affair. I could imagine them together. Slow as a pair of turtles.

I learned to say I was going out, and Esther knew what it meant. One time, she dryly commented that she was happy I'd discovered I was gay after all these years, since I was spending so much time with my pal.

"No such luck," I replied. "I'm going to keep fucking the daylights out of you, so you'd better get used to it." Though in truth, after our brief second honeymoon, things had chilled between us in the bedroom. If anything, maybe Esther was gay because over time she didn't seem to enjoy sex with me as much as tolerate it. It occurred to me that she simply didn't like men very much.

My friend's new wife, Melanie, was nice to me the few times I met her but accepted that guy time was guy time. I was not surprised when she turned out to be a plain-looking girl with unbecoming short hair and glasses. However, she was a nice person and presumably had a lot of money. He also could have done worse. They eloped at city hall, so there was no wedding to speak of. But, he told me, if there had been one I'd have been his best man. In spite of myself, I was touched.

His son was an unusual kid, what people called an "old soul." While little kids often lightened an atmosphere in a room, nine-year-old Scotty—or was he ten?—had a way of making it heavier. It was as though he knew when the world was going to end but wasn't about to tell anyone. I predicted he was either going to become a really good person or a really awful person, but would never be an average person. Scotty showed little interest in wanting to know other people and seemed to resent anyone who took his father's attention away from him. I never became his honorary "Uncle Jesse"—or I mean, "Uncle Randy"—so there were no issues about having to drag the kid along.

After engaging in what is obnoxiously called male bonding for a little while, I decided the time was right to pin my buddy down about Biff. Assuming he honestly didn't know where Biff was, he could still do computer shit to find him. My friend had no reason not to trust me. I arranged for a movie and drinks.

I let my pal pick the movie, and it sucked. It featured a B-list action hero who rescued his blah wife and obnoxious daughter from this insane sex slave trader. The good guy was a cop or a DA—I forgot which—and the bad guy wanted to get back at him for busting his bomb-happy brother. The hero's wife had to put out before getting rescued. But even psycho fantasies go only so far in these kinds of movies. Naturally, the awful teenage daughter was spared only moments before she was about to lose her cherry. There was a lot of predictable cutting back and forth between the screeching daughter and the hero's screeching car as he drove at a hundred miles an hour to the abandoned warehouse where his family members were held. After the bad guy fell to his death from a tall roof beam and a pool of blood formed around his head, the movie ended with the hero climbing into the ambulance with his wife and daughter. The daughter said something like, "I love you, Daddy," and the hero said something like, "I love you, too." The somber yet uplifting background music gave the cue for the closing credits. I supposed that the moral of the story was that the family that kept itself from getting sold into sex slavery was the family that stayed together.

"Wow, what a cool movie," said my buddy, as we got up from our seats. He took an obligatory last swallow of the melted ice in what had been his medium-sized Coke.

"I loved how the bad guy bled to death." I pretended to concur.

"Huh. I was sorry he died. He should've gone to prison for what he did."

"You have a point," I agreed, as if we were discussing some morally complex Ibsen play. "There are worse punishments than death."

"I guess I'll say, 'No comment.'"

It took me a moment to realize he was referring to his suicide attempt. One more thing to blame on Biff.

"Gee, I'm sorry. I didn't mean—"

"Hey, no sweat. Really, I'm glad I'm still around." He smiled at me in gratitude.

We stepped out into the blank night air. "A drink?" I suggested.

"Sure." Of course this meant he'd get a Coke or something. I asked him if he was in AA, and he told me no, he just didn't like to drink. But he had a good way of keeping up with drunk talk and never made me feel guilty for ordering yet another scotch straight up.

The first bar we came to was one of those places that looked very expensive from the outside, with almost no one on the inside. But it served alcohol, which meant it met my criteria. After feigning more interest in the movie and ordering a fresh drink, I got to the point. "I need to ask a huge favor." The radio or whatever was playing the dumb old song, "Torn between Two Lovers." I guessed I didn't like it because it seemed the kind of song Linda Goldstein would've liked.

He gamely squeezed his slice of lime into his Coke, took a sip, and shrugged. "Ask me. I'm all ears."

"It's Biff," I said. "I still can't find him. I was wondering if I gave you a cut of my locator's fee, could you do a little fancy computer stuff to track him down?"

My friend laughed. "Maybe someone bumped him off. He was such a shit." He frowned and added, "Seriously, I'm not a cop or anything. Hacking for any reason could get me arrested. Assuming I could even hack that well. I'm good, but I don't know if I'm *that* good."

I wore a mock expression of understanding. "I understand your reluctance. I promise, no harm will come to you. You're shielded. I swear on the lives of my wife and daughter." I held up my right hand for full impact. "And anyway, speaking of legal, don't you want to bring him to justice? When you've been a PI for as long as I have, you learn to do what you have to do."

He waved for the cocktail server and told her to bring him a scotch. He'd never before had anything to drink in my presence. (Except, of course, for the vodka he said he drank when he tried to off himself.) We sat there quietly, waiting for his drink to arrive. When it did, I smiled at the server and gestured with my hand that her bow tie was crooked. She grinned at me flirtatiously as she straightened it. While this was going on, my pal apparently swallowed his scotch in one gulp. Staring at his empty glass, he resisted, yet savored, the drink's burning taste.

Finally, he said, "Okay. I'll see if I can do it."

I gave him the most sincere expression I could muster. "I am truly grateful."

"Wow, this case must really mean a lot to you, my friend." He nudged my arm with his fist. "But anyway, that's what friends are for."

We sat there for a while. Finally, he said, "You're sure I won't be in any trouble? I have a wife, a son, and a mother who depend on me. I couldn't—"

"You're *fine*," I reiterated, raising my glass jovially. He might not have been fine at all. Besides the FBI possibly not being amused, Biff himself could retaliate. But it's not like I forced my friend to do anything. He agreed of his own free will. I was in pretty deeply myself, so I wasn't asking him to do something I wouldn't do if I had the computer skill.

He stood up and whomped me in the back. "I guess there's no time like the present. Let's get cracking on the case."

"Uh, isn't it getting kind of late? Besides, I'm sure I'd only be in the way." I was always nervous about spending much time at his place. If his mother was there, she might recognize me as Jesse Falcon, despite my changed appearance.

He smiled but looked confused. "I thought it would be fun. But I can start it tomorrow. No, wait a second. I can start next week. I just remembered some other stuff I have to do."

In the moment, I dangerously decided I didn't want to wait another week. "Maybe it's not that late after all. Sure, let's go do it now."

"Great. And for some of the real secret stuff, I'll have you look the other way." Distractedly, he took out his cell phone and texted a message. "A reminder to myself. Scotty wants a new book," he explained.

"Scotty reads a lot, doesn't he?" I asked. Technically, this was a mark of intelligence, but in the case of Scotty, it somehow seemed like a disability.

"Yeah, he sure does," my friend replied, as if understanding.

He and his wife and son had moved into a spanking new—if nondescript—home in an overpriced new development just outside of town called the Paradise Cul-de-Sac. It was a large horseshoe of identical homes that all had swimming pools, shared a clubhouse, tennis courts, and jogging trails; and were walking distance to a lake so pristine it looked artificial even though it wasn't. His mother was invited to live with them, but she said it was all a bunch of shit and was happier in her small condo. The one she'd bought from me. I got the impression she visited a lot, despite her protests.

It was even later by the time we got to the Cul-de-Sac, and I was old enough to not have to be told to be quiet upon entering because everyone was asleep. I had a passing thought about what Esther might think of the fact the entire home was done in black and white. Probably she would consider it another strike against my friend. For Esther, good taste made you a good person, and bad taste made you a bad person. But what did I know about that kind of stuff? Sabrina did those weird paintings in black and white and supposedly they were profound works of art. Maybe black and white were the new "in" colors or some shit.

We quietly walked to his office. The computer was already on. The screen saver featured a series of photos of Scotty. His glasses often produced a distracting camera glare, but my friend didn't seem to mind. He was a father who was proud of his kid. He clicked off the screen saver as he sat himself down.

"Oh, I see you're reading McShrink. Didn't I tell you it was great?" I was trying to keep things friendly.

He clicked out of McShrink.com and went to his home page. "Let's get to it," he said.

I sat next to him and watched as a series of computer screens I'd never seen before appeared one after another. My friend kept typing in all these codes like he knew exactly what he was doing, though once or twice he paused for a moment to think. One time he even said, "Fuck." But I couldn't tell what had gone wrong, and he made no effort to explain himself. I saw a different side of him—the work side. He was one of those people who, when working, did not pay attention to anyone or anything else. Just as I predicted, I felt like a useless kid.

"Please turn around." It was the first time he spoke to me in about half an hour.

"Uh, sure." I didn't like sitting there staring at the wall and had to remind myself he was doing me a favor.

"Okay, you can turn back around." I obeyed but resented anyone telling me what to do for even a moment.

"Bingo." My friend wore a sarcastic smile as he turned the screen in my direction.

Sure enough, I saw a long list of transactions by Biff, all from my various accounts into various accounts of his, and then from his account to a third list of accounts. The list didn't have any name on it—instead, there were these weird computer codes—but I recognized all the stolen amounts of money on certain dates. I thought I'd be happy to see this once and for all, but looking at it scared me a little, like when you think you want to see a dead person only it turns out you don't. My heart sank and a peculiar nervousness overtook me.

"Huh. So now he's using other people's accounts to launder money."

My friend shook his head sadly. "Unless they're all aliases."

"Can you find out who he's stealing from?" I asked, to make it seem like I had no idea.

"Hmm. I'd rather not. These innocent people have had enough violation to their privacy."

"And he's still off in the islands, banking away to his heart's content?"

"Yep. As of the other day, he was in the capital city." He typed in a few more codes and showed me an address for Biff.

I stood up and anxiously walked about the room. "I wonder who's in on it with him. You said he doesn't know computers, right?"

My buddy leaned back in his swivel chair to face me. "I've told you, Biff can't do anything without help."

I suddenly got a *new* sinking feeling. "Say, you're not—I mean, you're not in on it with him? You wouldn't do that to me, would you?"

He stared at me in disbelief and had to put his hand over his mouth to keep from laughing too hard. "I told you, Biff did me the biggest favor of my life by fucking Betsy. But I don't owe him a damn thing. Really, why would you even think that? And why is this case such a big deal to you, anyway?" Before I could say anything, he pointed at me. "Holy shit. You're fucking Betsy, aren't you?"

I had to hand it to him—I never thought he was that smart. I took a moment to answer. "It was a quickie," I finally replied. "I don't like her or anything, if that's what you're getting at."

He slapped his knee. "I knew it. That is so Betsy. She can't meet a dude without fucking him. I wonder if I'm supposed to be jealous? Anyway, what did you think?"

I kept visualizing all sorts of exotic forms of torture I wanted to perform on Biff. "Think? What did I think about what?"

He sighed with impatience. "Betsy, you dumb ass."

"Oh, right. She was . . . I mean, I didn't really . . ." I didn't know how to say that his ex-wife was such a turnoff that she just lay there like an ice sculpture. True, he hated her, but I didn't want him to think I knew what his sex life must've been like all those years.

He put his hand to his mouth. "Gee, I'm sorry, dude. If you couldn't—I guess that happens to everyone. I shouldn't have asked." The screen saver came back on. He tapped on the keyboard to bring the damning list of Biff's transactions back up, as if we had not yet finished going over an x-ray.

He thought the problem was *me*? Could I live with that and let the whole thing go?

"I performed fine. I always do." It was the God's honest truth, I'd never had a flop in my life. I worshipped sex. I lived for it. "We weren't compatible," I added.

"You'd have to be Godzilla to be compatible with Betsy. God, she was insatiable."

Betsy insatiable? Was my friend as lousy in bed as she was? I could see it was time to get back on topic. "Anyway, to answer your question, I treat every case seriously. It's my life."

There was a knock at the office door. "Dad?" said the sleepy voice of a child, which by process of elimination I knew had to be Scotty. He frankly hadn't made enough of an impression on me to recognize his voice.

My buddy looked at me as if to say, *Oh great, just what we need.* "What is it, son?"

"Can I talk to you?"

He swore under his breath and put a different screen on the

computer. "Okay." Rising to open the door, he scratched his son's head affectionately. "What is it, soldier?"

Scotty grabbed his father's legs. "I had a bad dream."

"How did you know I was in here? By the way, say hello to Mr. Van Sant."

"Hey, Scotty," I enthused.

"Hello, sir," he replied indifferently.

"You haven't answered my question, Scotty," said the boy's father.

"I heard you talking, okay? Not real well, but I heard voices."

"How could you hear voices if you were having a bad dream?" My friend was so scrupulously honest, he was on guard for the smallest fib from his son.

"I don't know. I just did, okay?" He grabbed his father's legs even tighter. "There was this giant *thing*. It kept eating people. It was after me."

"And I'll eat you myself," said a cranky old woman's voice, "if you don't get back to bed and leave your father alone."

An older woman padded to the doorway. I panicked as I recognized her as my friend's mother. I tried to sort of subtly look in another direction. *You've had plastic surgery*, I kept chanting to myself.

"Mom, this is my friend Randy whom I've been telling you about."

The woman looked at me with squinty, suspicious eyes. "I can't see a thing without my glasses, but how do you do?" She extended her hand. I had to walk over to shake it. As I did, I could smell liquor on her. Apparently familiar with this phenomenon, she said, "Yeah, I tied one on, Mr. Hoity-Toity. You got a problem with that?"

"Not at all. Done the same thing myself a million times." I made my speaking voice slightly hoarse.

"My hat goes off to you, Mr. Van Sant. You'll be a good influence on my son. He's such a wimp. What an asshole." As I politely laughed, she said, "You look kind of familiar."

"People say that all the time. I have that kind of face."

I was grateful on a cosmic level when she turned her attention to Scotty. "What the hell are you still doing up? Go to bed this instant. Bad dreams are good for you. They'll put hair on your chest. They'll make you a man."

Scotty scooted back toward his bedroom, but then paused. "What do bad dreams do to women, Grandma?"

"They give us tits," she replied. "Now go to sleep." She turned to the boy's father. "He's too old for that help-me-daddy bad dream bullshit. It's time you let him grow some balls. Oh, wait a minute. I'm sorry, forgot, you don't have any yourself." She winked at me. Though embarrassed for my friend, I winked back. It was best to not disturb her oblivion.

She bowed at us with a mock theatrical flourish. "Good night to you, gentlemen. I'm going to feel like shit tomorrow. What a bunch of shit."

As soon as his mother departed, my friend closed the door. "I'm glad you met my mom when she was in a good mood."

Seeing my friend humiliated and grateful to the universe that she did not recognize me, I felt humbled. "Don't feel bad. Everyone has a mother. Shrinks would go out of business without them. In fact, I—" I caught myself from saying something about my actual life.

"You what?" We walked back to the computer and sat down.

"Nothing, nothing at all. Only that my own mother and father . . . oh, never mind."

"No, really, go ahead." He seemed to be aimlessly surfing the web.

"They never looked happy. I don't know. It's hard to explain."

He stopped surfing. "My mom is affectionate with no one. I try not to take it personally. I'm sorry, though, about your mom and dad. Are they still alive? My dad was a really nice guy. Everyone said so."

This was starting to sound like a therapy session. At this rate, we were going to end up hugging. Which I could live without.

"Well, anyway, back to business. I guess I'll have to fly to the capital."

"No, don't," my friend said, with surprising force in his voice. "It will just . . . Biff is . . . look, let me go instead. Even after all that's happened, I know that Biff will listen to me and only me. It's this strange thing between us that's always been there. Even if you find him, I swear, he'll get out of it."

I thought about it. "Well, why don't we both go?"

"You mean like just up and fly somewhere?" I couldn't tell if the thought shocked or pleased him for its novelty. Some people never thought about seeing new places, and apparently, he was one of them. I can't say this took me by surprise. He was a man who gave off no aura at all of loving adventure.

"Sure. People do it all the time."

My buddy threw his hands in the air. "Okay, why not? But first I go see Biff alone. Really, trust me. It's the only way."

"You know, I hate to bring this up, but how much do you want for doing all this?"

He yawned as he checked his e-mail. "Nothing. Hell, pay my plane fare, I guess."

"Okay. I'll throw in meals and the hotel room, too."

"Deal." He raised his hands to high-five me, and I complied, though I'd never done it before and thought it was a dumb ritual.

We made plane and hotel reservations online, and I went home to pack a few things. The next day, we were on a plane to Biff's island paradise. It seemed to take forever, especially since my friend slept for almost the entire flight. I did, however, flirt with a couple of the flight attendants; one of them gave me her island phone number. I thought about getting a second girl for my friend, but he already told me he wasn't into cheating on Melanie. I liked how he didn't judge me, though, for making the suggestion.

Even before we landed, the island looked like a postcard. I could've cared less about the much-advertised deep, blue waters or sparkling, white sands. All I wanted was to find Biff. No sooner had we exited the plane than we ran into a mob of passengers who'd disembarked from a cruise ship. They all looked the same to me, with sunglasses and tote bags. I could hear a lot of mumblings about how beautiful the island was, but I also overheard that most of them were headed to the duty-free shopping district. The sun was blindingly intense, even with sunglasses on. I could tell there was a cooling ocean breeze by the swaying of the palm leaves. But I couldn't really feel it while trapped in this crowd of tourists. I hated how hot it was.

My friend didn't seem bothered at all, and though he walked at a leisurely pace, he still walked faster than me. He was several people ahead when I saw him turn and mouth the word, *Biff,* and point toward a bunch of bicycle riders about a block to the right. I stared into the bright sun and looked again at my friend, who was managing to deftly maneuver his way through the crowd. A couple of people told him to stop shoving. He ignored them and kept going toward Biff as fast as he could.

"Wait for me," I shouted, but I knew he couldn't hear. Besides, he'd been saying all along he needed to talk to Biff alone.

I saw him approach the bike riders, and then make a left-hand turn down a side street. (As I would later learn, it was the street that Biff lived on, according to the computer.)

I finally made it through the crowd. I was itching with sweat. Figuring I might as well check into the hotel, I asked a police officer for directions and before long had showered, shaved, and ordered coffee. I wasn't comfortable with sharing a space with another guy, so we each had our own room. What can I say? It was a hotel room. There was a double bed with a tropical-looking bedspread, a fake palm tree, leafy-green wallpaper, and—glory halleluiah—a small refrigerator with some tiny liquor bottles. I supposed there was a nice ocean view, though obviously I had no interest in the famous beaches. Popping a happy pill and washing it down with scotch, I called the flight attendant who gave me her number. There was no answer. I called for the bellboy. Before long, a girl was arranged to visit me. I had to do something while I waited for my friend to return, and sex was the best cure for impatience that I knew of.

I assumed I'd get an island girl. Instead, she was a bleach-blonde who spoke with a decided Brooklyn accent. I could tell it pissed her off when I told her she couldn't smoke. I also told her the booze was off-limits.

Still, I was amazed how cheap it was to get a full fuck. And this was without taking into account the going currency rate. I even gave her a tip, which I usually didn't do with hookers.

After she left, I called Esther to say I missed her. When she asked how my case was going—I had told her I was working on a case so she wouldn't worry—I said it was going great. She made a kissing sound; I made a kissing sound back.

I took another shower, put on clean underwear, turned up the air conditioner, and fell asleep on top of the bedspread. The obviously synthetic fibers were a little scratchy, but I couldn't get it together to unmake the bed.

Someone was shaking my shoulder; the light had been turned

on and my eyes saw spots for a moment before adjusting. It took a second to see my friend standing over me. I could see through the window that it was night. There was a full moon.

"Don't worry, I'm okay," he told me.

But he sure as hell didn't look okay. He sported two black eyes and a bleeding gash running down his face to match the bruises and cuts on his arms. His clothes were torn and muddy, with a few small spots of blood. "I got worked over a little," he said. "But really, I'm fine." He limped his way to the chair across the room. "Do you mind if I sit?"

I sat up in bed. "Of course not. It's a stupid hotel room. What happened?"

"I chased after Biff. I *knew* it was him. Just as I got up behind him, these thugs grabbed me from out of nowhere. They told me to mind my own business and go back home on the next plane."

"They spoke English?" I got up to pour him a drink. There was a tiny bottle of bourbon that I thought he might like.

He made no protests when offered the drink. "Yeah. They sounded American. There were three of them." He took a big swallow of his drink. "They said they knew who I was. They said that Betsy sent me, but that Biff wanted nothing more to do with her. Something about how he didn't believe the kid was his."

"What did you say?"

"Nothing." He nervously wiped the blood off his cheek and wiped his blood-stained hand on his shirt. "When you're getting the shit beaten out of you, it makes you kind of taciturn. They said that they'd . . . you know, kill me if I didn't stay away." He polished off the drink. "Then they said they'd go after Scotty."

"You need a doctor."

"No." He raised his voice. "No doctor. I'm fine. I want to get out of here." He stood up and fell to his knees. "Please, let's go. I'm really scared." He was such a torn and bloody mess, I couldn't tell if he was crying. "If it was just me—but Scotty. I can't let anything happen to him." He literally was begging.

I only thought for a moment, but it was one of the most important moments of my life. "Okay, we'll go back. I'll tell Betsy. I'll tell her something that leaves you out of it."

But what I really thought was that I'd fly back to the island alone, buy a gun, and take care of Biff myself.

"Thank you, thank you." My friend seemed immeasurably relieved. "I'll go to my room and clean myself up."

"Do you need help?"

"No, I'll be fine. I always pack a first aid kit."

"You were a Boy Scout, weren't you?"

"An Eagle Scout. Is it that obvious?" He smiled in spite of himself. "Anyway, let's fly back first thing in the morning."

I was right. He had no business getting this involved, though at least he took his beating like a man. Yet why did I feel as if I *could* handle it? My own life had been easier than his. I guessed it had to do with inner strength—either you had it or you didn't.

"Sure. Whatever you say."

He stopped in the doorway for a moment. "Randy?"

"Yeah?"

"Nothing, I guess. Just that you . . . you're really a nice guy."

I'd been called many things in my time, but a nice guy had never been one of them. I also never thought I'd want to be called one, yet it felt mighty nice.

"Get yourself cleaned up. You're a motherfucking mess."

Given how bloody and beaten up he was, his big smile looked sort of creepy. "You know, that's the nicest thing anyone's ever said to me."

Ironically, after he left, I ended up needing a bit of first aid myself. I got so pissed off thinking about Biff that I broke a drinking glass into my hand. Yet despite a rather ostentatious flow of blood, the cut itself was merely superficial.

11: AKA JESSE FALCON

IT WASN'T EASY BEING MANY DIFFERENT PEOPLE at the same time, but I did the best I could. In fact, if they gave Oscars for real-life performances, I would've won one after the magnificent piece of bullshit I pulled off at the island. It's not easy to beat yourself to a pulp. To slice your own face and punch yourself so hard that you give yourself two black eyes, and then ram yourself against a building until you are bruised and lacerated all over. It takes a lot of nerve. It takes an enormous amount of self-discipline.

Plus—let's face it—it takes having no choice.

I should point out that this was not the first time I beat myself up. Once when Biff and I were kids, I gave myself a bloody nose so that my mom and dad wouldn't punish me for staying out late. I guess you could say I already had the potential to be a self-mutilator.

Still, I liked Randy a lot. I looked up to him, and you could even say that I loved him. The more I lied to him, the more I kept hoping that one of the lies somehow would be powerful enough to erase all the other lies. The last thing I wanted to do was hurt this man who'd saved my life, taught me so much, and had been kind to me.

Nevertheless, lie after lie was keeping my son out of prison or the loony bin, take your pick.

One thing I did succeed in was keeping Sequoia protected. When I came back from my island trip—I told her I was going along to keep Randy company while he worked on a case—I told her I had gotten mugged by the island locals. I had not told her about the bungled suicide attempt or how Randy saved my life.

Given how fucked up her childhood was, I wanted her to feel secure. And when she pointed out that it was best she not meet Randy at all so that she wouldn't be more connected to the Biff angle than she already was, I readily saw her logic. She needed to keep her hands as clean as possible to be there for Scotty, in case things went really nutso.

We decided to create a phony wife who would meet Randy instead of my actual wife. After a bit of shopping around, we found the best of both worlds: a prostitute who was also studying to be an actress. She'd keep her mouth shut for obvious reasons, plus she could create a believable personality as my wife. We didn't tell her what was going on, and she had the street smarts not to ask. We named her Melanie and kind of frumped her up with a sexless short wig and glasses, so that she really didn't exist except when she met Randy a couple of times. After a couple of these meetings, we made sure Sequoia was never at home on those rare occasions I brought Randy over.

We decided to tell Scotty about Melanie. Not that we went into any details. Only that we had to play a game with Randy that I was really married to Melanie. When Randy came over, Scotty was to act like Melanie was his stepmom. Scotty, who talked more and more like an adult even though he was barely ten, replied that he knew it wasn't a game, but he'd play along with it anyway. He ignored everyone when Melanie and Randy were at the house, which was what he did with most everyone all the time anyway.

I continued to launder money through Biff's phony offshore accounts. I figured that if I got caught, I could tell the cops I was doing it to try to catch Dr. Jesse Falcon. I still couldn't find him, no matter how hard I tried. The serial killer thing never scared me. As that police detective said, Jesse Falcon only killed comatose or ex-comatose women. Plus, though it's hard to explain, I knew that I'd never die that easily.

I still worried about money all the time. I was making big bucks as McShrink, but I was afraid it would all get taken away if people learned that McShrink was not a real shrink. Sometimes I didn't think about the identity theft for hours at a time. It was like a dieter's urge to give in to doughnuts just this once. Inevitably, I had my lapses. I'd try in vain to get back into Jesse Falcon's accounts, and when I couldn't, I'd think about finding a new identity to steal from. I even looked up a few people that I would've enjoyed stealing from—an old grade school bully, or some of the people I used to work with—but none of them had much of anything to take. In the meantime, I made do with the stockpile of cash I'd put into the Biff accounts I had created.

In this totally insane way, I *missed* Dr. Jesse Falcon. As I thought about it, he and I were very close. I was sure he hated me, but hate is, after all, an intimate emotion. Though he didn't know my name, my existence mattered. I was possibly the most important person in his life. I missed that rush of power, and then the inevitable guilt, like adding a moldy slice of lemon to a Coke. Also, the thought of paying him back, so I could feel like a good person again. Adding Biff to the mix had been the finishing touch. At least in death, Biff would have a shitty reputation, which was better than nothing.

On the surface, everything was working out. Everything but me. Even though Melanie was my idea, once she was in place something else snapped inside me. It was one deception too many. I thought, *Surely life isn't this fucked up, surely you can't just keep going further and further over the top with your lies and still get away with it.* But apparently, you could. I was far from a beacon of virtue by this time, yet the fact that I kept getting away with it all made me increasingly cynical and despondent about other people. I retaliated with even more mischief, since apparently people deserved no better. It had become the only way to live, and with every deception, I became more convinced that the people I lied to were dumb fucks.

Even Randy. If he was such a great PI, why could I fool him so easily? And I had to admit, I was sick and tired of people treating me like I was this nice little nothing that obviously had never done anything wrong or had anything of substance happen to him. Even when people knew at least a few things, like getting fired or Betsy dumping me, they assumed I'd be perfectly fine because I was always nice and was never a bother. Good ol' me. I think this was one of the things that brought Sequoia and me together. We both knew what it was like to be treated as though we were invisible. One exception was Mom, who knew I was visible all right but wished I wasn't. I was determined that Scotty would never feel invisible—that he knew I would stop at nothing to protect him.

Speaking of Scotty being ten, per my earlier promise to him, he was now old enough to get a dog. I figured we'd go to the animal shelter and rescue one of the dogs. My motives were not completely altruistic; the dog already would be housebroken.

Sequoia being Sequoia, she was touched that I wanted to rescue an animal. We agreed that the dog shouldn't be too big. When we went to the local shelter a few days later, Scotty wanted to take home a Great Dane, but Sequoia talked him into the smallest dog there: a bulldog that Scotty named Astronaut. He was only a few years old, according to the shelter, though when we took him to the vet for a check-up, the vet said he was much older and that shelters sometimes say dogs are younger than they are to help them get adopted. I decided to ignore this piece of information. I was already getting very attached to Astronaut myself, and I wished him a long and happy life. Astronaut went totally crazed when he met Randy and wouldn't stop jumping up on him and licking his face.

Then, on top of that, Sequoia led me blindfolded to our bedroom, and when she took off the blindfold there was a cake with candles. The message on the cake was, "Congratulations, Daddy!" I literally wept for joy when I realized I'd be a father again. We fed each other the cake while having sex, making a big mess out of the bed sheets. The slash I gave to my face was leaving a faint scar that the doctor said would disappear over time. Sequoia kept kissing and kissing the scar, as if it had something to do with the baby we were going to have.

"How do you feel?" I asked her, burying my face between her breasts.

She giggled for the sensation. "Stop worrying. The doctor says I'm fine. There shouldn't be any—"

I lifted up my head. "I mean on the inside. How do you feel about having a baby after . . . you know, how your own childhood was."

She answered as if I'd asked the stupidest question in the world. "Obviously, I'm going to give this baby all the love I never got. What did you think I wanted to do, toss it in a dumpster?"

To lighten things up in a hurry, I made a goofy face and said, "Hell, yeah."

Fortunately, she was amused, and we had a pillow fight. Yet her reaction troubled me. I wondered if it really was going to work out. How do you give to someone else what you never got yourself? You could mean to do it, you could say you're going to do it, but could you do it? Still, Sequoia was truly elated. She never seemed more beautiful, and I put this fear out of my mind.

Scotty was so enamored of Astronaut that he barely stopped playing with him long enough to hear that he'd soon have a baby sister or brother. He was mildly confused.

"Why have a baby when we already have a dog?" he asked.

Soon he was asking to be homeschooled in order to play with Astronaut all the time. I said absolutely not, he needed to go to school and be with kids his own age. He'd started throwing these weird fits when he didn't get his way. Screaming, red-faced, his hands clenched into fists at his side, he would yell out all sorts of strange things before running off to his room. In this instance, it was: "If the baby wanted to be homeschooled, you'd let it!"

He talked to his psychiatrist about it, who said we should let him express himself because he otherwise might withdraw so far into himself there'd be no getting him out.

"Are you *sure* nothing else happened to traumatize him?" the doctor asked. Sequoia and I guiltily shook our heads and shrugged.

Sequoia said it would be a good idea to homeschool Scotty. She said she'd be home with the baby, anyway, and Scotty needed to know he was equally important. He wasn't making any friends in school, and if he could give and receive love with his dog, that at least was a start. The doctor agreed with her. Mom, though, took my side . . . sort of. She said it was clear who wore the pants in my family, and obviously, it wasn't me. But she also had a lot to say against taking Scotty out of school.

"Homeschooling is for the birds," she said. "If you don't teach your kid he's *normal*, you might as well forget it. You were the strangest kid I ever saw, but I always told you you were as good as everyone else."

I couldn't let that one go. "Mom, when have you ever told me I'm as good as everyone else?"

"I've certainly never criticized you. I've always supported everything you did."

"Fine, Mom. You're right. I don't know what came over me."

So, there I was, the suburban success I'd always pretended to be with Betsy: beautiful wife, a second kid on the way, money, a nice home that was paid for. All it took to achieve was pretending about everything else in my life and keeping my fingers crossed that I didn't end up in jail. Over time, I was getting used to my many fears, the way you got used to any troubling thought after a while.

When I learned Sequoia was pregnant, I called Mom, who said, "Great, just what I need, another kid to worry about when you're done flushing yourself down the toilet." She did go on to ask if Sequoia was getting enough rest. Oddly, she didn't ask to talk to Sequoia herself. "Do me one favor," Mom said. "If you find out the sex of the kid, don't tell me. It's weird, people knowing ahead of time if they're having a boy or a girl. The surprise is the only fun thing about getting knocked up, and now they even spoil that."

"Is that why I was an only child? Because you didn't like being pregnant?"

"Never you mind why I never had another screaming, shitting, pain-in-the-ass kid. It's none of your goddamn business. Kids don't have respect for their parents anymore."

I also called Randy, who said we should meet for drinks to celebrate. We met at what had become our usual haunt, a low-key neighborhood bar in the city.

"Here's to Dad." Randy offered up his shot glass. I raised mine to hit his in a toast. Since knowing Randy, I'd developed more of a taste for alcohol. I even got drunk once with Mom. "And here's to Godfather," I replied. "And I won't take no for an answer."

Randy seemed taken aback. "Godfather? Gee, I don't know. Don't you have someone else, like an old friend or cousin?"

I was hurt and confused. "Why, don't you want to?"

"Oh, it's not that I don't want to. It's only that we haven't known each other all that long. I wouldn't want someone else's feelings to get hurt."

I laughed bitterly. "Believe me, there is no one else."

"Okay then. So long as no one thinks I'm the other kind of godfather."

It took me a moment to get it: godfather, mafia, and so on. I pretended I thought it was funnier than I did. Next, because supposedly I was a know-nothing, I asked him if there was any news about Biff.

Randy's face turned red. "I'm leaving you out of all that. We agreed. Ever since the island."

I motioned for refills. "I know, but I deserve to know *something*, don't I? After everything Biff did to me."

The woman who always waited on us came to our table to take our orders. I heard her mutter "prick," under her breath. Randy explained that they'd had what he called a roll in the hay, and now she was upset because he never called her back.

"I don't get that about women," he said. "Everything is so serious all the time."

I thought about it. "In my experience, men are more serious. But speaking of men, what about Biff? You still haven't answered my question."

Our drinks were served with a scowl. Once we were alone again, Randy said, "Biff won't be bothering us anymore."

I tried to have no particular reaction. "What does that mean? Has he been arrested?"

Randy roared with laughter. "Not exactly. That's all I'm going to say."

I was concerned about what exactly Randy meant. I could feel that scared feeling coming over me. "Oh, c'mon. We're celebrating. As a father-to-be, I deserve a present, and I want it to be the latest on Biff. In fact, I insist."

Out of nowhere, Randy rose and grabbed me by my collar. "Nobody tells me what to do or when to do it." There was pure rage in his eyes, though his voice was quiet, which in a way made it more frightening than if he'd yelled. "I gotta go," he said, letting go of me.

I followed him outside. It had turned into a rainy night. And after a few seconds outside, a deluge. Our cars were parked next to each other only a few doors down, but we were both soaked to the skin by the time we reached them. As Randy was about to get into his car, I lunged toward him from behind and knocked him to the ground. We rolled around punching each other on the pavement as the rain pelted down, continually washing us both clean of blood.

I was on top of Randy and had him in a half nelson, which I knew surprised him. He didn't think I had it in me. A full nelson can break someone's neck. When I shouted at him, "What happened to Biff?" he realized he had to answer.

"Okay!" he shouted above the rainstorm, so loud he was hoarse. "I killed him. Are you happy now? I swear, if you tell anyone, I'll fucking kill you, too."

I let go of Randy and sat there on the sidewalk in the rain. "Killed him? We're talking about *Biff*, right?" It was one thing when crazy Betsy pretended to have killed Biff, but Randy wasn't someone whom I thought would make something like this up.

"Let's go in my car. This is stupid."

As we settled into the front seats of Randy's car, we took a moment to catch our breath before Randy told me what happened. The rain seemed to hit the windshield in waterfalls rather than in drops. I could see Randy's face and hands were pretty scratched up, as were mine.

"Wow, we really had a go at it," he said, giving me a friendly nudge. "I never fought with a man before."

"I did as a kid. And one time in high school, when someone called Biff a jerk."

We both sat there, breathing in and out. Our breath made frost on the windows.

"I went back to the island," Randy finally said. "It was the day after we returned. I had the address you gave me for Biff. It must've been a typo because the street ended before the number of his address. I started calling hotels. I started with the best ones, and the third place I called had a guest with his name. I went up to his room. He wasn't there, so I waited in the doorway to watch for him. I waited over five hours, but I was so jazzed up to find him I didn't mind. It seemed like five minutes. He was whistling down the hall when he entered his room, not a care in the world. I knocked on the door, asked for Biff, and said I was the concierge. I can't tell you what that was like, to finally see him face to face. After what he did to you."

"I really appreciate that, Randy," I felt forced to say. "And you're sure it was Biff?"

He stared at me quizzically. "Why wouldn't I be? He looked a little different from in his photos, Who doesn't?"

I remember being tempted to say that this was true, the camera adds ten pounds, but I let Randy continue instead.

"He let me in and said he was Biff. That was when I told him I was a PI, that there were people looking for him, and that I knew about the identity theft scam, and I also didn't appreciate his thugs beating up my friends. He said he didn't know what I was talking about and he wasn't really Biff after all. 'Let me show you my ID,' he said. I told him that if he could do all these other things, he certainly could get a fake ID. I grabbed him before he could say or do anything more. I completely lost it. I said he was a total fuck, and I was going to kill him. He pulled out a gun from his jacket. I reached for a paperweight. It was right next to me on the desk. It had the stupid hotel logo on it. But it was heavy. I hit him in the head with all my might. He fell to the floor. I kept hitting him and hitting him and his head cracked open and there was blood and brain shit everywhere. And he was like, you know. Dead."

I had no idea why someone would say he was Biff when he wasn't. I immediately suspected Betsy, only what was she trying to prove? Or maybe Biff's parents paid some look-alike to pose as their son? Only *why*? The only thing I knew for certain was that I had to stop stealing in Biff's name, especially in case this person had an ID that said he was Biff. And I could only hope that the guy who got killed was up to no good anyway. After all, he was carrying a gun.

"I never killed anyone before," Randy said. "No matter how big a shit. But Biff . . . I couldn't control myself."

"It was self-defense, Randy."

"I tell myself that. But I know it wasn't."

"Maybe it was the final straw," I offered helpfully. "You snapped because he was one creep too many."

Randy choked back a sob. "Yeah, maybe that was it. I wiped the place around to get rid of fingerprints and ran down the stairs as fast as I could, hoping no one would see me. The hotel was right on the beachfront, and it was dark by then. I took off most of my clothes and rinsed off in the ocean. Some other people were on the beach, but too far away to see me up close. So far, so good. And there haven't been any more . . ." He stopped himself.

"Any more what?"

"Nothing, just that I haven't heard anything more about it."

"Maybe the whole island hated Biff so much they hushed it up."

Randy laughed, in spite of himself. "Or maybe they don't want bad publicity. It would hurt the tourist trade. Or maybe his parents hushed it up. Who knows?"

We sat there and watched the rain. After a little while, it let up some. "Guess I should go home," I said. "Randy, you know I'll never tell, don't you?"

"I know," he said quietly. "You're the only person I trust."

"Same here. I mean, I guess I trust Melanie, but that's different, you know?"

"Trust me, I know."

I laughed. "You look like a motherfucking piece of shit." It was true. He was still sopping wet, and with his scrapes and bruises he looked like some street derelict.

"So do you."

It probably sounds crazy, but I felt very close to Randy in that moment. "This has to stop. All my best memories are of getting beaten up." He reached across the car, and we gave each other a bear hug. It kind of hurt, given the bruises we gave each other, yet it didn't matter.

"You're the best friend I ever had, Randy."

"Same here."

I drove straight to Betsy's. My old home. I couldn't do anything else until I knew if she was involved in more bullshit. This lack of patience was my weakness as a crook. I knew the best thing to do was sit back and wait, to play it cool. But sometimes I couldn't. As far as Betsy was concerned, the only thing I could think of was that she had the money to pay for a Biff look-alike, whom she now would marry and save face. And a lot of people had offshore accounts on the island, so maybe the guy was there, waiting for her. Still, what about the murder trial? Surely even Betsy would realize that by producing a fake Biff, she could be indicted for interfering with a criminal investigation or whatever the charge would be. Did Biff mean so much to her that even a fake Biff was worth it? Whatever. If Betsy wasn't involved, then I figured it would've been Biff's parents because there was no one else it could've been. At least I'd know that much.

I was hoping Betsy would've been too stupid to change the locks on the doors. I still had my old house key, but the one time I actually wanted Betsy to be stupid she was smart. My key wouldn't open the door. I picked up a garden stone and smashed it through the front window. It set off an alarm. I couldn't believe that I'd forgotten about the stupid alarm system. It was a dumb mistake, the kind that gets criminals caught but which you were bound to make sooner or later because . . . because nobody's perfect. I had to move fast and think fast.

Betsy had always been the heaviest sleeper I'd ever known, so I wasn't surprised when she was still asleep despite the racket.

I took a mean pleasure in noting that she was sleeping alone. I almost turned on the light but realized that would be stupid, too. I crept over to her. Looking around the room, I saw a fancy glass lamp I had always hated that cost me a whole lot of money. I smashed it to the floor. Betsy slightly stirred. I picked up a sharp-edged shard of glass and shook her awake. As always, she gave the impression of waking up as being the most difficult task in the world. She sounded drunk and drugged whether she was or not.

"What the . . . Fuck you." She tried to go back to sleep, and I shook her again.

This time she noticed the sharp glass in my hand. The house alarm grew louder. It sounded like a psychotic cat in heat. Or maybe a bomb about to destroy the world.

"Look, I'm done with you. Why are you killing me?" Betsy started crying, something I didn't know she was capable of doing, since crying required feelings and feelings required a heart. She was such a loud crier that she competed with the alarm for being the dominant sound. What was it about me that made people shocked to see that I got angry just like anyone else?

"I don't want to kill you. But I will if you don't tell me the truth about Biff and tell me now."

"What the fuck are you talking about?" she shrieked. "You've always been crazy, but my God, this is a new world's record."

"The cops will be here any second. Talk." I twisted her arm so she couldn't move. The glass was a millimeter away from her pride and joy—her face.

"It's that detective I hired, isn't it?" she replied, with unusual accuracy. It wasn't at all the main point, yet for once she intuited something that had something to do with something. "He put you up to it. I bet he controls your mind. Like some sort of shrink."

"Did you hire someone to be Biff?"

"Fuck, no."

I thought, *Shrink . . . Randy . . . Photo . . . Jesse Falcon . . .* Then everything got jumbled. It was hard to remember what really happened versus what I thought happened or maybe had a dream about.

You know those dreams where you never get to where you're supposed to go or nobody hears what you're saying? You can shout at them or push them off a cliff and still nothing penetrates the slow, gooey molasses we call life.

I realized that it was all the same. My life was no different from my bad dreams. Of course Betsy would never tell me the truth. Of course my mother would never change. Of course Jesse Falcon . . . I was stupid, I was noble, I was a crook, I was cruel, my enemy was my friend, I destroyed my friend.

I remember looking at Betsy, the pathological liar, as if she were an oracle of truth. I heard myself say, "I hate my . . ." But I didn't know how to finish the sentence. "I hate . . ."

There was a heavy thud to my head and that's the last thing I remember.

12: DR. JESSE FALCON

I TOLD ESTHER I GOT MUGGED, changed out of my dirty wet clothes, and ran under a hot shower. Esther insisted on putting some ointment on my scrapes. I kissed her in thanks and fell into a deep sleep. I slept for a full day, and by the time I woke up, it was night again. There's something weird about waking up at night. I suddenly remembered being a little kid and being upset when I woke up from a nap when it was dark outside. Though, of course, I didn't cry now.

I couldn't get a grip on anything. I was exhausted. I felt like I had woken up from a coma.

There was one obvious solution. I told Esther I had to go to the store for something. Yes, my excuse was that flaky. I went to where the whores hung out on the street. I couldn't even be bothered with going to a hotel. Driving through the rubble and closed up storefronts, I thought, *What a shitty neighborhood. What a shitty world.* I noticed one very pretty girl with big tits, and I was about to pull up next to her. But then I spotted another girl who wasn't nearly as hot to look at, yet for some reason captured my attention. I pulled up next to her.

"Hey, big guy," she smiled. "Like to go for a ride?"

"Get in."

She did as she was told. "You know, Mister, I . . ." She paused for some reason. "I really like your kind of man. You seem so—"

"How much for a blow job? How much for a fuck?" I was in no mood for her perfunctory bullshit.

She told me her rates.

I pulled the car over on a dead-end street, where our only company was a couple of abandoned warehouses. The streetlamp cover had been smashed, so there was a bright glare from the big naked bulb. Right in front of us, on the street, I could make out a piece of roadkill. It was a pregnant rat. Little pink rat fetuses oozed from its dead stomach.

"Blow me," I told her.

"Are you sure you don't want to fuck?" she asked hopefully, like any salesperson trying to make more money.

"Nah. I don't feel like looking at anybody."

We positioned ourselves so that she could get to work. "Wait," I decided, with a slight moan. "Don't blow me. Let me do it. Hold still, and let me fuck your face. Like your mouth is just another fuck hole."

After a moment, she said, "Sure. You're the boss."

I thrust into her mouth. "You're nothing but a fuck hole," I kept repeating, which really got me excited. In fact, to my profoundest disappointment, I had a premature ejaculation.

"I don't suppose that gives me fifty percent off?" I joked, zipping up my pants.

She smiled. "A man with a sense of humor. I like that." As she sat up in the car, her face got caught in the brightness of the light bulb high above.

"Hey, wait a second." I took her face in my hands and moved it side to side.

"Are you by any chance a Hollywood talent scout?" she said, though I could tell she was nervous. "My real dream is Broadway, because that's where the great acting is."

I fumbled for my reading glasses, then remembered they were in my shirt pocket. "Put these on."

"Uh, sure." She smiled wanly as she put on the glasses.

I grabbed her hair and pulled it back. "Holy motherfucking shit. You're Melanie."

She tried to act dumb. "My name's Amber, Mister. Amber La Rue. I mean, it's not my real name, but it's the name I use for . . . like, this stuff. I have different names I use as an actress. I think I'd better get going. I can walk back." She reached for the door handle. But I grabbed her by the throat. I reached over to my glove compartment and took out the handgun I'd bought after coming back from the is-land. I'd figured I should be on the safe side, in case anyone came af-ter me about Biff. I pulled back on her hair, and as her mouth opened in reflex, I stuck the gun inside it. She was whimpering in terror.

"Are you going to tell me everything?"

She frantically nodded her head.

"Okay, then." I slid the gun from her mouth, which made her say ouch. "Talk to me."

She stopped sniffling and grew calm, in the manner of some-one accustomed to talking her way out of trouble. "I don't know much, I swear. This guy and his wife asked me to pose as his wife a couple of times. No sex, just a performance. I'm a drama major, you know."

"I'm sure you'll win many awards."

"They say that's how a lot of big stars began . . . you know, like me."

"If that's true, I'm sure they at least knew who to fuck. Enough of this bullshit. Go on with your story, and I'll decide whether or not I believe you." I looked at her with all the intimidation in me, which I must admit was considerable.

"That's really about it. They didn't tell me why I had to do it, and I didn't ask. The only times I did were when you came over. I didn't recognize you at first, not until I got up next to you in the car. And by that time, it was too late. I had to hope for the best. Your name is Robby, right?"

"It's Randy," I said, with a conviction that took me by surprise.

She gave a wry grin. "I meet a lot of guys. Say, do you by any chance know anyone in show biz? You seem like an important man. No bullshit. You really do."

"Yeah, I'm the fucking President of the United States. Now get out of my car. And if you say anything to that couple—"

"Don't worry. I know when to shut up. Oh, and thanks. It was a pleasure doing business with you." Whores could be so sarcastic.

"My pleasure," I replied with equal sarcasm. But as she was about to leave, I told her to wait. I had one more question. "What did this guy's actual wife look like?"

"She was gorgeous. The most beautiful long hair I ever saw. A face like an angel. And she had this way about her. It's hard to describe. Like a princess."

"Shit." I saw she was staring at me. "Will you just *go?*"

I drove around aimlessly for a while, trying to figure out my next move. Then I remembered Esther. I called her from the car and said that I couldn't explain now, but I had to do something. She started asking about million questions at once. I told her I loved her and hung up the phone. When she called back, I didn't answer.

I mentally beat myself up about Astronaut, the bulldog. I thought he looked like Jeremy, and he was nuts about me. True, when I saw Jeremy at Sabrina's studio, he ignored me. Of course, a dog's emotional response to a human being can be unpredictable. And I should've realized that. Anyway, I had a lousy memory even for people, let alone a dog. I was so angry at myself for not noticing this that I literally punched myself in the face.

I couldn't believe that I'd let myself be betrayed again. By my own daughter. She'd married the guy at the bank robbery. How did he convince her to lead such a complicated double life? Of course if it was Biff, he could have paid her off or something. Or maybe he threatened her. Yes, that was the nicer possibility to ponder. She was doing all this to protect Esther and me.

But what about my so-called friend? He was in on it with Biff from Day One. No wonder he knew so much. When he hacked into those bank accounts, he'd been doing it all along. And *he* certainly was not trying to protect me. He took advantage of my daughter to keep her from coming forward. He even let Biff's thugs beat him up on the island to make it look good. All to keep me away from Biff. He was, after all, Biff's impoverished best friend for all those years, so it wasn't hard to see that he could be bought. Besides having some insane loyalty to Biff. Of course, super-rich people sometimes have that sort of power over people. I should've thought of this much sooner. Instead, I stupidly assumed he was living off of Melanie's money. What a numbskull I was. And *me*, a shrink.

Yet as my shrink self kicked into gear—I'd almost forgotten I wasn't always a PI—I thought of another way my fake friend could've gotten involved. His mother treated him like crap, and his father died—abandoned him. Then Betsy dumped him for Biff. Since Biff was a crook, my pal had to become one, too. It was a way of holding on to Betsy, to not feel abandoned. Beneath that vanilla exterior, he was a total lunatic. As a shrink, that should've made me feel sorry for him. But I was a human being first and foremost, and I hated him almost as much as Biff. I'd leave the forgiving to God, assuming there was a God.

I called the Paradise Cul-de-Sac. Sabrina answered the phone, and I said, "I'm on my way, Sabrina, don't you dare leave." I figured she needed to leave with me. If she simply left on her own, her creepy husband would go after her or even worse. Pulling up in front of Number 11, I pounded on the door and rang and rang the buzzer. There was no answer. I saw that there was an alarm system, so I prowled around the house to see if there was an open window. I lucked out. The sliding back door was unlocked. I touched the handgun in my pants pocket for a sense of security.

I made no effort to be quiet as I stepped inside the kitchen. "Anybody home?" I shouted. "Sabrina? Mr. Asshole?"

Since it was the middle of the night, I figured I'd find them upstairs. I was about to give a new definition to the term, "rude awakening." I didn't intend to kill anyone. Even killing Biff was making me crazy with guilt. I wanted to tell them I knew what was up and for my daughter to be able to leave him and get her life back.

It never occurred to me to call the cops. They probably wouldn't do anything even if they believed me. And I still worried about having pulled the plug on Linda Goldstein.

I opened the master bedroom door, though the thought of seeing them in bed together grossed me out.

The bed was empty. But it was unmade. I checked the master bath, and no one was there. Suddenly, I heard a voice and followed it down the hall.

"There's blood everywhere. Naked and so much blood. Dead."

After a pause, the voice said: "I . . . I never wanted this to happen." Obviously, someone was on the phone. I couldn't quite make out who it was because the person was talking very low, but I took a wild guess it was my daughter's theoretical husband. As I listened, it sounded like a 911 call:

"Oh God, oh God . . . Christ, please, hurry! . . . It's not just one—I mean, yes. I don't know. Just get an ambulance . . . I'm home, damn it. In my bedroom . . . I told you, it's not just one person. Why can't you listen? Can't you send an ambulance? . . . I'm in the Paradise Cul-de-sac, Number 11. I'm . . . I'm Dr. Jesse Falcon."

At the sound of my name, I opened the door with such force it came loose from its hinges.

"I'm not that kind of doctor, you dumb shit. I'm a—I'm a psychologist."

And there he was, before me. Scotty, talking in a deep voice to sound like an adult. At the sight of me, he said, "No . . . Please, no more," and hung up the phone.

It was only then I saw the bodies on the floor. Both were face down, but I recognized their hair. One was Betsy, and one was . . . I could see it was my beautiful daughter, Sabrina. The pools of blood around them told me they were dead. Betsy was naked. But I checked Sabrina's pulse to make sure; I felt something. I kissed her wrist in gratitude. Thank God help was on the way. Then I thought I might as well check Betsy's pulse. Nothing, nada. She was a goner.

"Please don't be mad at me, Mr. Van Sant." He said this as if I found out he broke my window playing baseball.

I grabbed the boy by the shoulders and lifted him off the ground, shaking him hard. "Scotty, you tell me everything right now, or I'll take you to jail. You'll be in prison for the rest of your life with rats and cockroaches and other prisoners who will—" I stopped myself. I wanted to kill him for what he did to Sabrina and maybe I would, but first I needed to know what happened. I owed it to my daughter. In a much calmer voice, I set him down and quietly said, "Just tell me what happened." I wasn't a shrink all those years for nothing. I knew how to coax the truth out of people. I might as well have had a multiple personality disorder. Life will do that to you. Yet a strange sense of peace flooded my body, as if my blood had turned to warm milk. Something that couldn't be helped was finally over.

Of course, looking back, I simply was in shock. I didn't even cry.

Scotty looked down at the floor as he spoke, as if too ashamed to look at me. "Mom came over. I was supposed to be asleep but I heard her. She told my stepmom that Dad had been hurt. She said he broke into her house and tried to kill her and this guy—who was, you know, like, a boyfriend—came out of the bathroom and hit him over the head really hard. Then the police came and arrested the guy. My dad is in a *coma*." He started to cry. "I knew it wasn't true because Dad would never kill Mom. Dad is the best guy in the world, and Mom is a liar. I knew my grandma had a gun in the house for when she stayed here. I wasn't supposed to know about it, but I saw her hide it. I climbed up on a chair and got it out of a box in back of the top shelf of the hallway closet. I cried out that I was having a bad dream. I do that sometimes. You know, for attention. I feel all the time like I'm not even *here*—like I'm invisible or something. The grown-ups are always talking about stuff they don't want me to know about. I hate being a kid."

"That's an awful way to feel, Scotty. Invisible. No wonder you get upset." I could see his little fists tightening, as if something inside him was exploding. It was a feeling I knew well. "Please go on, Scotty. I am very interested in what you have to say."

He actually smiled. "Thank you, Mr. Van Sant. I never knew before you were such a cool guy."

"Thank you. I think you're cool, too." Remembering that dumb high five his father did with me once, I repeated the gesture with Scotty, who grinned even wider.

"Well, both my moms came into the room. I turned to my real mom and pulled out the gun. 'You take back what you said about Dad, or I'll shoot.' She started to laugh, though my stepmom looked worried. My real mom said, 'Scotty, don't be dumb. Put down the gun and go back to sleep.' That made me mad. 'I'm not dumb,' I said. Then I started screaming. 'I'm not dumb, I'm not dumb.' And then the next thing I knew, I pulled the trigger and shot. The bullet missed my mom. But it . . . it hit my stepmom, right in the heart. She fell over. My real mom laughed and said, 'Jesus, what a lousy shot. Or should a say a great shot? I hated that bitch. Now, give Mommy the gun, Scotty.' I gave it to her, all right. I shot her through the neck. You should've seen the blood! I kept looking at my mom, I mean my real mom. I was so confused. Did I really just kill her? On TV, they examine the bodies, so I . . . I know it was naughty, but I took off her clothes. I wanted to see the bullet hole and just . . . I wanted to see her. I wanted her to be okay. I put my head between her . . . her, you know, uh, breasts. I don't know why, but I started crying. I put her arms around me. She never liked to hug me, and I . . . I just wanted to *feel* her, you know? Really feel her. Then I figured I'd call 911."

I nodded encouragingly throughout this confession, so that I did not scare him into stopping. "Why did you say you were Dr. Jesse Falcon?"

"From sneaking into Dad's computer, I knew there was this guy named Dr. Jesse Falcon that he was looking for. Dad was even in contact with the police. I figured Dr. Jesse Falcon was someone bad, so I gave his name. You know, so that I wouldn't get caught."

Obviously, Scotty misunderstood what was in the computer. I thought about asking him to show it to me. I heard the cop car sirens from a distance.

"Scotty, you like your grandmother, right?"

"Yes, sir."

"Give me the gun. Now, we're going to sneak out the back door very quietly. If you hear the cops breaking into the house, you keep following me and don't make a sound."

"What about my dog?"

"We'll get Jeremy—I mean, Astronaut later. Now, do as I say, young man."

We made it to my car with seconds to spare. From my rearview mirror I could see the cop cars entering the cul-de-sac. I drove to his grandmother's—my old condo—and banged on the door. Fortunately, the old bag was still awake. Drinking, I presumed.

"Mr. Van Sant," she said. "Scotty. What are you doing here?"

"Get Scotty a lawyer this very moment. Then make him tell you what happened. He needs . . . he needs *something*."

She was smart enough to know that whatever it was, she should do it. "Got it," she said, and as she closed the door, she added, "Thanks."

My reasons for getting Scotty to safety were quite calculated. I wanted to make sure neither of us were around when the cops came, to buy myself some time. He shot my daughter. Yeah, it was an accident. Yeah, he was only a kid. But I had to think of some way to avenge her death, and I needed to stay clear of the cops to do it.

I drove to the hospital and went to the emergency desk. The receptionist asked if I had a question.

"Yes. Do you have a patient named—" I stopped myself. "Do you have a patient named Dr. Jesse Falcon?"

The receptionist sighed. "I'm afraid we do. I remember him from that awful bank robbery. When I saw them bring him in again, I thought, 'That poor man has the worst luck in the world.' But it helped us get him checked in."

"I'm his doctor," I said. "His psychologist. I'd really like to see how he's doing."

"I shouldn't, but okay. There's a police officer outside his door, anyway. He may stop you from going in."

"I'm sure I can talk him into letting me see him." I winked as I took a slip of paper with the room number. The supposed cop at the doorway wasn't even there. How typical. But also, how lucky for me.

I saw my ex-son-in-law-ex-best-friend lying in a coma. He had fewer gadgets hooked up to him than Linda Goldstein had, but it was the same general idea. I sat down next to him. I really didn't know what to think anymore.

"So, buddy boy, you steal from me and marry my daughter and get her killed. After I saved your life. Those transactions on the computer . . . it was all part of your plan with Biff. In the bar, you sent that text message. Was it to Sabrina, telling her to leave because I was coming over? You were even willing to get beaten up to try to keep me away from Biff. Did it hurt you to know I killed him? Did it scare you? And now here you are. Oblivious to everything. Maybe you'll die never even knowing all that you did. Should I pull your plug and give you death? Or should I hope you wake up and face what you did? Which is worse? Which will stab you over and over with more of my rage?"

I was startled by a tap on my shoulder.

"In the mood for pulling another plug, Dr. Falcon?" It was a woman's voice.

"I don't know what you mean." I turned and saw this cop right in my face. The whole thing was some kind of setup. The cop not being on duty, the name of Jesse Falcon. Was Scotty right—or at least partially right—after all? Did the cops hire this fuckhead to find me? When? Why?

"Linda Goldstein ring any bells?"

"I . . . I want a lawyer."

She handcuffed me as she read me my rights. "Dr. Jesse Falcon, aka Randall Van Sant, you are under arrest for the murder of Linda Goldstein."

Just to have the last word, I said, "Why would a woman want to be a cop? Couldn't you get laid?"

"I have a thing for serial killers." She yawned, like she'd heard it all before.

I thought I must've heard wrong. "Serial killer? What the hell do you mean?"

"You asked to speak to a lawyer, sir. I'm sure it will all get straightened out at the station."

That was two years ago. At first they thought I killed a whole mess of people who woke up from comas, but finally they settled on just Linda Goldstein. I never said a word about killing Biff, though the charges against the mob guy and hit man were dropped due to lack of evidence, so they were free to go their merry way, killing more people. The cops really did ask my dumb-ass friend to find Jesse Falcon, and he truly didn't know that's who I was. There was a plea bargain I never knew about. The FBI guy who gave me my new name never told his superiors, so in typical fucked-up fashion, no one had any idea what anyone else was doing. I fell off the radar, until they finally added two and two.

Eventually, they also figured out that the asshole doctor who talked to me the night I pulled Linda's plug had killed the other patients. I guess you could say the squeaky wheel got the grease because he had a trial in about five minutes—guilty, the death penalty—while I've been rotting in prison for two years as my trial keeps getting postponed. God, I miss sex.

There really is no justice in this world.

13: Esther Vargas Falcon AKA Valerie Van Sant

WHEN I FIRST MET JESSE FALCON, I WAS SIXTEEN, and I thought he was a young god. He was so handsome, born to wear tuxedos and polo gear, but not in a self-aware way, like a conceited male model or movie star. Truly handsome men do not give off an aura of knowing how handsome they are. That was Jesse—oblivious perfection. And for a year or two, we were obliviously happy. Then . . . how do I say it? He looked in the mirror and liked what he saw. Indeed, he liked it way too much. The magic spell had been broken. He became narcissus; he couldn't stop looking at himself. The first time he cheated on me was the night of our engagement party. I remember thinking, "Oh, so he's only another man." But I put that realization in the back of my mind, like a beautiful garden that has a pile of mulch way in the back. I suppose you could say my life has been about trying to believe that men are not the way they really are.

Of course, at sixteen I believed that I was a young goddess to match his god. Not that I was stuck-up. But I was financially well-set, and I was pretty and young. And it never occurred to me that I would ever be anything else. I was *that* kind of sixteen-year-old girl. The kind who goes through life getting everything she wants or else nothing she wants. There is no in between. Either way, people hate her as she ages. They hate her for getting wrinkles like an old hag. They hate her for getting fat, and they hate her for staying skinny. They hate her for failing, and they hate her for succeeding. When she succeeds, they want her to fail. When she fails, they want her to fail more. Once I overheard these girls talking on the bus about some young movie star, and one of them said, "I look forward to reading about her fifth divorce." The girl who said this was wearing a T-shirt that read: *World*

Peace Now. I'm sure that there were many who knew the true story of my marriage and gloated from afar.

When we married at eighteen, there were whispers that I was pregnant, which rumors of course were not dignified with a response. But to distract attention away from this possibility, it was decided that there would be a double wedding with my brother, Clement, and his wife-to-be, Gabrielle. My family was relieved that I wouldn't be going to college. They thought young ladies needed limited education. They gave Jesse and me a starter house while he studied to become a psychologist. (For all the good it did him.)

In truth, I *was* pregnant. One night when Jesse was drunk, I suppose you could say he raped me, though I didn't think of it that way at the time. He broke into my room where I was sleeping, and next thing I knew, I woke up from a dream with him on top of me. I still remember, it was a dream about being invited to the White House. And that was how I lost my virginity. Jesse was very turned on by this surprise-attack approach and was sorely disappointed when, after we were married, I told him he must never do it again.

Yet while the rest of the world was finally adjusting to the fact that girls got pregnant before they were married, my own family would have none of it. They did not blame me, but they did make it clear that I was to do certain things to preserve the family reputation. Which, of course, I was happy to do. I graduated from prep school before I started to show, and then went traveling as a graduation present. Specifically, I traveled to a private hospital run by nuns in Switzerland.

I gave birth to twin girls. They were fraternal—one was slightly more elongated—but they still looked quite a bit alike. The plan was for the nuns to raise them for about a year, and at which time Jesse and I would "adopt" them. But by the time we were ready to come back for them, Jesse only wanted one girl. He said he didn't want children at all, and I should be grateful for this compromise. He said children were expensive to raise, and he wanted to be worth a certain sum of money by a certain age. He would not make his goal with even one child, let alone two. I put up as much of a fight as I could, but Jesse said he would walk out on me if I insisted on taking both. I hoped that seeing them would change his mind, but it didn't. In the end, he literally flipped a coin to decide which one to take. Heads won, which meant we took the baby on the right, while my brother and his wife agreed to adopt the other. Some people might think, "How could a mother let this happen?" With a lifetime of tears, that's how. Jesse complained about how distant I was, but it was guilt weighing me down all day, every day. It never let up. Guilt and rage. I hated Jesse, but I hated myself more.

What was strange was that Clement and Gabrielle decided not to tell Sequoia she was adopted, while Jesse made sure we told our own Sabrina that she was. As she got older, Sabrina was not happy with the thought that she was adopted, and Jesse couldn't understand why. Though Sabrina has sworn on a stack of Bibles that her father never did anything inappropriate with her, Jesse surely committed a form of mental incest with her for years. She was his princess, his true love. Their relationship nauseated me at times because they were quite flirtatious with each other until Sabrina got old enough to understand. As Sabrina grew into a beauty, I could see her father getting aroused at the sight of her.

So Jesse's cheating wasn't even the worst of it. After a while, all that seemed pathetic. That is, until we had to move away or risk scandal. And he could've done more with our nest egg, but he insisted on making namby-pamby investments. My family knew how to make money really happen—how to go out on a limb and land on your feet because you knew how to play the market and you believed in your right to the bigger piece of the pie. Jesse, for all his conceit and bravado, always played it safe. I got used to not being as well-off as we could've been. One should not live ostentatiously, anyway.

He hit me a few times over the years, and once when I inquired too deeply into our investments, he said he'd kill me if I kept interfering. Yet, I took that in my stride. I forgave. I prayed he would get help.

No, his true foulness lay elsewhere. With Sequoia, with so many things.

As Fate would have it, Sequoia came back to live with us when the rest of her family died. There we were, with an adopted daughter who was really our blood daughter and an adopted niece who also was really our blood daughter. Twins who didn't even know they were twins. Clement, Gabrielle, and two of their children were killed in an awful fire. My brother was a doctor who dedicated himself to helping others and had lived a blameless life. I'd gone to boarding school with Gabrielle.

At first, the fire seemed to have been caused by an electrical malfunction, but it turned out to have been arson. I am not saying that Jesse lit the match or even that he paid someone else to do it. Though I must admit these possibilities ran through my mind over the years. After all, I was first in line after Sequoia to inherit Clement's estate. Jesse knew I wondered about this. He was very good at knowing what people were thinking, though he seldom used this gift in a positive way.

"I didn't start the fire," he told me. "Get that foolish idea out of your head."

I was in the middle of arranging some flowers in a vase, and I pretended to be absorbed in my task. "Did you say something, dear?"

"Christ, you drive me crazy, woman. Why do you shut me out? Hell, you're not even a woman. You're an iceberg with a smile carved into it."

Jesse never ran out of vivid ways of describing how heartless I was. Naturally, I pretended to have no reaction.

Still, *his* reaction to the fire—now, that was heartless. Throughout the ordeal, he offered me no comfort. Zero. Not even a hug. On the first morning we heard about it, he left me alone to go have sex with one of his whores. Jesse laughed out loud when the news story on TV showed a small corpse with a sheet over its head.

"Guess that's one less Yalie," he said.

You see, in my family the men went to Yale, while in his family they went to Princeton. There was a silly feud about it for years. My family took it as a joke, Jesse took it seriously. He actually told me to cheer up because fire was a good thing. Surely I was in my brother's will—which I was—and that in case Gabrielle kept a diary, it was best it was destroyed. Because he hated to think what it would do to my reputation if people found out that he'd had sex with my sister-in-law. Or, as he put it, people would know how unfuckable I was. When I started to cry, he yelled at me. "I'm only thinking of you," he said. "What's the big deal?"

After that, I could feel myself harden. For the sake of Sabrina, for the sake of appearances, I'd stay married as best I could. And I wasn't a weakling. I stood up to him many times. I made threats. But in the end, I was my parents' daughter. I did not divorce. Eventually, I found some measure of happiness in my interior design business, and Sabrina got a great deal of affection from me. Perhaps too much; we did not prepare her for the Colton Coles of this world. Indeed, I find considerable comfort in the notion that Sequoia was the lucky one. She got to live her own life, and she got away from Jesse and me.

Jesse made sure Sequoia's days with us were heartbreakingly few. Sequoia looked the same as Sabrina and had many of the same personality traits. But she simply could not compete, as far as Jesse was concerned. Not only was Sabrina the apple of her father's eye, but poor Sequoia had lost what she believed to be her parents and siblings and so naturally did not have the vivacity of her sister. It was a vicious cycle; Sequoia felt under-appreciated. This made her withdraw and act less loving, so she was ignored all the more. I did not want to lose my daughter again, but Jesse insisted we ship her back to Switzerland—this time to a finishing school.

She never forgave Jesse, and I had to send her letters in secret for many years. I secretly visited her twice. The positive side to Jesse's self-absorption was that sometimes I could do things without his knowing it. I also sent her many gifts, not the least of which were large amounts of cash and some stock options. She'd always lived comfortably anyway, but as she often joked, it was the thought that counted. She had great wit, as many people who know tragedy when they are young do.

I need to make one thing clear. That identity thief disgusted me, and he deserved much worse than he got. No one deserves to have their identity stolen, not to mention their money and their sanity. Inexcusable. Unforgivable. When I met the man, I found him off-putting, to say the least. He was like a fly that wouldn't go away. He wanted and he wanted and he wanted. I could see why he and Jesse got along so well. And yet good always comes from bad, don't you agree? That awful thief produced a marvelous child, Scotty, who has brought such sunshine into my life.

And yet . . . and yet I was thrilled to watch Jesse finally suffer. Had it been a movie, I would've stood up and cheered. I thought that at last, Jesse might develop some compassion. He would need me again, like he did when we first met. As it turned out, Jesse was incapable of suffering and therefore could not develop compassion. He was only capable of self-pity. And there is a world of difference between the two. At times, it almost did seem like he was learning something from it all. But he'd go and do something else behind my back that was awful, like that poor Goldstein woman.

When Sequoia and Sabrina turned eighteen, I arranged for all three of us to meet. I told them the truth. God, how we all cried. And how we all hated Jesse. Sequoia looked *slightly* different from her sister. I was reminded of those beauty pageants where, unless you looked carefully, one contestant looked pretty much like another. But Sabrina's features were slightly softer, while Sequoia's were slightly sharper. They had the same glorious manes of hair, and both had beautiful faces and figures. If I may brag a little, I come from a damn good gene pool. They also were both talented artists, who—independent of each other—developed a fascination for black and white instead of colors. (I've read that in studies of separated twins, these kinds of similarities happen.) But black and white took on a special significance when I told them that they were seeking each other through these opposite colors. It was a proof they always knew the truth in their hearts about being sisters, each seeking her complement in the other.

"It's a sign of your love for each other," I said. "For all three of us."

"Let's keep it our secret," Sequoia said.

"All I have to do is paint in black and white, and we're together like we are now," said Sabrina.

We toasted with champagne, and oh how we laughed. I thought, *I will get back at you, Jesse. Something will come along, and I will crush you with it.*

Sequoia was at the bank robbery. She called me as soon as it was over and told me not only about the robbers but about the man who said he was Dr. Jesse Falcon. Was that an odd coincidence, or did it mean something else? Then, in the meantime, Jesse and I learned about the identity thief. I didn't trust how he would take the news about the thief probably being at the bank robbery, so I asked Sequoia if she'd find out if this guy survived the bank robbery and to let me know. I must say, she did me one better—she met him and pretended to fall in love with him. I worried for her. Sequoia assured me that he was just a computer geek and posed no threat. I also expressed alarm when she told me she bedded down with a man she loathed. I knew all too well about those emotional scars. Sequoia was such a good sport. She laughed and said that he was a lame lover, and she composed art projects in her head while he got his business over with.

Still feeling terrible about the way Sequoia's father abandoned her, I told her in that case she should help herself to her father's money, which she did. I think it enabled Sequoia to feel better about herself. Sometimes all you can do with a man is get back at him. She really did care about Scotty—which is not at all hard to do—and she skimmed a great deal off the top for herself when the supposed love of her life struck gold as McShrink. He was an utter fool who found good luck here, bad luck there, and never grew any the wiser. Obviously, Sequoia never believed his bull about working for the government, and she found his mother to be intolerable. What Jesse didn't know was that he really wasn't losing as much money as he thought. Most of it was getting recycled through Sequoia. I think she wanted to prove to her father she was worthy of his love. Children can't help but want approval from their parents, even when they are as dreadful at the job as Jesse.

Yet I was torn. In all fairness, Jesse did deserve to know something. So I arranged for Sabrina to come out to visit us. Sabrina told her father that *she* was at the bank robbery, to give him a piece of the puzzle. Given how he reacted, it may have been a mistake.

You see, Sabrina had her own burden to bear. She had a boyfriend named Colton Cole who neglected to tell her he was HIV positive. He convinced her to have unprotected sex. And now she was HIV positive herself, or POZ, as the young people say. Fortunately, she was doing well, though her life would never be the same. It was a terrible, terrible thing to do to someone against her will. I knew her father could not handle knowing this. But as we dug further into things, we found a way to deal with Colton Cole.

There was a missing young man named Biff— a rich bum, from what I understand. He didn't look exactly like Colton Cole, but he was the same general type. The real Biff, Sequoia eventually told me, had been murdered, though she did not specify how or by whom. She said she did this to protect me. Legally, the less I knew, the better. I took her word for it. But it did involve the identity thief—I imagine he killed him—and as part of the ruse, she encouraged her loving husband to shift the blame of the identity theft onto the missing Biff. Eventually, the real thief staged a trip to the island—getting him to help our cause was like shooting ducks in a barrel—and he came back all beaten up from God knows what. Sequoia said she thought he did it to himself. He certainly was weird enough to have done something like that.

Naturally, her father, Jesse, was not about to take this lying down. So Sabrina pretended to forgive Colton and said she'd meet him on the island. She said that they'd be using a room being loaned to them by her old friend Biff, so to check in as Biff. Colton said wasn't that the guy who was missing or dead? Sabrina said that he was trying to get away from his family, and it would all be straightened out soon. She also intimated that it was in Colton's best interests to help Biff finish what he started, as there would be a reward at the end of the rainbow. Like most cruel people, Colton wasn't really very bright, so he went along with it.

We expected Jesse to beat him up. Killing him was like an added bonus. We paid off the corrupt island police to get rid of the body with no questions asked. It was quite a pay off, but it was worth it. The whole episode brought Sabrina and Sequoia much closer together. I can't tell you how it moved me, finally seeing my lovely daughters be true sisters. We can only wonder if Colton got a chance to tell Jesse who he really was, though Jesse probably wouldn't have believed him anyway. He always had a terrible memory for names. Not that we really care. But Jesse certainly cannot say we never did anything to help him. He murdered someone, for God's sake, and we cleaned up his mess.

There isn't too much else to tell. Scotty did accidentally shoot his whore mother, and we try not to dwell on that. Sequoia wasn't shot at all. Jesse, the big dope, called to say he was on his way over there. Thinking quickly, Sequoia told Scotty to help her make it look like she'd been shot, too, and to say that he did it. She promised him a special treat if he cooperated, but he is such a cooperative boy anyway. I imagine they had to scoop up the other woman's blood, but I choose not to think about it. Though Sequoia did do an admirable job of holding her breath to seem dead. She said she learned a special way of doing this in a drama class in Paris. I was so proud of her. She inherited her mother's smarts. We paid some—shall we say—less-than-ideal young men to clean up the mess.

We'd long orchestrated it for Jesse to think it was Sabrina who was involved with his identity thief, saying just enough here and there for him to believe this. Jesse was such a stupid man. It's like his other daughter didn't even exist to him. So again, we wanted to teach him a lesson. But again, Fate had something else in store. He ended up thinking his beloved Sabrina had been killed. When he first was arrested, Jesse told his lawyer that Sabrina was dead, but his lawyer said that was ridiculous. He had spoken to Sabrina himself. Jesse let the matter drop, dumbfounded as ever. It was immeasurably funny watching Jesse go crazy when Sabrina led him on about being at the bank robbery and seeing that awful man get shot. But you see, we had to confuse him as much as possible.

Really, the only mistake we made was that smelly old bulldog, Jeremy. Sabrina thought it best that he get a different home, in case she got sick. So she brought him to the pound, and in exchange for a donation, we were allowed to arrange for Sequoia and Scotty and that other creep to adopt the animal. When Sequoia knew Jesse was coming over, she was going to take the dog with her when she left. But Scotty made such a fuss, she felt sorry for him. Fortunately, the dog didn't make any difference one way or the other. God was on our side.

Neither of Jesse's daughters has been to see him or has had any contact with him. From what I've gathered, it hasn't occurred to him to even ask about Sequoia, and he's still afraid to ask about Sabrina. Despite her years of being pampered, Sabrina cannot forgive her father for what he did to Sequoia and to me, for I have shared with my daughters at least some things about their father.

I did finally go see Jesse myself. There were no greetings or re-criminations. He merely sat down in the visiting area, picked up the telephone, and through the sheet of glass between us he told me, "I used to watch those true crime shows on TV and think how crazy it was when some serial killer would say how now his life was in a much better place. But I understand it. Something *is* better. Nothing anybody does makes sense. But you live as best you can until you die." Then he got up and went back to his cell. I never saw him again.

Sequoia was never pregnant. That was part of the scheme to make her husband more nervous about getting caught. Had he not been hit over the head and fallen into a coma, she would've faked a miscar-riage down the road. As it was, the doctor said he'd never wake up, so as his wife, Sequoia pulled the plug. The three of us toasted with champagne. Why pay money to keep someone like that alive? We all felt a little bad for Scotty losing both his mother and father. But really, with parents like that, aren't you better off being an orphan? We were disappointed, though, that the scumbag died knowing so little of what really happened and how much damage he did.

It wasn't hard to convince Scotty's paternal grandmother to let us have custody over the child. And yes, we made it a joint, three-way custody, in case anything should happen to any of us. So he has Sequoia Mom and Sabrina Mom and of course, Grandma Esther. He is such a bright boy, witty and sensitive and polite. Yet he had a screwball teacher who said she was worried about him, that he didn't fit in with other children and supposedly displayed violent tendencies. If she only *saw* how devastated he was after shooting his mother, she would've known better.

"I don't have to listen to this," I told the teacher. "Boys will be boys, and Scotty couldn't be nicer most of the time."

"Everyone is nice sometimes," said the impertinent teacher. "Adolph Hitler was nice sometimes. That doesn't prove anything."

"If you're comparing my grandson to Hitler, he has no place in your classroom. We'll homeschool him, since clearly we're the only people who appreciate all he has to offer."

The teacher said that wasn't what she meant, but it made no difference. We started homeschooling Scotty the next day. He keeps us company all the time. Some awful, obnoxious new neighbor accused poor Scotty of poisoning her cat. I assured this know-nothing that Scotty loved animals. He and that bulldog are inseparable.

The last thing I'll say is that because the McShrink column had done so well, the three of us made an effort to keep it going. But the readership dropped off. When we lost sponsorship, we called it quits. One of the former advertisers said that McShrink had lost his touch.

Now he was telling people to try to talk out their differences with other people, and nobody wanted to hear . . . I might as well say it. He said nobody anymore wanted to hear a bunch of nice shit. Nice, he said, was out of style. Only self-survival mattered now.

I don't believe a word of it and neither do my daughters or my grandson. We are four nice people. The nicest people you'd ever want to meet. I expect we'll be around a long, long time.

ACKNOWLEDGMENTS

SPECIAL THANKS to Michele Orwin of Bacon Press and my editor Lorraine Fico-White of Magnifico Manuscripts, for taking on the daunting task of trying to understand me.

Thanks also to the many people who taught me that their identities were not worth stealing, whereby I was stuck with my own.

ABOUT THE AUTHOR

JP BLOCH has a PhD but hopes people won't hold it against him. His last name is pronounced "Block," not "Blotch," but he's gotten used to it. He has been called far worse. He has lived all over the country, and so far the feds have not busted him. He finally settled in Connecticut, where he is an indentured servant to his dog. JP writes on his king-size bed with the fan on. His hobbies include eating cashews while watching TV and overdosing on film noir favorites.

Doc Bloch, as he affectionately calls himself, teaches criminology, gender, and other things. He has appeared on TV and radio numerous times. Having grown up in different households, he became interested at a young age in the fragility of self-identity. On his own since age 15, he also developed a lifelong interest in finding food and shelter. Thus he hopes you will buy this book. He has discarded many identities himself over the years before sticking with chocolate mint chip. JP is also a victim of identity theft, which is ironic since he has no money.

He enjoys people who have gained wisdom from hardship, and ask questions more than they assume answers. His turn-offs include Brussels sprouts, bigotry, and people who think life is simple.

Besides novels, he writes poetry, nonfiction and scholarly articles. JP's paintings have been hailed as naïve folk art. Tumultuous skies are preferred over sunny ones.